FIVE LITTLE PEPPERS AND HOW THEY GREW

Margaret Sidney

AN
APPLE
PAPERBACK

SCHOLASTIC INC.
New York Toronto London Auckland Sydney

ISBN 0-590-42520-X

Five Little Peppers and How They Grew was first published in 1881. All rights reserved. Published by Scholastic Inc. APPLE PAPERBACKS is a registered trademark of Scholastic Inc.

12 11 10 9 8 7 6 5 4 3 2 1   9/8 0 1 2 3 4/9

Printed in the U.S.A.
First Scholastic printing, April 1989   28

CONTENTS

A HOME VIEW

THE little old kitchen had quieted down from the bustle and confusion of midday, and now, with its afternoon manners on, presented a holiday aspect that, as the principal room in the brown house, it was eminently proper it should have. It was just on the edge of the twilight, and the little Peppers, all except Ben, the oldest of the flock, were enjoying a breathing spell, as their mother called it, which meant some quiet work suitable for the hour. All the breathing spell they could remember, however, poor things, for times were always hard with them nowadays; and since the father died when Phronsie was a baby, Mrs. Pepper had had hard work to scrape together money enough to put bread into her children's mouths and to pay the rent of the little brown house.

But she had met life too bravely to be beaten down now. So with a stout heart and a cheery face, she had worked away day after day at making coats and tailoring and mending of all descriptions; and she had seen with pride that couldn't be concealed her noisy, happy brood growing up around her and filling her heart with comfort, and making the little brown house fairly ring with jollity and fun.

"Poor things!" she would say to herself. "They haven't had any bringing up; they've just scrambled up!" And then she would set her lips together tightly and fly at her work faster than ever. "I must get schooling for them some way, but I don't see how!"

Once or twice she had thought, "Now the time is coming!" but it never did: for winter shut in very cold, and it took so much more to feed and warm them that the money went faster than ever. And then, when the way seemed clear again, the store changed hands, so that for a long time she failed to get her usual supply of sacks and coats to make, and that made sad havoc in the quarters and half-dollars laid up as her nest egg. But — "Well, it'll come sometime," she would say to herself, "because it must!" And so at it again she would fly, brisker than ever.

"To help mother" was the great ambition of all the children, older and younger; but in Polly's and Ben's souls, the desire grew so overwhelmingly great as to absorb all lesser thoughts. Many and vast were their secret plans by which they were to astonish her at some future day, which they would only confide — as they did everything else — to one another. For this brother and sister were everything to each other and stood loyally together through thick and thin.

Polly was ten, and Ben one year older; and the younger three of the Five Little Peppers, as they were always called, looked up to them with the intensest admiration and love. What *they* failed to do couldn't very well be done by anyone!

"Oh, dear!" exclaimed Polly as she sat over in the corner by the window helping her mother pull out basting threads from a coat she had just finished, and giving an impatient twitch to the sleeve. "I do wish we could ever have any light — just as much as we want!"

"You don't need any light to see these threads," said Mrs. Pepper, winding up hers carefully on an old spool as she spoke, "Take care, Polly, you broke that; thread's dear now."

"I couldn't help it," said Polly vexedly. "It snapped. Everything's dear now, it seems to me! I wish we could have — oh, ever an' ever so many candles; as many as we wanted. I'd light 'em all, so there! And have it light here one night, anyway!"

"Yes, and go dark all the rest of the year, like as anyway," observed Mrs. Pepper, stopping to untie a knot. "Folks who do so never have any candles," she added sententiously.

"How many'd you have, Polly?" asked Joel curiously, laying down his hammer and regarding her with the utmost anxiety.

"Oh, two hundred!" said Polly decidedly. "I'd have two hundred, all in a row!"

"*Two hundred candles!*" echoed Joel in amazement. "My whockety! What a lot!"

"Don't say such dreadful words, Joel," put in Polly nervously, stopping to pick up her spool of basting thread that was racing away all by itself. " 'Tisn't nice."

" 'Tisn't worse than to wish you'd got things you haven't," retorted Joel. "I don't believe you'd light 'em all at once," he added incredulously.

"Yes, I would too!" replied Polly recklessly. "Two

hundred of 'em, if I had a chance; all at once, so there, Joey Pepper!"

"Oh," said little Davie, drawing a long sigh. "Why, 'twould be just like heaven, Polly! But wouldn't it cost money, though!"

"I don't care," said Polly, giving a flounce in her chair, which snapped another thread. "Oh, dear me! I didn't mean to, mammy; well, I wouldn't care how much money it cost. We'd have as much light as we wanted, for once; so!"

"Mercy!" said Mrs. Pepper. "You'd have the house afire! Two hundred candles! Who ever heard of such a thing!"

"Would they burn?" asked Phronsie anxiously, getting up from the floor where she was crouching with David, overseeing Joel nail on the cover of an old box; and going to Polly's side, she awaited her answer patiently.

"Burn?" said Polly. "There, that's done now, mamsie dear!" And she put the coat, with a last little pat, into her mother's lap. "I guess they would, Phronsie pet." And Polly caught up the little girl and spun round and round the old kitchen till they were both glad to stop.

"Then," said Phronsie, as Polly put her down, and stood breathless after her glorious spin, "I do so wish we might, Polly; oh, just this very one minute!"

And Phronsie clasped her fat little hands in rapture at the thought.

"Well," said Polly, giving a look up at the old clock in the corner, "deary me! It's half-past five, and most time for Ben to come home!"

Away she flew to get supper. So for the next few moments nothing was heard but the pulling out of the old

4

table into the middle of the floor, the laying of the cloth, and all the other bustle attendant upon the being ready for Ben. Polly went skipping around, cutting the bread, and bringing dishes, only stopping long enough to fling some scraps of reassuring nonsense to the two boys, who were thoroughly dismayed at being obliged to remove their traps into a corner.

Phronsie still stood just where Polly left her. *Two hundred candles!* Oh! What could it mean! She gazed up to the old beams overhead, and around the dingy walls, and to the old black stove, with the fire nearly out, and then over everything the kitchen contained, trying to think how it would seem. To have it bright and winsome and warm! To suit Polly — *"Oh!"* she screamed.

"Goodness!" said Polly, taking her head out of the old cupboard in the corner. "How you scared me, Phronsie!"

"Would they *ever* go out?" asked the child gravely, still standing where Polly left her.

"What?" asked Polly, stopping with a dish of cold potatoes in her hand. "What, Phronsie?"

"Why, the candles," said the child. "The ever an' ever so many pretty lights!"

"Oh, my senses!" cried Polly with a little laugh. "Haven't you forgotten that! Yes — no, that is, Phronsie, if we could have 'em at all, we wouldn't *ever* let 'em go out!"

"Not once?" asked Phronsie, coming up to Polly with a little skip and nearly upsetting her, potatoes and all. "Not once, Polly, truly?"

"No, not forever an' ever," said Polly. "Take care, Phronsie, there goes a potato! No, we'd keep 'em always!"

"No, you don't want to," said Mrs. Pepper, coming out of the bedroom in time to catch the last words. "They won't be good tomorrow; better have them tonight, Polly."

"Ma'am!" said Polly, setting down her potato dish on the table and staring at her mother with all her might. "Have *what*, mother?"

"Why, the potatoes, to be sure," replied Mrs. Pepper. "Didn't you say you better keep them, child?"

" 'Twasn't potatoes — at all," said Polly with a little gasp. " 'Twas — dear me! Here's Ben!" For the door opened, and Phronsie, with a scream of delight, bounded into Ben's arms.

"It's just jolly," said Ben, coming in, his chubby face all aglow and his big blue eyes shining so honest and true. "It's just jolly to get home! Supper ready, Polly?"

"Yes," said Polly. "That is, all but — " And she dashed off for Phronsie's eating apron.

"Sometime," said Phronsie, with her mouth half full, when the meal was nearly over, "we're going to be *awful* rich. We are, Ben, truly?"

"No?" said Ben, affecting the most hearty astonishment. "You don't say so, chick!"

"Yes," said Phronsie, shaking her yellow head very wisely at him and diving down into her cup of very weak milk and water to see if Polly had put any sugar in by mistake — a proceeding always expectantly observed. "Yes, we are really, Bensie, very dreadful rich!"

"I wish we could be rich now, then," said Ben, taking another generous slice of the brown bread. "In time for mamsie's birthday." And he cast a sorrowful glance at Polly.

6

"I know," said Polly. "Oh, dear! If we only *could* celebrate it!"

"I don't want any other celebration," said Mrs. Pepper, beaming on them so that a little flash of sunshine seemed to hop right down on the table, "than to look round on you all. I'm rich now, and that's a fact!"

"Mamsie don't mind her five bothers," cried Polly, jumping up and running to hug her mother, thereby producing a like desire in all the others, who immediately left their seats and followed her example.

"Mother's rich enough," ejaculated Mrs. Pepper, her bright black eyes glistening with delight as the noisy troop filed back to their bread and potatoes. "If we can only keep together, dears, and grow up good, so that the little brown house won't be ashamed of us, that's all I ask."

"Well," said Polly in a burst of confidence to Ben after the table had been pushed back against the wall, the dishes nicely washed, wiped, and set up neatly in the cupboard, and all traces of the meal cleared away. "I don't care; let's *try* and get a celebration, somehow, for mamsie!"

"How are you going to do it?" asked Ben, who was of a decidedly practical turn of mind and thus couldn't always follow Polly in her flights of imagination.

"I don't know," said Polly, "but we *must* some way."

"Phoh! That's no good," said Ben disdainfully. Then, seeing Polly's face, he added kindly, "Let's think, though, and perhaps there'll be some way."

"Oh, I know," cried Polly in delight. "I know the very thing, Ben! Let's make her a cake — a big one, you know, and — "

"She'll see you bake it," said Ben, "or else she'll smell it, and that'd be just as bad."

"No, she won't either," replied Polly. "Don't you know she's going to help Mrs. Henderson tomorrow; so there!"

"So she is," said Ben. "Good for you, Polly. You always think of everything!"

"And then," said Polly with a comfortable little feeling at her heart at Ben's praise, "why, we can have it all out of the way splendidly, you know, when she comes home — and besides, Grandma Bascom'll tell me how. You know we've only got brown flour, Ben; I mean to go right over and ask her now."

"Oh, no, you mustn't," cried Ben, catching hold of her arm as she was preparing to fly off. "Mammy'll find it out; better wait till tomorrow. And besides, Polly — " And Ben stopped, unwilling to dampen this propitious beginning. "The stove'll act like everything tomorrow! I know 'twill; then what'll you do!"

"It *shan't!*" said Polly, running up to look it in the face. "If it does, I'll shake it, the mean old thing!"

The idea of Polly's shaking the lumbering old black affair sent Ben into such a peal of laughter that it brought all the other children running to the spot. And nothing would do but they must one and all be told the reason. So Polly and Ben took them into confidence, which so elated them that half an hour after, when long past her bedtime, Phronsie declared, "I'm not going to bed! I want to sit up like Polly!"

"Don't tease her," whispered Polly to Ben, who thought she ought to go. So she sat straight up on her little stool, winking like everything to keep awake.

At last, as Polly was in the midst of one of her liveliest

sallies, over tumbled Phronsie, a sleepy little heap, upon the floor.

"I want — to go — to bed!" she said. "Take me — Polly!"

"I thought so," laughed Polly, and bundled her off into the bedroom.

MAKING HAPPINESS
FOR MAMSIE

AND so, the minute her mother had departed for the minister's house next morning and Ben had gone to his day's work, chopping wood for Deacon Blodgett, Polly assembled her force around the old stove and proceeded to business. She and the children had been up betimes that morning to get through with the work; and now, as they glanced around with a look of pride on the neatly swept floor, the dishes all done, and everything in order, the moment their mother's back was turned they began to implore Polly to hurry and begin.

"It's most 'leven o'clock," said Joel, who, having no work to do outside that day, was prancing around, wild to help along the festivities. "It's most 'leven o'clock, Polly Pepper! You won't have it done."

"Oh, no, 'tisn't either, Joe," said Polly with a very flushed face, and her arms full of kindlings, glancing up at the old clock as she spoke: " 'Tisn't but quarter of nine; there, take care, Phronsie! You can't lift off the cover. Do help her, Davie."

"No, let me!" cried Joel, springing forward. "It's my

turn. Dave got the shingles; it's my turn, Polly."

"So 'tis," said Polly. "I forgot, there," as she flung in the wood and poked it all up in a nice little heap coaxingly. "It can't help but burn; what a cake we'll have for mamsie!"

"It'll be so big," cried Phronsie, hopping around on one set of toes, "that mamsie won't know what to do, will she, Polly?"

"No, I don't believe she will," said Polly gaily, stuffing in more wood. "Oh, *dear!* There goes Ben's putty; it's all come out!"

"So it has," said Joel, going around back of the stove to explore. And then he added cheerfully, "It's bigger'n ever. Oh! It's an awful big hole, Polly!"

"Now, whatever shall we do!" said Polly in great distress. "That *hateful* old crack! And Ben's clear off to Deacon Blodgett's!"

"I'll run and get him," cried Joel briskly. "I'll bring him right home in ten minutes."

"Oh, no, you must not, Joe," cried Polly in alarm. "It wouldn't ever be right to take him off from his work; mamsie wouldn't like it."

"What will you do, then?" asked Joel, pausing on his way to the door.

"I'm sure I don't know," said Polly, getting down on her knees to examine the crack. "I shall have to stuff it with paper, I s'pose."

" 'Twon't stay in," said Joel scornfully. "Don't you know you stuffed it before, last week?"

"I know," said Polly with a small sigh. And sitting down on the floor, she remained quite still for a minute, with her two black hands thrust out straight before her.

"Can't you fix it?" asked Davie soberly, coming up. "Then we can't have the cake."

"Dear me!" exclaimed Polly, springing up quickly. "Don't be afraid; we're going to *have* that cake! There, you ugly old thing, you!" (This to the stove.) "See what you've done!" Two big tears flew out of Phronsie's brown eyes at the direful prospect, and the sorrowful faces of the two boys looked up into Polly's own for comfort. "I can fix it, I most know. Do get some paper, Joe, as quick as you can."

"Don't know where there is any," said Joel, rummaging around. "It's all tore up, 'xcept, the almanac. Can't I take that?"

"Oh, dear, no!" cried Polly. "Put it right back, Joe. I guess there's some in the woodshed."

"There isn't either," said little Davie quickly. "Joel and I took it to make kites with."

"Oh, dear," groaned Polly. "I don't know what we *shall* do; unless" — as a bright thought struck her — "you let me have the kites, boys."

"Can't," said Joel. "They're all flew away and torn up."

"Well, now, children," said Polly, turning round impressively upon them, the effect of which was heightened by the extremely crocky appearance she had gained in her explorations, "we *must* have some paper, or something to stop up that old hole with — some way, there!"

"I know," said little Davie, "where we'll get it; it's upstairs." And without another word he flew out of the room, and in another minute he put into Polly's hand an old leather boot top, one of his most treasured possessions. "You can chip it," he said, "real fine, and then 'twill go in."

"So we can," said Polly. "And you're a real good boy, Davie, to give it. That's a splendid present to help celebrate for mamsie!"

"I'd a-given a boot top," said Joel, looking grimly at the precious bit of leather which Polly was rapidly stripping into little bits, "if I'd a-hed it; I don't have anything!"

"I know you would, Joey," said Polly kindly. "There now, you'll stay, I guess!" as with the united efforts of the two boys, cheered on by Phronsie's enthusiastic little crow of delight, the leather was crowded into place, and the fire began to burn.

"Now, boys," said Polly, getting up and drawing a long breath, "I'm going over to Grandma Bascom's to get her to tell me how to make the cake; and you must stay and keep house."

"I'm going to nail," said Joel. "I've got lots to do."

"All right," said Polly, tying on her hood. "Phronsie'll love to watch you; I won't be gone long," and she was off.

"Grandma Bascom" wasn't really the children's grandmother, only everybody in the village called her so by courtesy. Her cottage was over across the lane and just a bit around the corner; and Polly flew along and up to the door, fully knowing that now she would be helped out of her difficulty. She didn't stop to knock, as the old lady was so deaf she knew she wouldn't hear her, but opened the door and walked in. Grandma was sweeping up the floor, already as neat as a pin. When she saw

Polly coming, she stopped and leaned on her broom.

"How's your ma?" she asked, when Polly had said "good morning," and then hesitated.

"Oh, mammy's pretty well," shouted Polly into the old lady's ear. "And tomorrow's her birthday!"

"Tomorrow'll be a bad day!" said grandma. "Oh, don't never say that. You mustn't borrow trouble, child."

"I didn't," said Polly. "I mean — it's her *birthday*, grandma!" This last so loud that grandma's cap border vibrated perceptibly.

"The land's sakes 'tis!" cried Mrs. Bascom delightedly. "You don't say so!"

"Yes," said Polly, skipping around the old lady and giving her a small hug. "And we're going to give her a surprise."

"What is the matter with her eyes?" asked grandma sharply, turning around and facing her. "She's been a-sewin' too stiddy, hain't she?"

"A *surprise!*" shouted Polly, standing upon tiptoe, to bring her mouth on a level with the old lady's ear. "A *cake*, grandma, a big one!"

"A *cake!*" exclaimed grandma, dropping the broom to settle her cap, which Polly in her extreme endeavors to carry on the conversation had knocked slightly awry. "Well, that'll be fine."

"Yes," said Polly, picking up the broom and flinging off her hood at the same time. "And, oh! Won't you please tell me how to make it, grandma!"

"To be sure, to be sure," cried the old lady, delighted beyond measure to give advice. "I've got splendid re-ceets; I'll go get 'em right off," and she ambled to the door of the pantry.

14

"And I'll finish sweeping up," said Polly, which grandma didn't hear; so she took up the broom and sent it energetically and merrily flying away to the tune of her own happy thoughts.

"Yes, they're right in here," said grandma, waddling back with an old tin teapot in her hand. "Goodness, child! What a dust you've kicked up! That ain't the way to sweep." And she took the broom out of Polly's hand, who stood quite still in mortification.

"There," she said, drawing it mildly over the few bits she could scrape together and gently coaxing them into a little heap. "That's the way; and then they don't go all over the room."

"I'm sorry," began poor Polly.

" 'Tain't any matter," said Mrs. Bascom kindly, catching sight of Polly's discomfited face. " 'Tain't a mite of matter; you'll sweep better next time. Now let's go to the cake." And putting the broom into the corner, she waddled back again to the table, followed by Polly, and proceeded to turn out the contents of the teapot, in search of just the right "receet."

But the right one didn't seem to appear; not even after the teapot was turned upside down and shaken by both grandma's and Polly's anxious hands. Every other "receet" seemed to tumble out gladly and stare them in the face — little dingy rolls of yellow paper, with an ancient odor of spice still clinging to them. But all efforts to find this particular one failed utterly.

"Won't some other one do?" asked Polly in the interval of fruitless searching, when grandma bewailed and lamented and wondered, "Where I could a-put it!"

"No, no, child," answered the old lady. "Now, where

do you s'pose 'tis!" And she clapped both hands to her head to see if she could possibly remember. "No, no, child," she repeated. "Why, they had it down to my niece Mirandy's weddin' — 'twas just elegant! Light as a feather; and 'twan't rich either," she added. "No eggs, nor — "

"Oh, I couldn't have *eggs,*" cried Polly in amazement at the thought of such luxury. "And we've only brown flour, grandma, you know."

"Well, you can make it of brown," said Mrs. Bascom kindly. "When the raisins is in 'twill look quite nice."

"Oh, we haven't any raisins," answered Polly.

"Haven't any raisins!" echoed grandma, looking at her over her spectacles. "What are you goin' to put in?"

"Oh — cinnamon," said Polly briskly. "We've got plenty of that, and — it'll be good, I guess, grandma!" she finished anxiously. "Anyway, we must have a cake; there isn't any other way to celebrate mamsie's birthday."

"Well, now," said grandma, bustling around. "I shouldn't be surprised if you had real good luck, Polly. And your ma'll set ever so much by it. Now, if we only could find that receet!" And returning to the charge, she commenced to fumble among her bits of paper again. "I never shall forget how they eat on it. Why, there wasn't a crumb left, Polly!"

"Oh, dear," said Polly, to whom "Mirandy's wedding cake" now became the height of her desires. "If you only can find it! Can't I climb up and look on the pantry shelves?"

"Maybe 'tis there," said Mrs. Bascom slowly. "You might try. Sometimes I do put things away, so's to have 'em safe."

16

So Polly got an old wooden chair, according to direction, and then mounted up on it, with grandma below to direct. She handed down bowl after bowl, interspersed at the right intervals with cracked teacups and handleless pitchers. But at the end of these explorations, "Mirandy's wedding cake" was further off than ever.

" 'Tain't a mite o' use," at last said the old lady, sinking down in despair, while Polly perched on the top of the chair and looked at her. "I must a-give it away."

"Can't I have the next best one, then?" asked Polly despairingly, feeling sure that "Mirandy's wedding cake" would have celebrated the day just right. "And I must hurry right home, please," she added, getting down from the chair and tying on her hood, "or Phronsie won't know what to do."

So another "receet" was looked over and selected. And with many charges, and bits of advice not to let the oven get too hot, etc., etc., Polly took the precious bit in her hand and flew over home.

"Now, we've got to — " she began, bounding in merrily, with dancing eyes. But her delight had a sudden stop, as she brought up so suddenly at the sight within that she couldn't utter another word. Phronsie was crouching, a miserable little heap of woe, in one corner of the mother's big calico-covered rocking chair, and crying bitterly, while Joel hung over her in the utmost concern.

"What's the matter?" gasped Polly. Flinging the "receet" on the table, she rushed up to the old chair and was down on her knees before it, her arms around the little figure. Phronsie turned and threw herself into Polly's protecting arms, who gathered her up, and sitting

17

down in the depths of the chair, comforted her as only she could.

"What is it?" she asked of Joel, who was nervously begging Phronsie not to cry. "Now, tell me all that's happened."

"I was a-nailing," began Joel. "Oh, dear! Don't cry, Phronsie! Do stop her, Polly."

"Go on," said Polly hoarsely.

"I was a-nailing," began Joel slowly, "and — and — Davie's gone to get the peppermint," he added, brightening up.

"Tell me, Joe," said Polly, "all that's been going on," and she looked sternly into his face, "or I'll get Davie to," as little Davie came running back with a bottle of castor oil, which in his flurry he had mistaken for peppermint. This he presented with a flourish to Polly, who was too excited to see it.

"Oh no!" cried Joel in intense alarm. "Davie isn't going to! I'll tell, Polly; I will truly."

"Go on, then," said Polly, "tell at once" (feeling that if somebody didn't tell pretty quick, she would tumble over).

"Well," said Joel, gathering himself up with a fresh effort, "the old hammer was a-shaking and Phronsie stuck her foot in the way — and — I couldn't help it, Polly — no, I just couldn't, Polly."

Quick as a flash, Polly tore off the little old shoe and well-worn stocking and brought to light Phronsie's fat little foot. Tenderly taking hold of the white toes, the boys clustering around in the greatest anxiety, she worked them back and forth and up and down. "Nothing's broken," she said at last, and drew a long breath.

18

"It's there," said Phronsie through a rain of tears, "and it hurts, Polly." And she began to wiggle the big toe, where around the nail was settling a small black spot.

"Poor little toe," began Polly, cuddling up the suffering foot. Just then a small and peculiar noise struck her ear, and looking up, she saw Joel, with a very distorted face, making violent efforts to keep from bursting out into a loud cry. All his attempts, however, failed, and he flung himself into Polly's lap in a perfect torrent of tears. "I didn't — mean to — Polly," he cried. " 'Twas the — ugly, old hammer! *Oh, dear!*"

"There, there, Joey, dear," said Polly, gathering him up in the other corner of the old chair, close to her side. "Don't feel bad. I know you didn't mean to," and she dropped a kiss on his stubby black hair.

When Phronsie saw that anybody else could cry, she stopped immediately and, leaning over Polly, put one little fat hand on Joel's neck. "Don't cry," she said. "Does *your* toe ache?"

At this Joel screamed louder than ever, and Polly was at her wit's end to know what to do, for the boy's heart was almost broken. That he should have hurt Phronsie — the baby, the pet of the whole house, upon whom all their hearts centered — it was too much. So for the next few moments, Polly had all she could do by way of comforting and consoling him. Just as she had succeeded, the door opened, and Grandma Bascom walked in.

"Settin' down?" said she. "I hope your cake ain't in, Polly," looking anxiously at the stove, "for I've found it." And she waved a small piece of paper triumphantly toward the rocking chair as she spoke.

"Do tell her," said Polly to little David, "what's happened, for I can't get up."

So little Davie went up to the old lady and, standing on tiptoe, screamed into her ear all the particulars he could think of concerning the accident that had just happened.

"Hey?" said grandma, in a perfect bewilderment. "What's he a-sayin', Polly — I can't make it out."

"You'll have to go all over it again, David," said Polly despairingly. "She didn't hear one word, I don't believe."

So David tried again, this time with better success. And then he got down from his tiptoes and escorted grandma to Phronsie in flushed triumph.

"Land alive!" said the old lady, sitting down in the chair which he brought her. "You got pounded, did you?" looking at Phronsie as she took the little foot in her ample hand.

"Yes'm," said Polly quickly. " 'Twasn't anyone's fault. What'll we do for it, grandma?"

"Wormwood," said the old lady, adjusting her spectacles in extreme deliberation and then examining the little black-and-blue spot, which was spreading rapidly, "is the very best thing; and I've got some to home — you run right over," she said, turning round on David quickly, "an' get it; it's a-hangin' by the chimbley."

"Let me, let me!" cried Joel, springing out of the old chair so suddenly that grandma's spectacles nearly dropped off in fright. "Oh! I want to do it for Phronsie!"

"Yes, let Joel, please," put in Polly. "He'll find it, grandma."

So Joel departed with great speed, and presently returned with a bunch of dry herbs, which dangled comfortingly by his side as he came in.

"Now I'll fix it," said Mrs. Bascom, getting up and taking off her shawl. "There's a few raisins for you, Polly; I don't want 'em, and they'll make your cake go better." And she placed a little parcel on the table as she spoke. "Yes, I'll put it to steep; an' after it's put on real strong, and tied up in an old cloth, Phronsie won't know as she's got any toes!" and grandma broke up a generous supply of the herb and put it into an old tin cup, which she covered up with a saucer and placed on the stove.

"Oh!" said Polly. "I can't thank you! For the raisins and all — you're so good!"

"They're awful hard," said Joel, investigating into the bundle with Davie, which, however, luckily the old lady didn't hear.

"There, don't cry," she said cheerily. "An' I found cousin Mirandy's weddin' cake receet, for — "

"Did you?" cried Polly. "Oh! I'm so glad!" feeling as if that were comfort enough for a good deal.

"Yes, 'twas in my Bible," said Mrs. Bascom. "I remember now; I put it there to be ready to give John's folks when they come in. They wanted it. So you'll go all straight now. And I must get home, for I left some meat a-boilin'." So grandma put on her shawl, and waddled off, leaving a great deal of comfort behind her.

"Now, says I," said Polly to Phronsie, when the little foot was snugly tied up in the wet wormwood, "you've got to have on one of mamsie's old slippers."

"Oh, ho," laughed Phronsie. "Won't that be funny, Polly!"

21

"I should think it would," laughed Polly, back again, pulling on the big cloth slipper that Joel produced from the bedroom, the two boys joining uproariously as the old black thing flapped dismally up and down and showed strong symptoms of flying off. "We shall have to tie it on."

"It looks like a pudding bag," said Joel as Polly tied it securely through the middle with a bit of twine. "An old black pudding bag!" he finished.

"Old black pudding bag!" echoed Phronsie, with a merry little crow; and then all of a sudden she grew very sober and looked intently at the foot thrust out straight before her as she still sat in the chair.

"What is it, Phronsie?" asked Polly, who was bustling around, making preparations for the cake making.

"Can I *ever* wear my new shoes again?" asked the child gravely, looking dismally at the black bundle before her.

"Oh, yes; my goodness, yes!" cried Polly. "As quick again as ever. You'll be around again as smart as a cricket in a week — see if you aren't!"

"Will it go on?" asked Phronsie, still looking incredulously at the bundle. "And button up?"

"Yes, indeed!" cried Polly again. "Button into every one of the little holes, Phronsie Pepper, just as elegant as ever!"

"Oh!" said Phronsie. And then she gave a sigh of relief, and thought no more of it, because Polly had said that all would be right.

MAMSIE'S BIRTHDAY

"RUN down and get the cinnamon, will you, Joey?" said Polly. "It's in the Provision Room."

The Provision Room was a little shed that was tacked on to the main house and reached by a short flight of rickety steps; so called, because, as Polly said, " 'Twas a good place to keep provisions in, even if we haven't any. And besides," she always finished, "it sounds nice!"

"Come on, Dave! Then we'll get something to eat!"

So the cinnamon was handed up, and then Joel flew back to Davie.

And now Polly's cake was done and ready for the oven. With many admiring glances from herself and Phronsie, who with Seraphina, an extremely old but greatly revered doll, tightly hugged in her arms, was watching everything with the biggest of eyes from the depths of the old chair, it was placed in the oven, the door shut to with a happy little bang, and then Polly gathered Phronsie up in her arms and sat down in the chair to have a good time with her and to watch the process of cooking.

There was a bumping noise that came from the Provision Room that sounded ominous, and then a smothered sound of words, followed by a scuffling over the old floor.

"Boys!" called Polly. No answer; everything was just as still as a mouse. *"Joel and David!"* called Polly again, in her loudest tones.

"Yes," came up the crooked stairs, in Davie's voice.

"Come up here, right away!" went back again from Polly. So up the stairs trudged the two boys, and presented themselves rather sheepishly before the big chair.

"What was that noise?" she asked. "What have you been doing?"

" 'Twasn't anything but the pail," answered Joel, not looking at her.

"We had something to eat," said Davie, by way of explanation. "You always let us."

"I know," said Polly. "That's right, you can have as much bread as you want to. But what have you been doing with the pail?"

"Nothing," said Joel. " 'Twouldn't hang up, that's all."

"And you've been bumping it," said Polly. "Oh, Joel, how could you! You might have broken it; then what would mamsie say?"

"I didn't," said Joel stoutly, with his hands in his pockets, "bump it worse'n Davie, so there!"

"Why, Davie," said Polly, turning to him sorrowfully, "I shouldn't have thought *you* would!"

"Well, I'm tired of hanging it up," said little Davie vehemently. "And I said I wasn't a-goin' to. Joel always makes me; I've done it for two million times, I guess!"

"Oh, dear," said Polly, sinking back into the chair, "I don't know what I ever shall do. Here's Phronsie hurt,

24

and we want to celebrate tomorrow, and you two boys are bumping and banging out the bread pail, and — "

"Oh! We won't!" cried both of the children, perfectly overwhelmed with remorse. "We'll hang it right up."

"I'll hang it," said Davie, clattering off down the stairs with a will.

"No, *I* will!" shouted Joel, going after him at double pace. And presently both came up with shining faces and reported it nicely done.

"And now," said Polly after they had all sat around the stove another half hour, watching and sniffing expectantly, "the cake's done — dear me! It's turning black!"

And quickly as possible Polly twitched it out with energy and set it on the table.

Oh, dear. Of all things in the world! The beautiful cake over which so many hopes had been formed — that was to have given so much happiness on the morrow to the dear mother — presented a forlorn appearance as it stood there in anything but holiday attire. It was quite black on the top, in the center of which was a depressing little dump, as if to say, "My feelings wouldn't allow me to rise to the occasion."

"Now," said Polly, turning away with a little fling and looking at the stove, "I hope you're satisfied, you old thing. You've spoiled our mamsie's birthday!" and without a bit of warning she sat right down in the middle of the floor and began to cry as hard as she could.

"Well I never!" said a cheery voice that made the children skip.

"It's Mrs. Beebe. Oh, it's Mrs. Beebe!" cried Davie. "See, Polly."

Polly scrambled up to her feet, ashamed to be caught thus, and whisked away the tears; the others explaining to their new visitor the sad disappointment that had befallen them; and she was soon oh-ing and ah-ing enough to suit even their distressed little souls.

"You poor creeters, you!" she exclaimed at last, for about the fiftieth time. "Here, Polly, here's some posies for you, and — "

"Oh, thank you!" cried Polly with a radiant face. "Why, Mrs. Beebe, we can put them in here, can't we? The very thing!"

And she set the little know of flowers in the hollow of the cake, and there they stood and nodded away to the delighted children like brave little comforters, as they were.

"The very thing!" echoed Mrs. Beebe, tickled to death to see their delight. "It looks beautiful, I declare! And now I must run right along, or pa'll be worrying." And so the good woman trotted out to her waiting husband, who was impatient to be off. Mr. Beebe kept a little shoe shop in town. And always being of the impression if he left it for ten minutes that crowds of customers would visit it, he was the most restless of companions on any pleasure excursion.

"And Phronsie's got hurt," said Mrs. Beebe, telling him the news as he finished tucking her up and started the old horse.

"Ho? You don't say so!" he cried. *"Whoa!"*

"Dear me!" said Mrs. Beebe. "How you scat me, pa! What's the matter?"

"What? The little girl that bought the shoes?" asked her husband.

"Yes," replied his wife. "She's hurt her foot."

"Sho, now," said the old gentlemen, "that's too bad," and he began to feel in all his pockets industriously. "There, can you get out again and take her that?" And he laid a small piece of peppermint candy, thick and white, in his wife's lap.

"Oh, yes," cried Mrs. Beebe good-naturedly, beginning to clamber over the wheel.

So the candy was handed in to Phronsie, who insisted that Polly should hold her up to the window to thank Mr. Beebe. So amid nods and shakings of hands, the Beebes drove off, and quiet settled down over the little brown house again.

"Now, children," said Polly after Phronsie had made them take a bite of her candy all around, "let's get the cake put away safe, for mamsie may come home early."

"Where'll you put it?" asked Joel, wishing the world was all peppermint candy.

"Oh — in the cupboard," said Polly, taking it up. "There, Joe, you can climb up and put it clear back in the corner — oh! Wait. I must take the posies off, and keep them fresh in water." So the cake was finally deposited in a place of safety, followed by the eyes of all the children.

"Now," said Polly as they shut the door tight, "don't you go to looking at the cupboard, Joey, or mammy'll guess something."

"Can't I just open it a little crack and take one smell when she isn't looking?" asked Joel. "I should think you might, Polly; just *one*."

"No," said Polly firmly. "Not one, Joe; she'll guess if you do."

But Mrs. Pepper was so utterly engrossed with her baby when she came home and heard the account of the accident that she wouldn't have guessed if there'd been a dozen cakes in the cupboard. Joel was consoled, as his mother assured him in a satisfactory way that she never should think of blaming him; and Phronsie was comforted and coddled to her heart's content. And so the evening passed rapidly and happily away, Ben smuggling Phronsie off into a corner, where she told him all the doings of the day — the disappointment of the cake, and how it was finally crowned with flowers; all of which Phronsie, with no small pride in being the narrator, related gravely to her absorbed listener. "And don't you think, Bensie," she said, clasping her little hand in a convincing way over his two bigger, stronger ones, "that Polly's stove was *very* naughty to make poor Polly cry?"

"Yes, I do," said Ben, and he shut his lips tightly together. To have Polly cry hurt him more than he cared to have Phronsie see.

"What are you staring at, Joe?" asked Polly a few minutes later as her eyes fell upon Joel, who sat with his back to the cupboard, persistently gazing at the opposite wall.

"Why, you told me yourself not to look at the cupboard," said Joel in the loudest of stage whispers.

"Dear me. That'll make mammy suspect worse'n anything else if you look like that," said Polly.

"What did you say about the cupboard?" asked Mrs. Pepper, who caught Joe's last word.

"We can't tell," said Phronsie, "shaking her head at her mother, " 'cause there's a ca — "

"Ugh!" and Polly clapped her hand on the child's

mouth. "Don't you want Ben to tell us a story?"

"Oh, yes!" cried little Phronsie, in which all the others joined with a whoop of delight. So a most wonderful story, drawn up in Ben's best style, followed till bedtime.

The first thing Polly did in the morning was to run to the old cupboard, followed by all the others, to see if the cake was safe; and then it had to be drawn out, and dressed anew with the flowers, for they had decided to have it on the breakfast table.

"It looks better," whispered Polly to Ben, "than it did yesterday. And aren't the flowers pretty?"

"It looks good enough to eat, anyway," said Ben, smacking his lips.

"Well, we tried," said Polly, stifling a sigh. "Now, boys, call mamsie; everything's ready."

Oh! How surprised their mother appeared when she was ushered out to the feast, and the full glory of the table burst upon her. Her delight in the cake was fully enough to satisfy the most exacting mind. She admired and admired it on every side, protesting that she shouldn't have supposed Polly could possibly have baked it as good in the old stove; and then she cut it, and gave a piece to every child, with a little posy on top. Wasn't it good, though! For like many other things, the cake proved better on trial than it looked, and so turned out to be really quite a good surprise all around.

"Why can't I ever have a birthday?" asked Joel, finishing the last crumb of his piece. "I should think I might," he added reflectively.

"Why, you have, Joe," said Ben. "Eight of 'em."

"What a story!" ejaculated Joel. "When did I have 'em? I *never* had a cake, did I, Polly?"

"Not a cake birthday, Joel," said his mother. "You haven't got to that yet."

"When's it coming?" asked Joel, who was decidedly of a matter-of-fact turn of mind.

"I don't know," said Mrs. Pepper, laughing, "but there's plenty of time ahead."

TROUBLE FOR THE LITTLE BROWN HOUSE

"Oн, I do wish," said Joel a few mornings after, pushing back his chair and looking discontentedly at his bowl of mush and molasses, "that we could ever have something new besides this everlasting old breakfast! Why can't we, mammy?"

"Better be glad you've got that, Joe," said Mrs. Pepper, taking another cold potato, and sprinkling on a little salt. "Folks shouldn't complain so long as they've anything to eat."

"But I'm so tired of it — same old thing!" growled Joel. "Seems as if I sh'd turn into a meal bag or a molasses jug!"

"Well, hand it over, then," proposed Ben, who was unusually hungry and had a hard day's work before him.

"No," said Joel, alarmed at the prospect, and putting in an enormous mouthful. "It's better than nothing."

"Oh, dear," said little Phronsie, catching Joel's tone. "It isn't nice; no, it isn't." And she put down her spoon so suddenly that the molasses spun off in a big drop that trailed off the corner of the table and made Polly jump up and run for the floor cloth.

"Oh, Phronsie," she said reprovingly, "you ought not to. Never mind, pet," as she caught sight of two big tears trying to make a path in the little molasses-streaked face. "Polly'll wipe it up."

"Shan't we ever have anything else to eat, Polly?" asked the child gravely, getting down from her high chair to watch the operation of cleaning the floor.

"Oh, yes," said Polly cheerfully. "Lots and lots — when our ship comes in."

"What'll they be?" asked Phronsie, in the greatest delight, prepared for anything.

"Oh, I don't know," said Polly. "Ice cream, for one thing, Phronsie, and maybe little cakes."

"With pink on top?" interrupted Phronsie, getting down by Polly's side.

"Oh, yes," said Polly, warming to her subject. "Ever and ever so much pink, Phronsie Pepper; more than you could eat!"

Phronsie just clasped her hands and sighed. More than she could eat was beyond her!

"Hoh!" said Joel, who caught the imaginary bill of fare. "That's nothing, Polly. I'd speak for a plum puddin'."

"Like the one mother made us for Thanksgiving?" asked Polly, getting up and waiting a minute, cloth in hand, for the answer.

"Yes, sir," said Joel, shutting one eye and looking up at the ceiling musingly while he smacked his lips in remembrance. "Wasn't that prime, though!"

"Yes," said Polly thoughtfully. "Would you have 'em all like that, Joe?"

"Every one," replied Joe promptly. "I'd have seventy-five of 'em."

"Seventy-five what?" asked Mrs. Pepper, who had gone into the bedroom, and now came out, a coat in hand, to sit down in the west window, where she began to sew rapidly. "Better clear up the dishes, Polly, and set the table back. Seventy-five what, Joel?"

"Plum puddings," said Joel, kissing Phronsie.

"Dear me!" ejaculated Mrs. Pepper. "You don't know what you're saying, Joel Pepper. The house couldn't hold 'em!"

"Wouldn't long," responded Joel. "We'd eat 'em."

"That would be foolish," interposed Ben. "I'd have roast beef and fixings — and oysters — and huckleberry pie."

"Oh, dear," cried Polly. "How nice, Ben! You always do think of the very best things."

But Joel phoohed and declared he wouldn't waste his time "over old beef; he'd have something nice!" And then he cried, "Come on, Dave, what'd you choose?"

Little Davie had been quietly eating his breakfast amid all this chatter, and somehow thinking it might make the mother feel badly, he had refrained from saying just how tiresome he had really found this "everlasting breakfast," as Joel called it. But now he looked up eagerly, his answer all ready. "Oh, I know," he cried, "what would be most beautiful! Toasted bread — white bread — and candy."

"What's candy?" asked Phronsie.

"Oh, don't you know, Phronsie," cried Polly. "What Mrs. Beebe gave you the day you got your shoes — the pink sticks; and — "

"And the peppermint stick Mr. Beebe gave you, Phronsie," finished Joel, his mouth watering at the remembrance.

"That day when you got your toe pounded," added Davie, looking at Joel.

"Oh!" cried Phronsie. "I want some now, I do!"

"Well, Davie," said Polly, "you shall have that for breakfast when our ship comes in, then."

"Your ships aren't ever coming," broke in Mrs. Pepper wisely, "if you sit there talking. Folks don't ever make any fortunes by wishing."

"True enough," laughed Ben, jumping up and setting back his chair. "Come on, Joe. You've got to pile today."

"Oh, dear," said Joel dismally. "I wish Mr. Blodgett's wood was all afire."

"Never say that, Joel," said Mrs. Pepper, looking up sternly. "It's biting your own nose off to wish that wood was afire — and besides, it's dreadfully wicked."

Joel hung his head, for his mother never spoke in that way unless she was strongly moved. But he soon recovered and hastened off for his jacket.

"I'm sorry I can't help you do the dishes, Polly," said David, running after Joel.

"I'm going to help her," said Phronsie. "I am."

So Polly got the little wooden tub that she always used, gave Phronsie the well-worn cup napkin, and allowed her to wipe the handleless cups and cracked saucers, which afforded the little one intense delight.

"Don't you wish, Polly," said little Phronsie, bustling around with a very important air, nearly smothered in the depths of a big brown apron that Polly had carefully tied under her chin, "that you didn't ever an' ever have so many dishes to do?"

"Um — maybe," said Polly thoughtlessly. She was thinking of something else besides cups and saucers just then — of how nice it would be to go off for just one day and do exactly as she had a mind to in everything. She even envied Ben and the boys who were going to work hard at Deacon Blodgett's woodpile.

"Well, I tell you," said Phronsie confidentially, setting down a cup that she had polished with great care, "I'm going to do 'em all tomorrow for you, Polly — I can truly. Let me now, Polly, *do*."

"Nonsense!" said Polly, giving a great splash with her mop in the tub, ashamed of her inward repinings. "Phronsie, you're no bigger than a mouse!"

"Yes, I am," retorted Phronsie very indignantly. Her face began to get very red, and she straightened up so suddenly to show Polly just how very big she was that her little head came up against the edge of the tub. Over it went! A pile of saucers followed.

"There, now," cried Polly, "see what you've done!"

"Ow!" whimpered Phronsie, breaking into a subdued roar. "Oh, Polly! It's all running down my back."

"Is it?" said Polly, bursting out into a laugh. "Never mind, Phronsie, I'll dry you."

"Dear me, Polly!" said Mrs. Pepper, who had looked up in time to see the tub racing along by itself toward the Provision Room door, a stream of dishwater following in its wake. "She will be wet clear through; do get off her things, quick."

"Yes'm," cried Polly, picking up the tub and giving

two or three quick sops to the floor. "Here you are, Pussy," grasping Phronsie, crying as she was, and carrying her into the bedroom.

"Oh, dear," wailed the child, still holding the wet dish towel. "I won't ever do it again, if you'll only let me do 'em all tomorrow."

"When you're big and strong," said Polly, giving her a hug, "you shall do 'em every day."

"May I really?" said little Phronsie, blinking through the tears and looking radiant.

"Yes, truly — every day."

"Then I'll grow right away, I will," said Phronsie, bursting out merrily. And she sat down and pulled off the well-worn shoes, into which a big pool of dishwater had run, while Polly went for dry stockings.

"So you shall," said Polly, coming back, a big piece of gingerbread in her hand. "And this'll make you grow, Phronsie."

"*O-o-h!*" And Phronsie's little white teeth shut down quickly on the comforting morsel. Gingerbread didn't come often enough into the Pepper household to be lightly esteemed.

"Now," said Mrs. Pepper when order was restored, the floor washed up brightly, and every cup and platter in place, hobnobbing away to themselves on the shelves of the old corner cupboard, and Polly had come as usual with needle and thread to help mother — Polly was getting so that she could do the plain parts on the coats and jackets, which filled her with pride at the very thought. "Now," said Mrs. Pepper, "you needn't help me this morning, Polly; I'm getting on pretty smart. But you may just run down to the parson's and see how he is."

"Is he sick?" asked Polly in awe.

To have the parson sick was something quite different from an ordinary person's illness.

"He's taken with a chill," said Mrs. Pepper, biting off a thread, "so Miss Huldy Folsom told me last night, and I'm afraid he's going to have a fever."

"Oh, dear," said Polly in dire distress. "Whatever'd we do, mammy!"

"Don't know, I'm sure," replied Mrs. Pepper, setting her stitches firmly. "The Lord'll provide. So you run along, child, and see how he is."

"Can't Phronsie go?" asked Polly, pausing halfway to the bedroom door.

"Well, yes, I suppose she might," said Mrs. Pepper assentingly.

"No, she can't either," said Polly, coming back with her sun bonnet in her hand and shutting the door carefully after her, " 'cause she's fast asleep on the floor."

"Is she?" said Mrs. Pepper. "Well, she's been running so this morning, she's tired out, I 'spose."

"And her face is dreadfully red," continued Polly, tying on her bonnet. "Now, what'll I say, mammy?"

"Well, I should think 'twould be," said Mrs. Pepper, replying to the first half of Polly's speech. "She cried so. Well, you just tell Mrs. Henderson your ma wants to know how Mr. Henderson is this morning, and if 'twas a chill he had yesterday, and how he slept last night, and — "

"Oh, ma," said Polly, "I can't ever remember all that."

"Oh, yes, you can," said Mrs. Pepper encouragingly. "Just put your mind on it, Polly; 'tisn't anything to what I used to have to remember when I was a little girl, no bigger than you are."

Polly sighed, and feeling sure that something must be the matter with her mind, gave her whole attention to the errand; till at last after a multiplicity of messages and charges not to forget any one of them, Mrs. Pepper let her depart.

Up to the old-fashioned green door, with its brass knocker, Polly went, running over in her mind just which of the messages she ought to give first. She couldn't for her life think whether "if 'twas a chill he had yesterday" ought to come before "how he slept." She knocked timidly, hoping Mrs. Henderson would help her out of her difficulty by telling her without asking. All other front doors in Badgertown were ornaments, only opened on grand occasions, like a wedding or a funeral. But the minister's was accessible alike to all. So Polly let fall the knocker and awaited the answer.

A scuffling noise sounded along the passage, and then Polly's soul sank down in dire dismay. It was the minister's sister and not gentle little Mrs. Henderson. She never could get on with Miss Jerusha in the least. She made her feel, as she told her mother once, "as if I don't know what my name is." And now here she was; and all those messages.

Miss Jerusha unbolted the door, slid back the great bar, opened the upper half, and stood there. She was a big woman, with sharp black eyes, and spectacles over which she looked, which to Polly was much worse, for that gave her four eyes.

"Well, and what do you want?" she asked.

"I came to see — I mean my ma sent me," stammered poor Polly.

"And who is your ma?" demanded Miss Jerusha, as much like a policeman as anything. "And where do you live?"

"I live in Primrose Lane," replied Polly, wishing very much that she was back there.

"I don't want to know where you live before I know who you are," said Miss Jerusha. "You should answer the question I asked first; always remember that."

"My ma's Mrs. Pepper," said Polly.

"Mrs. who?" repeated Miss Jerusha.

By this time Polly was so worn that she came very near turning and fleeing, but she thought of her mother's disappointment in her, and the loss of the news, and stood quite still.

"What is it, Jerusha?" a gentle voice here broke upon Polly's ear.

"I don't know," responded Miss Jerusha tartly, still holding the door much as if Polly were a robber. "It's a little girl, and I can't make out what she wants."

"Why, it's Polly Pepper!" exclaimed Mrs. Henderson pleasantly. "Come in, child." She opened the other half of the big door and led the way through the wide hall into a big, old-fashioned room with painted floor and high, old sideboard and some stiff-backed rocking chairs.

Miss Jerusha stalked in also and seated herself by the window, and began to knit. Polly had just opened her mouth to tell her errand when the door also opened suddenly and Mr. Henderson walked in.

"*Oh!*" said Polly, and then she stopped, and the color flushed up into her face.

"What is it, my dear?" And the minister took her hand kindly and looked down into her flushed face.

"You are not going to have a fever, and be sick and die!" she cried.

"I hope not, my little girl." He smiled back encouragingly, and then Polly gave her messages, which now she managed easily enough.

"There," broke in Miss Jerusha, "a cat can't sneeze in this town but everybody'll know it in quarter of an hour."

And then Mrs. Henderson took Polly out to see a brood of new little chicks that had just popped their heads out into the world; and to Polly, down on her knees, admiring, the time passed very swiftly indeed.

"Now I must go, ma'am," she said at last, looking up into the lady's face regretfully, "for mammy didn't say I was to stay."

"Very well, dear. Do you think you could carry a little pat of butter? I have some very nice my sister sent me, and I want your mother to share it."

"Oh, thank you, ma'am!" cried Polly, thinking, "How glad Davie'll be, for he does so love butter! Only — "

"Wait a bit, then," said Mrs. Henderson, who didn't seem to notice the objection. So she went into the house, and Polly went down again in admiration before the fascinating little puffballs.

But she was soon on the way with a little pat of butter in a blue bowl, tied over with a clean cloth; happy in her gift for mammy and in the knowledge of the minister being all well.

40

"I wonder if Phronsie's awake," she thought to herself, turning in at the little brown gate. "If she is, she shall have a piece of bread with lots of butter."

"*Hush!*" said Mrs. Pepper from the rocking chair in the middle of the floor. She had something in her arms. Polly stopped suddenly, almost letting the bowl fall.

"It's Phronsie," said the mother, "and I don't know what the matter is with her. You'll have to go for the doctor, Polly, and just as fast as you can."

Polly still stood, holding the bowl, and staring with all her might. *Phronsie sick.*

"Don't wake her," said Mrs. Pepper.

Poor Polly couldn't have stirred to save her life for a minute. Then she said, "Where shall I go?"

"Oh, run to Dr. Fisher's — and don't be gone long."

Polly set down the bowl of butter and sped on the wings of the wind for the doctor. Something dreadful was the matter, she felt, for never had a physician been summoned to the hearty Pepper family since she could remember; only when the father died. Fear lent speed to her feet, and soon the doctor came and bent over poor little Phronsie, who still lay in her mother's arms, in a burning fever.

"It's measles," he pronounced, "that's all. No cause for alarm. You ever had it?" he asked, turning suddenly around on Polly, who was watching with wide-open eyes for the verdict.

"No, sir," answered Polly, not knowing in the least what "measles" was.

"What shall we do!" said Mrs. Pepper. "They haven't any of them had it."

The doctor was over by the little old table under the window, mixing up some black-looking stuff in a tumbler, and he didn't hear her.

"There," he said, putting a spoonful into Phronsie's mouth. "She'll get along well enough; only keep her out of the cold." Then he pulled out a big silver watch. He was a little thin man, and the watch was immense. Polly for her life couldn't keep her eyes off it; if Ben could only have one so fine!

"Polly," whispered Mrs. Pepper, "run and get my purse; it's in the top bureau drawer."

"Yes'm," said Polly, by a violent wrench taking her eyes off the fascinating watch; and she ran quickly and got the little old stocking leg, where the hard earnings that stayed long enough to be put anywhere always found refuge. She put it into her mother's lap and watched while Mrs. Pepper counted out slowly one dollar in small pieces.

"Here, sir," said Mrs. Pepper, holding them out toward the doctor. "And thank you for coming."

"Hey!" said the little man, spinning round. "That dollar's the Lord's!"

Mrs. Pepper looked bewildered and still sat holding it out.

"And the Lord has given it to you to take care of these children with; see that you do it." And without another word he was gone.

"Wasn't he good, mammy?" asked Polly after the first surprise was over.

"I'm sure he was," said Mrs. Pepper. "Well, tie it up again, Polly; tie it up tight. We shall want it, I'm sure," sighing at her little sick girl.

"Mayn't I take Phronsie, ma?" asked Polly.

"No, *no*," said Phronsie. She had got mammy, and she meant to improve the privilege.

"What is 'measles' anyway, mammy?" asked Polly, sitting down on the floor at their feet.

"Oh, 'tis something children always have," replied Mrs. Pepper. "But I'm sure I hoped it wouldn't come just yet."

"*I* shan't have it," said Polly decisively. "I know I shan't! Nor Ben — nor Joe — nor — nor Davie — I guess," she added, hesitatingly, for Davie was the delicate one of the family; at least not nearly so strong as the others.

Mrs. Pepper looked at her anxiously; but Polly seemed as bright and healthy as ever as she jumped up and ran to put the kettle on the stove.

"What'll the boys say I wonder?" she thought to herself, feeling quite important that they really had sickness in the house. As long as Phronsie wasn't dangerous, it seemed quite like rich folks; and she forgot the toil and the grind of poverty. She looked out from time to time as she passed the window, but no boys came.

"I'll put her in bed, Polly," said Mrs. Pepper in a whisper as Phronsie closed her eyes and breathed regularly.

"And then will you have your dinner, ma?"

"Yes," said Mrs. Pepper. "I don't care — if the boys come."

"The boys'll never come," said Polly impatiently. "I don't believe — why, here they are now!"

"Oh, dear," said Joel, coming in crossly, "I'm so hungry — oh, butter! Where'd you get it? I thought we never should get here!"

"I thought so too," said Polly. "Hush! Why, where's Ben?"

"He's just back," began Joel, commencing to eat, "and Davie. Something is the matter with Ben — he says he feels funny."

"Something the matter with Ben!" repeated Polly. She dropped the cups she held, which broke in a dozen pieces.

"Oh, whocky!" cried Joel. "See what you've done, Polly Pepper!"

But Polly didn't hear; over the big, flat door stone she sped and met Ben with little David, coming in the gate. His face was just like Phronsie's! And with a cold, heavy feeling at her heart, Polly realized that this was no play.

"Oh, Ben!" she cried, flinging her arms around his neck and bursting into tears. *"Don't!* Please — I wish you wouldn't. Phronsie's got 'em, and that's enough!"

"Got what?" asked Ben, while Davie's eyes grew to their widest proportions.

"Oh, measles!" cried Polly, bursting out afresh. "The *hatefulest, horridest measles!* And now you're taken!"

"Oh, no, I'm not," responded Ben cheerfully, who knew what measles were. "Wipe up, Polly, I'm all right. Only my head aches, and my eyes feel funny."

But Polly, only half reassured, controlled her sobs, and the sorrowful trio repaired to mother.

"Oh, dear!" ejaculated Mrs. Pepper, sinking into a chair in dismay at sight of Ben's red face. "Whatever'll we do now!"

The prop and stay of her life would be taken away if Ben should be laid aside. No more stray half- or quarter-

44

dollars would come to help her out when she didn't know where to turn.

Polly cleared off the deserted table — for once Joel had all the bread and butter he wanted. Ben took some of Phronsie's medicine and crawled up into the loft to bed; and quiet settled down on the little household.

"Polly," whispered Ben as she tucked him in, "it'll be hard buckling-to now for you, but I guess you'll do it."

MORE TROUBLE

"OH, dear," said Polly to herself the next morning, trying to get a breakfast for the sick ones out of the inevitable mush. "Everything's just as bad as it *can* be! They can't ever eat this. I wish I had an *ocean* of toast!"

"Toast some of the bread in the pail, Polly," said Mrs. Pepper.

She looked worn and worried. She had been up nearly all night, back and forth from Ben's bed in the loft to restless, fretful little Phronsie in the big four-poster in the bedroom, for Phronsie wouldn't get into the crib. Polly had tried her best to help her and had rubbed her eyes diligently to keep awake, but she was wholly unaccustomed to it, and her healthy, tired little body succumbed. And then when she awoke, shame and remorse filled her very heart.

"That isn't nice, ma," she said, glancing at the poor old pail, which she had brought out of the Provision Room. "Old brown bread! I want to fix 'em something nice."

"Well, you can't, you know," said Mrs. Pepper with a sigh. "But you've got butter now; that'll be splendid!"

"I know it," said Polly, running to the corner cupboard where the precious morsel in the blue bowl remained. "Whatever should we do without it, mammy?"

"Do *without* it!" said Mrs. Pepper. "Same's we *have* done."

"Well, 'twas splendid in Mrs. Henderson to give it to us, anyway," said Polly, longing for just one taste. "Seems as if 'twas a year since I was there. Oh, ma!" And here Polly took up the thread that had been so rudely snapped: "Don't you think she's got ten of the prettiest — yes, the sweetest little chickens you ever saw! Why can't we have some, mammy?"

"Costs money," replied Mrs. Pepper. "We've got too many *in* the house to have any *outside*."

"Oh, dear," said Polly with a red face that was toasting about as much as the bread she was holding on the point of an old fork. "We never have had *anything*. There," she added at last. "That's the best I can do; now I'll put the butter on this little blue plate. Ain't that cunning, ma?"

"Yes," said Mrs. Pepper approvingly. "It takes you, Polly."

So Polly trotted first to Ben, up the crooked, low stairs to the loft. And while she regaled him with the brown toast and butter, she kept her tongue flying on the subject of the little chicks and all that she saw on the famous Henderson visit. Poor Ben pretended hard to eat but ate nothing really; and Polly saw it all, and it cut her to the heart, so she talked faster than ever.

"Now," she said, starting to go back to Phronsie, "Ben Pepper, just as soon as you get well, *we'll* have some chickens — so there!"

"Guess we shan't get 'em very soon," said Ben despondently, "if I've got to lie here. And, besides, Polly, you know every bit we can save has *got* to go for the new stove."

"Oh, dear," said Polly. "I forgot that; so it has. Seems to me everything's giving out!"

"You can't bake any longer in the old thing," said Ben, turning over and looking at her. "Poor girl, I don't see how you've stood it so long."

"And we've been stuffing it," cried Polly merrily, "till 'twon't stuff anymore."

"No," said Ben, turning back again. "That's all worn out."

"Well, you must go to sleep," said Polly, "or mammy'll be up here. And Phronsie hasn't had her breakfast either."

Phronsie was wailing away dismally, sitting up in the middle of the old bed. Her face pricked, she said, and she was rubbing it vigorously with both fat little hands and then crying worse than ever.

"Oh, me! Oh, my!" cried Polly. "How you look, Phronsie!"

"I want my mammy!" cried poor Phronsie.

"Mammy can't come now, Phronsie dear; she's sewing. See what Polly's got for you — butter: isn't that *splendid!*"

Phronsie stopped for just one moment and took a mouthful; but the toast was hard and dry, and she cried harder than before.

"Now," said Polly, curling up on the bed beside her, "if you'll stop crying, Phronsie Pepper, I'll tell you about the cunningest, yes, the *very* cunningest little chickens you ever saw. One was white, and he looked just like this," said Polly, tumbling over on the bed in a heap. "He couldn't stand up straight, he was so fat."

"Did he *bite?*" asked Phronsie, full of interest.

"No, he didn't bite *me,*" said Polly. "But his mother put a bug in his mouth — just as I'm doing, you know." And she broke off a small piece of the toast, put on a generous bit of butter, and held it over Phronsie's mouth.

"Did he swallow it?" asked the child, obediently opening her little red lips.

"Oh, *snapped* it," answered Polly, "quick as ever he could, I tell you. But 'twasn't good like this, Phronsie."

"Did he have *two* bugs?" asked Phronsie, eyeing suspiciously the second morsel of dry toast that Polly was conveying to her mouth.

"Well, he would have had," replied Polly, "if there'd been bugs enough; but there were nine other chicks, Phronsie."

"Poor chickies," said Phronsie, and looked lovingly at the rest of the toast and butter on the plate; and while Polly fed it to her, listened with absorbed interest to all the particulars concerning each and every chick in the Henderson hen coop.

"Mother," said Polly toward evening, "I'm going to sit up with Ben tonight. Say I may, do, mother."

"Oh, no, you can't," replied Mrs. Pepper. "You'll get worn out, and then what shall I do? Joel can hand him his medicine."

"Oh, Joe would tumble to sleep, mammy," said Polly, "the first thing. Let me."

"Perhaps Phronsie'll let me go tonight," said Mrs. Pepper reflectively.

"Oh, no, she won't, I know," replied Polly decisively. "She wants you all the time."

"*I* will, Polly," said Davie, coming in with an armful of wood in time to hear the conversation. "I'll give him his medicine, mayn't I, mammy?" And David let down his load and came over where his mother and Polly sat sewing, to urge his rights.

"I don't know," said his mother, smiling on him. "Can you, do you think?"

"Yes, *ma'am!*" said Davie, straightening himself up.

When they told Ben, he said he knew a better way than for Davie to watch. He'd have a string tied to Davie's arm, and the end he'd hold in bed, and when 'twas time for medicine, he'd pull the string, and that would wake Davie up!

Polly didn't sleep much more on her shakedown on the floor than if she *had* watched with Ben. For Phronsie cried and moaned and wanted a drink of water every two minutes, it seemed to her. As she went back into her nest after one of these travels, Polly thought, "Well, I don't care if nobody else gets sick, if Ben'll only get well. Tomorrow I'm goin' to do mammy's sack she's begun for Mr. Jackson. It's all plain sewin', just like a bag; and I can do it, I know — " And so she fell into a troubled sleep, only to be awakened by Phronsie's fretful little voice. "I want a drink of water, Polly, I *do.*"

"Don't she drink awfully, mammy?" asked Polly after one of these excursions out to the kitchen after the necessary draft.

"Yes," said Mrs. Pepper. "And she mustn't have any more; 'twill hurt her." But Phronsie fell into a delicious sleep after that and didn't want any more, luckily.

"Here, Joe," said Mrs. Pepper the next morning. "Take this coat up to Mr. Peters, and be sure you get the money for it."

"How'll I get it?" asked Joe, who didn't relish the long, hot walk.

"Why, tell 'em we're sick — Ben's sick," added Mrs. Pepper as the most decisive thing, "and we must have it; and then wait for it."

" 'Tisn't pleasant up at the Peterses'," grumbled Joel, taking the parcel and moving slowly off.

"No, no, Polly," said Mrs. Pepper, "you needn't do that," seeing Polly take up some sewing after doing up the room and finishing the semi-weekly bake. "You're all beat out with that tussle over the stove. That sack'll have to go till next week."

"It can't, mammy," said Polly, snipping off a basting thread. "We've got to have the money; how much'll he give you for it?"

"Thirty cents," replied Mrs. Pepper.

"Well," said Polly, "we've got to get all the thirty centses we can, mammy dear; and I know I can do it, truly — try me once," she implored.

"Well." Mrs. Pepper relented slowly.

"Don't feel bad, mammy dear," comforted Polly, sewing away briskly. "Ben'll get well pretty soon, and then we'll be all right."

"Maybe," said Mrs. Pepper, and went back to Phronsie, who could scarcely let her out of her sight.

Polly stitched away bravely. "Now if I do this good, mammy'll let me do it other times," she said to herself.

Davie, too, worked patiently out of doors, trying to do Ben's chores. The little fellow blundered over things that

51

Ben would have accomplished in half the time, and he had to sit down often on the steps of the little old shed where the tools were kept, to wipe his hot face and rest.

"Polly," said Mrs. Pepper, "hadn't you better stop a little? Dear me! How fast you sew, child!"

Polly gave a delighted little hum at her mother's evident approval.

"I'm going to do 'em all next week, mammy," she said. "Then Mr. Atkins won't take 'em away from us, I guess."

Mr. Atkins kept the store and gave out coats and sacks of coarse linen and homespun to Mrs. Pepper to make; and it was the fear of losing the work that had made the mother's heart sink.

"I don't believe anybody's got such children as I have," she said, and she gave Polly a motherly little pat that the little daughter felt clear to the tips of her toes with a thrill of delight.

About half past two, long after dinner, Joe came walking in, hungry as a beaver but flushed and triumphant.

"Why, where have you been all this time?" asked his mother.

"Oh, Joe, you *didn't* stop to play?" asked Polly from her perch where she sat sewing, giving him a reproachful glance.

"Stop to play!" retorted Joe indignantly. "No, I guess I didn't! I've been to Old Peters's."

"Not all this time!" exclaimed Mrs. Pepper.

"Yes, I have too," replied Joel, sturdily marching up to her. "And there's your money, mother." And he counted out a quarter of a dollar in silver pieces and pennies, which he took from a dingy wad of paper stowed away in the depths of his pocket.

"Oh, Joe," said Mrs. Pepper, sinking back in her chair and looking at him. "What do you mean?"

Polly put her work in her lap and waited to hear.

"Where's my dinner, Polly?" asked Joel. "I hope it's a big one."

"Yes, 'tis," said Polly. "You've got lots today. It's in the corner of the cupboard, covered up with the plate. So tell on, Joe."

"That's elegant!" said Joel, coming back with the well-filled plate, Ben's and his own share.

"*Do* tell us, Joey," implored Polly. "Mother's waiting."

"Well," said Joel, his mouth half full, "I waited — and he said the coat was all right — and — and — Mrs. Peters said 'twas all right — and Mirandy Peters said 'twas all right; but they didn't any of 'em say anythin' about payin', so *I* didn't think 'twas all right — and — and — can't I have some more butter, Polly?"

"No," said Polly, sorry to refuse him, he'd been so good about the money. "The butter's got to be saved for Ben and Phronsie."

"Oh," said Joe, "I wish Mrs. Henderson would send us some more, I *do!* I think she might!"

"For shame, Joe," said Mrs. Pepper. "She was very good to send this, I think. Now what else did you say?" she asked.

"Well," said Joel, taking another mouthful of bread, "so I waited — you told me to, mother, you know — and they all went to work; and they didn't mind me at all, and — there wasn't anything to look at, so I sat — and sat — Polly, can't I have some gingerbread?"

"No," said Polly, "it's all gone. I gave the last piece to Phronsie the day she was taken sick."

"Oh, dear," said Joel. "Everything's gone."

"Well, do go on, Joe, *do*."

"And — then they had dinner; and Mr. Peters said, 'Hasn't that boy gone home yet?' and Mrs. Peters said, 'No' — and he called me in and asked me why I hadn't run along home; and I said, Phronsie was sick, and Ben had the squeezles — "

"The *what*?" said Polly.

"The *squeezles*," repeated Joel irritably. "That's what you said."

"It's measles, Joey," corrected Mrs. Pepper. "Never mind, I wouldn't feel bad."

"Well, they all laughed and laughed, and then I said you told me to wait till I *did* get the money."

"Oh, Joe," began Mrs. Pepper, "you shouldn't have told 'em so — what did he say?"

"Well, he laughed and said I was a smart boy, and he'd see; and Mirandy said, 'Do pay him, pa, he must be tired to death.' And don't you think, he went to a big desk in the corner, and took out a box, and 'twas full most of money — *lots!* Oh! And he gave me mine — and — that's all; and I'm tired to death." And Joel flung himself down on the floor, expanded his legs as only Joel could, and took a comfortable roll.

"So you must be," said Polly pityingly, "waiting at those Peterses'."

"Don't ever want to *see* any more Peterses'," said Joel, "never, never, *never!*"

"Oh, dear," thought Polly as she sewed on into the afternoon, "I wonder what does ail my eyes! Feels just like sand in 'em." And she rubbed and rubbed to thread her needle. But she was afraid her mother would see, so she kept at her sewing. Once in a while the bad feeling would go away, and then she would forget all about it. "There, now, who says I can't do it! That's most done," she cried, jumping up and spinning across the room to stretch herself a bit. "And tomorrow I'll finish it."

"Well," said Mrs. Pepper, "if you can do that, Polly, you'll be the greatest help I've had yet."

So Polly tucked herself into the old shakedown with a thankful heart that night, hoping for morning.

Alas! When morning did come, Polly could hardly move. The measles! What should she do! A faint hope of driving them off made her tumble out of bed and stagger across the room to look in the old cracked looking glass. All hope was gone as the red reflection met her gaze. Polly was on the sick list now!

"I *won't* be sick," she said. "At any rate, I'll keep around." An awful feeling made her clutch the back of a chair, but she managed somehow to get into her clothes and go groping blindly into the kitchen. Somehow Polly couldn't see very well. She tried to set the table, but 'twas no use. "Oh, dear," she thought, "whatever'll mammy do?"

"Hulloa!" said Joel, coming in. "What's the matter, Polly?"

Polly started at his sudden entrance and, wavering a minute, fell over in a heap.

"Oh, ma! Ma!" screamed Joel, running to the foot of the stairs leading to the loft, where Mrs. Pepper was with Ben. "Something's taken Polly, and she fell, and I guess she's in the woodbox!"

HARD DAYS FOR POLLY

"MA," said David, coming softly into the bedroom, where poor Polly lay on the bed with Phronsie, her eyes bandaged with a soft old handkerchief, "I'll set the table."

"There isn't any table to set," said Mrs. Pepper sadly. "There isn't anybody to eat anything, Davie. You and Joel can get something out of the cupboard."

"Can we get whatever we've a mind to, ma?" cried Joel, who followed Davie, rubbing his face with a towel after his morning ablutions.

"Yes," replied his mother absently.

"Come on, Davie!" cried Joel. "We'll have a breakfast!"

"We mustn't," said little Davie doubtfully, "eat the *whole*, Joey."

But that individual already had his head in the cupboard, which soon engrossed them both.

Dr. Fisher was called in the middle of the morning to see what was the matter with Polly's eyes. The little man looked at her keenly over his spectacles; then he said, "When were you taken?"

"This morning," answered Polly, her eyes smarting.

"Didn't you feel badly before?" questioned the doctor.

Polly thought back, and then she remembered that she *had* felt very badly. That when she was baking over the old stove the day before her back had ached dreadfully; and that somehow, when she sat down to sew, it didn't stop; only her eyes had bothered her so, she didn't mind her back so much.

"I thought so," said the doctor when Polly answered. "And those eyes of yours have been used too much. What has she been doing, ma'am?" He turned around sharply on Mrs. Pepper as he asked this.

"Sewing," said Mrs. Pepper, "and everything. Polly does everything, sir."

"Humph!" said the doctor. "Well, she won't again in one spell; her eyes are very bad."

At this a whoop, small but terrible to hear, came from the middle of the bed; and Phronsie sat bolt upright. Everybody started while Phronsie broke out, "Don't make my Polly sick! Oh! *Please* don't!"

"Hey!" said the doctor, and he looked kindly at the small object with a very red face in the middle of the bed. Then he added gently, "We're going to make Polly well, little girl, so that she can see splendidly."

"Will you *really?*" asked the child doubtfully.

"Yes," said the doctor. "We'll try hard. And you mustn't cry, 'cause then Polly'll cry, and that will make her eyes *very* bad, *very* bad indeed," he repeated impressively.

"I won't cry," said Phronsie. "No, not one bit." And she wiped off the last tear with her fat little hand and watched to see what next was to be done.

And Polly was left, very rebellious indeed, in the big bed with a cooling lotion on the poor eyes that somehow didn't cool them one bit.

"If 'twas anythin' but my eyes, mammy, I could stand it," she bewailed, flouncing over and over in her impatience. "And who'll do all the work now?"

"Don't think of the work, Polly," said Mrs. Pepper.

"I can't do anything *but* think," said poor Polly.

Just at that moment a queer noise out in the kitchen was heard.

"Do go out, mother, and see what 'tis," said Polly.

"I've come," said a cracked voice close up by the bedroom door, followed by a big black cap, which could belong to no other than Grandma Bascom, "to set by you a spell. What's the matter?" she asked, and stopped, amazed to see Polly in bed.

"Oh, Polly's taken," screamed Mrs. Pepper in her ear.

"Taken!" repeated the old lady. "What is it — a fit?"

"No," said Mrs. Pepper. "The same as Ben's got, and Phronsie — the *measles*."

"The measles, has she?" said grandma. "Well, that's bad. And Ben's away, you say."

"No, he isn't either," screamed Mrs. Pepper. "He's got them too!"

"Got two *what?*" asked grandma.

"Measles! He's got the measles too," repeated Mrs. Pepper, loud as she could; so loud that the old lady's cap trembled at the noise.

"Oh! The dreadful!" said grandma. "And this girl too?" laying her hand on Phronsie's head.

"Yes," said Mrs. Pepper, feeling it a little relief to tell over her miseries. "All three of them!"

"*I* haven't," said Joel, coming in in hopes that grandma had a stray peppermint or two in her pocket, as she sometimes did. "And I'm not going to, either."

"Oh, dear," groaned his mother. "That's what Polly said, and she's got 'em bad. It's her eyes," she screamed to grandma, who looked inquiringly.

"Her eyes, is it?" asked Mrs. Bascom. "Well, I've got a receet that cousin Samanthy's folks had when John's children had 'em; and I'll run right along home and get it," and she started to go.

"No, you needn't," screamed Mrs. Pepper. "Thank you, Mrs. Bascom, but Dr. Fisher's been here, and he put something on Polly's eyes, and he said it mustn't be touched."

"Hey?" said the old lady. So Mrs. Pepper had to go all over it again, till at last she made her understand that Polly's eyes were taken care of and they must wait for time to do the rest.

"You come along of me," whispered grandma, when at last her call was done, to Joel, who stood by the door. "I've got some peppermints to home; I forgot to bring 'em."

"Yes'm," said Joel, brightening up.

"Where you going, Joe?" asked Mrs. Pepper, seeing him move off with Mrs. Bascom. "I may want you."

"Oh, I've got to go over to grandma's," said Joel briskly. "She wants me."

"Well, don't be gone long, then," replied his mother.

"There," said grandma, going into her "keeping room" to an old-fashioned chest of drawers. Opening one, she took therefrom a paper, from which she shook out before Joe's delighted eyes some red and white peppermint drops. "There, now, you take these home. You may have some, but be sure you give the most to the sick ones, and Polly — let Polly have the biggest."

"She won't take 'em," said Joel, wishing he had the measles.

"Well, you try her," said grandma. "Run along now." But it was useless to tell Joel that, for he was halfway home already. He carried out grandma's wishes and distributed conscientiously the precious drops. But when he came to Polly, she didn't answer; and looking at her in surprise, he saw two big tears rolling out under the bandage and wetting the pillow.

"I don't want 'em, Joe," said Polly when he made her understand that " 'twas peppermints, real peppermints." "You may have 'em."

"Try one, Polly; they're real good," said Joel, who had an undefined wish to comfort. "There, open your mouth."

So Polly opened her mouth, and Joel put one in with satisfaction.

"Isn't it good?" he asked, watching her crunch it.

"Yes," said Polly, "real good. Where'd you get 'em?"

"Over to Grandma Bascom's," said Joel. "She gave me lots for all of us. Have another, Polly?"

"No," said Polly, "not yet. You put two on my pillow where I can reach 'em, and then you keep the rest, Joel."

"I'll put three," said Joel, counting out one red and two white ones and laying them on the pillow. "There!"

"And I want another, Joey, I *do*," said Phronsie from the other side of the bed.

"Well, you may have one," said Joel. "A red one,

Phronsie. Yes, you may have two. Now come on, Dave, we'll have the rest out by the woodpile."

How they ever got through that day, I don't know. But late in the afternoon carriage wheels were heard; and then they stopped right at the Peppers' little brown gate.

"Polly," said Mrs. Pepper, running to the bedroom door, "it's Mrs. Henderson!"

"Is it?" said Polly from the darkened room. "Oh, I'm so glad! Is Miss Jerushy with her?" she asked fearfully.

"No," said Mrs. Pepper, going back to ascertain. "Why, it's the parson himself! Deary! How we look!"

"Never mind, mammy," called back Polly, longing to spring out of bed and fix up a bit.

"I'm sorry to hear the children are sick," said Mrs. Henderson, coming in, in her sweet, gentle way.

"We didn't know it," said the minister, "until this morning. Can we see them?"

"Oh, yes, sir," said Mrs. Pepper. "Ben's upstairs, and Polly and Phronsie are in here."

"Poor little things!" said Mrs. Henderson compassionately. "Hadn't you better" — turning to the minister — "go up and see Ben first, while I will visit the little girls?"

So the minister mounted the crooked stairs, and Mrs. Henderson went straight up to Polly's side. And the first thing Polly knew, a cool, gentle hand was laid on her hot head, and a voice said, "I've come to see *my* little chicken now!"

"Oh, ma'am," said Polly, bursting into a sob, "I don't care about my eyes — only mammy — " And she broke right down.

"I know," said the minister's wife soothingly. "But it's

for you to bear patiently, Polly. What do you suppose the chicks were doing when I came away?" And Mrs. Henderson, while she held Polly's hand, smiled and nodded encouragingly to Phronsie, who was staring at her from the other side of the bed.

"I don't know, ma'am," said Polly. "Please tell us."

"Well, they were all fighting over a grasshopper — yes, ten of them."

"Which one got it?" asked Polly in intense interest. "Oh, I hope the white one did!"

"Well, he looked as much like winning as any of them," said the lady, laughing.

"Bless her!" thought Mrs. Pepper to herself out in the kitchen, finishing the sack Polly had left. "*She's* a parson's wife, *I* say!"

And then the minister came down from Ben's room and went into the bedroom, and Mrs. Henderson went upstairs into the loft.

"So," he said kindly, as after patting Phronsie's head he came over and sat down by Polly, "this is the little girl who came to see me when I was sick."

"Oh, sir," said Polly, "I'm *so* glad you wasn't!"

"Well, when I come again," said Mrs. Henderson, rising after a merry chat, "I see I shall have to slip a book into my pocket and read for those poor eyes."

"Oh, thank *you*!" cried Polly, and then she stopped and blushed.

"Well, what is it?" asked the minister encouragingly.

"Ben loves to hear reading," said Polly.

"Does he? Well, by that time, my little girl, I guess Ben will be downstairs. He's all right, Polly; don't you worry about him. And I'll sit in the kitchen, by the bedroom door, and you can hear nicely."

So the Hendersons went away. But somehow, before they went, a good many things found their way out of the old-fashioned chaise into the Peppers' little kitchen.

But Polly's eyes didn't get any better, with all the care, and the lines of worry on Mrs. Pepper's face grew deeper and deeper. At last she just confronted Dr. Fisher in the kitchen one day after his visit to Polly and boldly asked him if they ever could be cured. "I know she's — and there isn't any use keeping it from me," said the poor women — "she's going to be stone blind!"

"My good woman." Dr. Fisher's voice was very gentle, and he took the hard, brown hand in his own. "Your little girl will *not* be blind; I tell you the truth. But it will take some time to make her eyes quite strong — time, and rest. She has strained them in some way, but she will come out of it."

"Praise the Lord!" cried Mrs. Pepper, throwing her apron over her head. And then she sobbed on. "And you, sir — I can't ever thank you — for — for — if Polly was blind, we might as well give up!"

The next day Phronsie, who had the doctor's permission to sit up, only she was to be kept from taking cold, scampered around in stocking feet in search of her shoes, which she hadn't seen since she was first taken sick.

"Oh, I want on my very *best* shoes," she cried. "Can't I, mammy?"

"Oh, no, Phronsie. You must keep *them* nice," remonstrated her mother. "You can't wear 'em every day, you know."

" 'Tisn't every day," said Phronsie slowly. "It's only *one* day."

"Well, and then you'll want 'em on again tomorrow," said her mother.

"Oh, no, I won't!" cried Phronsie. "Never, no more tomorrow, if I can have 'em today. *Please*, mammy dear!"

Mrs. Pepper went to the lowest drawer in the high bureau and took therefrom a small parcel done up in white tissue paper. Slowly unrolling this before the delighted eyes of the child, who stood patiently waiting, she disclosed the precious red-topped shoes, which Phronsie immediately clasped to her bosom.

"My own, *very* own shoes! *Whole* mine!" she cried, and trudged out into the kitchen to put them on herself.

"Hulloa!" cried Dr. Fisher, coming in about a quarter of an hour later to find her tugging laboriously at the buttons. "*New* shoes! I declare!"

"My own!" cried Phronsie, sticking out one foot for inspection, where every button was in the wrong buttonhole. "And they've got red tops too!"

"So they have," said the doctor, getting down on the floor beside her. "Beautiful red tops, aren't they?"

"Be-*yew*-*ti*-ful," sang the child delightedly.

"Does Polly have new shoes every day?" asked the doctor in a low voice, pretending to examine the other foot.

Phronsie opened her eyes very wide at this.

"Oh, no, she don't have anything, Polly don't."

"And what does Polly want most of all, do you know? See if you can tell me." And the doctor put on the most alluring expression that he could muster.

"Oh, I know!" cried Phronsie with a very wise look.

"There now," cried the doctor, "you're the girl for me! To think you know! So, what is it?"

Phronsie got up very gravely, and with one shoe half on, she leaned over and whispered in the doctor's ear: "A *stove!*"

"A *what?*" said the doctor, looking at her and then at the old, black thing in the corner that looked as if it were ashamed of itself. "Why, she's got one."

"Oh," said the child, "it won't burn. And sometimes Polly cries, she does, when she's all alone — and I see her."

"Now," said the doctor very sympathetically, "that's too bad, that is! And then what does she do?"

"Oh, Ben stuffs it up," said the child, laughing. "And so does Polly, too, with paper; and then it all tumbles out quick, oh! Just as quick!" And Phronsie shook her yellow head at the dismal remembrance.

"Do you suppose," said the doctor, getting up, "that you know of any smart little girl around here, about four years old and that knows how to button on her own red-topped shoes, that would like to go to ride tomorrow morning in my carriage with me?"

"Oh, I do!" cried Phronsie, hopping on one toe. "It's *me!*"

"Very well, then," said Dr. Fisher, going to the bedroom door, "we'll look out for tomorrow, then."

To poor Polly, lying in the darkened room, or sitting up in the big rocking chair — for Polly wasn't really very sick in other respects, the disease having all gone into the merry brown eyes — the time seemed interminable. Not to *do* anything! The very idea at any time would have filled her active, wide-awake little body with horror; here she was!

"Oh, dear, I *can't* bear it!" she said when she knew by

the noise in the kitchen that everybody was out there, so nobody heard except a fat old black spider in the corner, and he didn't tell anyone!

"I *know* it's a week," she said, "since dinnertime! If Ben were only well, to talk to me."

"Oh, I say, Polly," screamed Joel at that moment, running in. "Ben's a-comin' down the stairs!"

"Stop, Joe," said Mrs. Pepper. "You shouldn't have told. He wanted to surprise Polly."

"Oh, is he!" cried Polly, clapping her hands in rapture. "Mammy, can't I take off this horrid bandage and *see* him?"

"Dear me, no!" said Mrs. Pepper, springing forward. "Not for the world, Polly! Dr. Fisher'd have our ears off!"

"Well, I can hear, anyway," said Polly, resigning herself to the remaining comfort. "Here he is! Oh, Ben!"

"There," said Ben, grasping Polly, bandage and all, "now we're all right. And I say, Polly, you're a brick!"

"Mammy told me not to say that the other day," said Joel with a very virtuous air.

"Can't help it," said Ben, who was a little wild over Polly, and besides, he had been sick himself and had borne a good deal too.

"Now," said Mrs. Pepper after the first excitement was over, "you're so comfortable together, and Phronsie don't want me now, I'll go to the store; I must get some more work if Mr. Atkins'll give it to me."

"I'll be all right now, mammy, that Ben's here," cried Polly, settling back into her chair, with Phronsie on the stool at her feet.

"I'm goin' to tell her stories, ma," cried Ben, "so you needn't worry about us."

"Isn't it funny, Ben," said Polly as the gate clicked after the mother, "to be sitting still and telling stories in the daytime?"

"Rather funny!" replied Ben.

"Well, do go on," said Joel, as usual rolling on the floor in a dreadful hurry for the story to begin. Little David looked up quietly as he sat on Ben's other side, his hands clasped tight together, just as eager, though he said nothing.

"Well, once upon a time," began Ben delightfully, and launched into one of the stories that the children thought perfectly lovely.

"Oh, Bensie," cried Polly, entranced, as they listened with bated breath, "however do you think of such nice things!"

"I've had time enough to think, the last week," said Ben, laughing, "to last a lifetime!"

"Do go *on*," put in Joel, impatient at the delay.

"Don't hurry him so," said Polly reprovingly. "He isn't strong."

"Ben," said David, drawing a long breath, his eyes very big. "Did he *really* see a bear?"

"No," said Ben. "Oh! Where was I?"

"Why, you said Tommy heard a noise," said Polly, "and he *thought* it was a bear."

"Oh, yes," said Ben, "I remember. 'Twasn't a — "

"Oh, *make* it a bear, Ben!" cried Joel, terribly disappointed. "Don't let it be not a bear."

"Why, I can't," said Ben. " 'Twouldn't sound true."

"Never mind, *make* it sound true," insisted Joel. "You can make anything true."

"Very well," said Ben, laughing. "I suppose I must."

"Make it *two* bears, Ben," begged little Phronsie.

"Oh, no. Phronsie, that's too much," cried Joel. "That'll spoil it. But make it a *big* bear, do, Ben, and have him bite him somewhere, and 'most kill him."

"Oh, Joel!" cried Polly, while David's eyes got bigger than ever.

So Ben drew upon his powers as storyteller to suit his exacting audience and was making his bear work havoc upon poor Tommy in a way captivating to all, even Joel, when —

"Well, I declare," sounded Mrs. Pepper's cheery voice coming in upon them, "if this isn't comfortable!"

"Oh, mammy!" cried Phronsie, jumping out of Polly's arms, whither she had taken refuge during the thrilling tale, and running to her mother, who gathered her baby up. "We've had a bear! A *real, live bear, we have!* Ben made him!"

"Have you!" said Mrs. Pepper, taking off her shawl and laying her parcel of work down on the table. "Now, that's nice!"

"Oh, mammy!" cried Polly. "It does seem so good to be all together again!"

"And I thank the Lord!" said Mrs. Pepper, looking down on her happy little group; and the tears were in her eyes. "And children, we ought to be very good and please Him, for He's been so good to us."

THE CLOUD OVER THE
LITTLE BROWN HOUSE

WHEN Phronsie, with many crows of delight and much chattering, had gotten fairly started the following morning on her much-anticipated drive with the doctor, the whole family excepting Polly drawn up around the door to see them off, Mrs. Pepper resolved to snatch the time and run down for an hour or two to one of her customers who had long been waiting for a little "tailoring" to be done for her boys.

"Now, Joel," she said, putting on her bonnet before the cracked looking glass, "you stay along of Polly. Ben must go up to bed, the doctor said, and Davie's going to the store for some molasses, so you and Polly must keep house."

"Yes'm," said Joel. "May I have somethin' to eat, ma?"

"Yes," said Mrs. Pepper. "But don't you eat the new bread. You may have as much as you want of the old."

"Isn't there *any* molasses, mammy?" asked Joel as she bade Polly good-bye and gave her numberless charges "to be careful of your eyes" and "not to let a crack of light in through the curtain," as the old green paper shade was called.

"No. If you're very hungry, you can eat bread," said Mrs. Pepper sensibly.

"Joel," said Polly after the mother had gone, "I *do* wish you could read to me."

"Well, I can't," said Joel, glad he didn't know how. "I thought the minister was comin'."

"Well, he was," said Polly, "but mammy said he had to go out of town to a consequence."

"A *what!*" asked Joel, very much impressed.

"A con — " repeated Polly. "Well, it began with a *con* — and I am sure — yes, *very* sure it was a consequence."

"That must be splendid," said Joel, coming up to her chair and slowly drawing a string he held in his hand back and forth, "to go to consequences, and everything! When I'm a man, Polly Pepper, *I'm* going to be a minister, and have a nice time, and go — just everywhere!"

"Oh, Joel!" exclaimed Polly, quite shocked. "You couldn't be one; you aren't good enough."

"I don't care," said Joel, not at all dashed by her plainness. "I'll be good, then — when I'm a big man. Don't you suppose, Polly," as a new idea struck him, "that Mr. Henderson *ever* is naughty?"

"No," said Polly very decidedly. "Never, *never, never!*"

"Then I don't want to be one," said Joel, veering round with a sigh of relief. "And besides, I'd rather have a pair of horses like Mr. Slocum's, and *then* I could go everywheres, I guess!"

"And sell tin?" asked Polly. "Just like Mr. Slocum?"

"Yes," said Joel. "This is the way I'd go — gee-*whop!* Gee-*whoa!*" And Joel pranced with his imaginary steeds all around the room, making about as much noise as any

70

other four boys, as he brought up occasionally against the four-poster or the high old bureau.

"Well!" said a voice close up by Polly's chair that made her skip with apprehension, it was so like Miss Jerusha Henderson's. Joel was whooping away behind the bedstead to his horses that had become seriously entangled, so he didn't hear anything. But when Polly said bashfully, "I can't see anything, ma'am," he came up red and shining to the surface and stared with all his might.

"I came to see you, little girl," said Miss Jerusha severely, seating herself stiffly by Polly's side.

"Thank you, ma'am," said Polly faintly.

"Who's this boy?" asked the lady, turning around squarely on Joel and eyeing him from head to foot.

"He's my brother Joel," said Polly.

Joel still stared.

"Which brother?" pursued Miss Jerusha, like a census taker.

"He is next to me," said Polly, wishing her mother was home. "He's nine, Joel is."

"He's big enough to do something to help his mother," said Miss Jerusha, looking him through and through. "Don't you think you might do something, when the others are sick and your poor mother is working so hard?" she continued in a cold voice.

"I *do* do something," blurted out Joel sturdily. "Lots and lots!"

"You shouldn't say 'lots,' " reproved Miss Jerusha with a sharp look over her spectacles. " 'Tisn't proper for boys to talk so. What do you do all day long?" she asked, turning back to Polly after a withering glance at Joel, who still stared.

"I can't do anything, ma'am," replied Polly sadly. "I can't see to do anything."

"Well, you might knit, I should think," said her visitor. "It's dreadful for a girl as big as you are to sit all day idle. I had sore eyes once when I was a little girl — how old are you?" she asked abruptly.

"Eleven last month," said Polly.

"Well, I wasn't only nine when I knit a stocking; and I had sore eyes, too; you see I was a very little girl, and — "

"Was you ever little?" interrupted Joel in extreme incredulity, drawing near and looking over the big square figure.

"Hey?" said Miss Jerusha, so Joel repeated his question before Polly could stop him.

"Of course," answered Miss Jerusha, and then she added tartly, "Little boys shouldn't speak unless they're spoken to. Now," and she turned back to Polly again, "didn't you ever knit a stocking?"

"No, ma'am," said Polly, "not a *whole* one."

"Dear me!" exclaimed Miss Jerusha. "Did I ever!" And she raised her black mitts in intense disdain. "A big girl like you never to knit a stocking! To think your mother should bring you up so! And — "

"She didn't bring us up," screamed Joel in indignation, facing her with blazing eyes.

"Joel," said Polly, "be still."

"And you're very impertinent too," said Miss Jerusha. "A good child *never* is impertinent."

Polly sat quite still, and Miss Jerusha continued. "Now, I hope you will learn to be industrious; and when I come again, I will see what you have done."

"You aren't ever coming again," said Joel defiantly. "No, *never!*"

"Joel!" implored Polly, and in her distress she pulled up her bandage as she looked at him. "You know mammy'll be so sorry at you! Oh, ma'am, and" — she turned to Miss Jerusha, who was now thoroughly aroused to the duty she saw before her of doing these children good — "I don't know what is the reason, ma'am; Joel never talks so. He's real good, and — "

"It only shows," said the lady, seeing her way quite clear for a little exhortation, "that you've all had your own way from infancy, and that you don't do what you might to make your mother's life a happy one."

"Oh, ma'am," cried Polly, and she burst into a flood of tears. "Please, *please* don't say that!"

"And I say," screamed Joel, stamping his small foot, "if you make Polly cry, you'll *kill* her! *Don't*, Polly, *don't!*" And the boy put both arms around her neck and soothed and comforted her in every way he could think of. And Miss Jerusha, seeing no way to make herself heard, disappeared, feeling pity for children who *would* turn away from good advice.

But still Polly cried on; all the pent-up feelings that had been so long controlled had free vent now. She really couldn't stop! Joel, frightened to death, at last said, "I'm going to wake up Ben."

That brought Polly to, and she sobbed out, "Oh, no, Jo-ey, I'll stop."

"I will," said Joel, seeing his advantage. "I'm going, Polly," and he started to the foot of the stairs.

"No, I'm done now, Joe," said Polly, wiping her eyes and choking back her thoughts. "Oh, Joe! I *must* scream!

My eyes ache so!" and poor Polly fairly writhed all over the chair.

"What'll I do?" said Joel, at his wit's end, running back. "Do you want some water?"

"Oh, no," gasped Polly. "Doctor wouldn't let me. Oh! I wish mammy'd come!"

"I'll go and look for her," suggested Joel, feeling as if he must do something, and he'd rather be out at the gate than to see Polly suffer.

"That won't bring her," said Polly, trying to keep still. "I'll try to wait."

"Here she is now!" cried Joel, peeping out of the window. "Oh! goody!"

JOEL'S TURN

"WELL" — Mrs. Pepper's tone was unusually blithe as she stepped into the kitchen — "you've had a nice time, I suppose — what in the world!" And she stopped at the bedroom door.

"Oh, mammy, if you'd been here!" said Joel, while Polly sat still, only holding on to her eyes as if they were going to fly out. "There's been a big woman here; she came right in — and she talked awfully! And Polly's been a-cryin', and her eyes ache dreadfully — and — "

"Been crying!" repeated Mrs. Pepper, coming up to poor Polly. "Polly been crying!" she still repeated.

"Oh, mammy, I couldn't help it," said Polly, "She said" — and in spite of all she could do, the rain of tears began again, which bade fair to be as uncontrolled as before. But Mrs. Pepper took her up firmly in her arms as if she were Phronsie and sat down in the old rocking chair and just patted her back.

"There, there," she whispered soothingly. "Don't think of it, Polly; mother's got home."

"Oh, mammy," said Polly, crawling up to the comfortable neck for protection, "I ought not to mind, but 'twas Miss Jerusha Henderson, and she said — "

"What *did* she say?" asked Mrs. Pepper, thinking perhaps it to be the wiser thing to let Polly free her mind.

"Oh, she said that we ought to be doing something; and I ought to knit, and — "

"Go on," said her mother.

"And then Joel got naughty; oh, mammy, he never did so before, and I couldn't stop him," cried Polly, in great distress. "I really couldn't, mammy — and he talked to her, and he told her she wasn't ever coming here again."

"Joel shouldn't have said that," said Mrs. Pepper, and under her breath something was added that Polly even failed to hear. "But no more she isn't!"

"And, mammy," cried Polly, and she flung her arms around her mother's neck and gave her a grasp that nearly choked Mrs. Pepper, "ain't I helpin' you *some,* mammy? Oh! I wish I could do something big for you. Ain't you happy, mammy?"

"For the land's sakes!" cried Mrs. Pepper, straining Polly to her heart. "Whatever has that woman — whatever *could* she have said to you? Such a girl as you are, too?" cried Mrs. Pepper, hugging Polly and covering her with kisses so tender that Polly, warmed and cuddled up to her heart's content, was comforted to the full.

"Well," said Mrs. Pepper when at last she thought she had formed between Polly and Joel about the right idea of the visit. "Well, now we won't think of it ever anymore; 'tisn't worth it, Polly, you know."

But poor Polly! And poor mother! They both were obliged to think of it. Nothing could avert the suffering of the next few days caused by that long flow of burning tears.

"Nothing feels good on 'em, mammy," said Polly at last, twisting her hands in the vain attempt to keep from rubbing the aching, inflamed eyes that drove her nearly wild with their itching. "There isn't any use in trying anything."

"There *will* be use," energetically protested Mrs. Pepper, bringing another cool bandage, "as long as you've got an eye in your head, Polly Pepper!"

Dr. Fisher's face, when he first saw the change that the fateful visit had wrought, and heard the accounts, was very grave indeed. Everything had been so encouraging on his last visit that he had come very near promising Polly speedy freedom from the hateful bandage.

But the little Pepper household soon had something else to think of more important even than Polly's eyes, for now the heartiest, the jolliest, of all the little group was down — Joel. How he fell sick they scarcely knew, it all came so suddenly. The poor, bewildered family had hardly time to think before delirium and perhaps death stared them in the face.

When Polly first heard it, by Phronsie's pattering downstairs and screaming, "Oh, Polly, Joey's dre-ad-ful sick, he *is!*" she jumped right up and tore off the bandage.

"Now, I *will* help mother! I *will*, so *there!*" and in another minute she would have been up in the sickroom. But the first thing she knew, a gentle but firm hand was laid upon hers, and she found herself back again in the old rocking chair, and listening to the doctor's words, which were quite stern and decisive.

"Now, I tell you," he said, "you must *not* take off that bandage again. Do you know the consequences? You will be blind! And then you will be a care to your mother all your life!"

"I shall be blind anyway," said Polly despairingly, "so 'twon't make any difference."

"No, your eyes will come out of it all right, only I did hope" — and the good doctor's face fell — "that the other two boys would escape. But" — and he brightened up at the sight of Polly's forlorn visage — "see you do *your* part by keeping still."

But there came a day soon when *everything* was still around the once happy little brown house; when only whispers were heard from white lips, and thoughts were fearfully left unuttered.

On the morning of one of these days, when Mrs. Pepper felt she could not exist an hour longer without sleep, kind Mrs. Beebe came to stay until things were either better or worse.

Still the cloud hovered, dark and forbidding. At last, one afternoon when Polly was all alone, she could endure it no longer. She flung herself down by the side of the old bed and buried her face in the gay patched bed quilt.

"Dear God," she said, "*make* me willing to have anything" — she hesitated — "yes, *anything* happen; to be blind forever, and to have Joey sick, only make me good."

How long she stayed there she never knew, for she fell asleep — the first sleep she had had since Joey was taken sick. And little Mrs. Beebe coming in found her thus.

"Polly," the good woman said, leaning over her, "you

poor, pretty creeter, you. I'm goin' to tell you some-thin' — there, there, just to think! Joel's goin' to get well!"

"Oh, Mrs. Beebe!" cried Polly, tumbling over in a heap on the floor, her face, as much as could be seen under the bandage, in a perfect glow. "Is he *really?*"

"Yes, to be sure; the danger's all over now," said the little old lady, inwardly thinking, "If I *hadn't* a-come!"

"Well, then, the Lord wants him to," cried Polly in rapture, "don't he, Mrs. Beebe?"

"To be sure, to be sure," repeated the kind friend, only half understanding.

"Well, I don't care about my eyes, then," cried Polly, and to Mrs. Beebe's intense astonishment and dismay, she spun round and round in the middle of the floor.

"Oh, Polly, *Polly!*" the little old lady cried, running up to her. "*Do* stop! The doctor wouldn't let you! He wouldn't really, you know! It'll all go to your eyes."

"I don't care," repeated Polly in the middle of a spin, but she stopped obediently. "Seems as if I just as soon be blind as not, it's *so* beautiful Joey's going to get well!"

SUNSHINE AGAIN

BUT as Joel was smitten down suddenly, so he came up quickly, and his hearty nature asserted itself by rapid strides toward returning health. And one morning he astonished them all by turning over suddenly and exclaiming, "I want something to eat!"

"Bless the Lord!" cried Mrs. Pepper. "Now he's going to live!"

"But he *mustn't* eat," protested Mrs. Beebe in great alarm, trotting for the cup of gruel. "Here, you pretty creeter you, here's something nice." And she temptingly held the spoon over Joel's mouth, but with a grimace he turned away.

"Oh, I want something to *eat!* Some gingerbread or some bread and butter."

"Dear me!" ejaculated Mrs. Beebe. "Gingerbread!"

Poor Mrs. Pepper saw the hardest part of her trouble now before her, as she realized that the returning appetite must be fed only on strengthening food: For where it was to come from she couldn't tell.

"The Lord only knows where we'll get it," she groaned within herself.

Yes, He knew. A rap at the door, and little David ran down to find the cause.

"Oh, mammy," he said. "Mrs. Henderson sent it — see! See!"

And in the greatest excitement he placed in her lap a basket that smelled savory and nice even before it was opened. When it was opened, there lay a little bird delicately roasted, and folded in a clean napkin; also a glass of jelly, crimson and clear.

"Oh, Joey," cried Mrs. Pepper, almost overwhelmed with joy. "See what Mrs. Henderson sent you! Now you can eat fit for a king!"

That little bird certainly performed its mission in life, for as Mrs. Beebe said, "It just touched the spot!" and from that very moment Joel improved so rapidly, they could hardly believe their eyes.

"Hoh! I haven't been sick!" he cried on the third day, true to his nature. "Mammy, I want to get up."

"Oh, dear, no! You mustn't, Joel," cried Mrs. Pepper in a fright, running up to him as he was preparing to give the bedclothes a lusty kick. "You'll send 'em in."

"Send *what* in?" asked Joel, looking up at his mother in terror as the dreadful thought made him pause.

"Why, the measles, Joey. They'll all go in if you get out."

"How they goin' to get in again, I'd like to know?" asked Joel, looking at the little red spots on his hands in incredulity. "Say, ma!"

"Well, they *will*," said his mother, "as you'll find to your sorrow if you get out of bed."

"Oh, dear," said Joel, beginning to whimper as he drew into bed again. "When *can* I get up, mammy!"

"Oh, in a day or two," responded Mrs. Pepper cheerfully. "You're getting on so finely, you'll be as smart as a cricket! Shouldn't you say he might get up in a day or two, Mrs. Beebe?" she appealed to that individual who was knitting away cheerily in the corner.

"Well, if he keeps on as he's begun, I shouldn't know *what* to think," replied Mrs. Beebe. "It beats all how quick he's picked up. I never seen anything like it, I'm sure!"

And as Mrs. Beebe was a great authority in sickness, the old, sunny cheeriness began to creep into the brown house once more and to bubble over as of yore.

"Seems as if 'twas just good to *live*," said Mrs. Pepper thankfully once, when her thoughts were too much for her. "I don't believe I shall ever care how poor we are," she continued, "as long as we're together."

"And that's just what the Lord meant, maybe," replied good Mrs. Beebe, who was preparing to go home.

Joel kept the house in a perfect uproar all through his getting well. Mrs. Pepper observed one day, when he had been more turbulent than usual, that she was "almost worn to a thread."

" 'Twasn't anything to take care of you, Joe," she added, "when you were real sick, because then I knew where you were; but — well, you won't ever have the measles again, I s'pose, and that's some comfort!"

Little David, who had been nearly stunned by the sickness that had laid aside his almost constant companion, could express his satisfaction and joy in no other way than by running every third minute and begging to do something for him. And Joel, who loved dearly to be waited on, improved every opportunity that offered, which Mrs. Pepper, observing, soon put a stop to.

"You'll run his legs off, Joel," at last she said when he sent David the third time down to the woodpile for a stick of just the exact thickness, and which the little messenger declared wasn't to be found. "Haven't you any mercy? You've kept him going all day, too," she added, glancing at David's pale face.

"Oh, mammy," panted David, "don't. I love to go. Here, Joe, is the best I could find," handing him a nice smooth stick.

"I know you do," said his mother. "But Joe's getting better now, and he must learn to spare you."

"I don't want to spare folks," grumbled Joel, whittling away with energy. "I've been sick — *real* sick," he added, lifting his chubby face to his mother to impress the fact.

"I know you have," she cried, running to kiss her boy, "but now, Joe, you're most well. Tomorrow I'm going to let you go downstairs; what do you think of *that!*"

"*Hooray!*" screamed Joel, throwing away the stick and clapping his hands, forgetting all about his serious illness. "That'll be *prime!*"

"Aren't you too sick to go, Joey?" asked Mrs. Pepper mischievously.

"No, I'm not sick," cried Joel in the greatest alarm, fearful his mother meant to take back the promise. "I've never been sick. Oh, mammy! You *know* you'll let me go, won't you?"

"I guess so," laughed his mother.

"Come on, Phron," cried Joel, giving her a whirl.

David, who was too tired for active sport, sat on the floor and watched them frolic in great delight.

"Mammy," said he, edging up to her side as the sport went on, "do you know, I think it's just good — it's —

oh, it's so *frisky* since Joe got well, isn't it, mammy?"

"Yes, indeed," said Mrs. Pepper, giving him a radiant look in return for his. "And when Polly's around again with her two eyes all right — well, I don't know what we *shall* do, I declare!"

"Boo!" cried a voice next morning, close to Polly's elbow, unmistakably Joel's.

"Oh, Joel Pepper!" she cried, whirling around. "Is that really *you!*"

"Yes," cried that individual confidently, "it's I. Oh, I say, Polly, I've had fun upstairs, I tell you what!"

"Poor boy!" said Polly compassionately.

"I wasn't a poor boy," cried Joel indignantly. "I had splendid things to eat. Oh, my!" And he closed one eye and smacked his lips in the delightful memory.

"I know it," said Polly, "and I'm so glad, Joel."

"I don't suppose I'll ever get so many again," observed Joel reflectively after a minute's pause, as one and another of the wondrous delicacies rose before his mind's eye. "Not unless I have the measles again — say, Polly, can't I have 'em again?"

"Mercy, no!" cried Polly in intense alarm. "I hope not."

"Well, I don't," said Joel. "I wish I could have 'em sixty — no — two hundred times, so there!"

"Well, mammy couldn't take care of you," said Ben. "You don't know what you're sayin', Joe."

"Well, then, I wish I could have the things *without* the measles," said Joel, willing to accommodate. "Only folks won't send 'em," he added in an injured tone.

"Polly's had the hardest time of all," said her mother, affectionately patting the bandage.

"I think so too," put in Ben. "If my eyes were hurt I'd give up."

"So would I," said David. And Joel, to be in the fashion, cried also, "I know *I* would," while little Phronsie squeezed up to Polly's side. "And *I* too."

"Would what, Puss?" asked Ben, tossing her up high.

"Have good things," cried the child in delight at understanding the others. "I would really, Ben," she cried gravely when they all screamed.

"Well, I hope so," said Ben, tossing her higher yet.

"Don't laugh at her, boys," put in Polly. "We're all going to have good times now, Phronsie, now we've got well."

"Yes," laughed the child from her high perch. "We aren't ever goin' to be sick again, ever — anymore," she added impressively.

The good times were coming for Polly — coming pretty near, and she didn't know it! All the children were in the secret, for as Mrs. Pepper declared, "They'd have to know it, and if they were let into the secret they'd keep it better."

So they had individually and collectively been entrusted with the precious secret and charged with the extreme importance of "never letting anyone know," and they had been nearly bursting ever since with the wild desire to impart their knowledge.

"I'm afraid I *shall* tell," said David, running to his mother at last. "Oh, mammy, I don't dare stay near Polly, I do want to tell *so bad*."

"Oh, no, you won't, David," said his mother encouragingly, "when you know mother don't want you to. And besides, think how Polly'll look when she sees it."

"I know," cried David in the greatest rapture. "I wouldn't tell for all the world! I guess she'll look nice, don't you, mother?" And he laughed in glee at the thought.

"Poor child! I guess she will!" And then Mrs. Pepper laughed, too, till the little old kitchen rang with delight at the accustomed sound.

The children all had to play "clap in and clap out" in the bedroom while *it* came, and "stagecoach," too — "anything to make a noise," Ben said. And then after they got nicely started in the game, he would be missing to help about the mysterious thing in the kitchen, which was safe, since Polly couldn't see him go on account of her bandage. So she didn't suspect in the least. And although the rest were almost dying to be out in the kitchen, they conscientiously stuck to their bargain to keep Polly occupied. Only Joel *would* open the door and peep once, and then Phronsie behind him began, "Oh, I see the sto — " but David swooped down on her in a twinkling and smothered the rest by tickling her.

Once they came very near having the whole thing pop out.

"Whatever is that noise in the kitchen?" asked Polly as they all stopped to take breath after the scuffle of "stagecoach." "It sounds just like grating."

"I'll go and see," cried Joel promptly, and then he flew out where his mother and Ben and two men were at work on a big, black thing in the corner. The old stove, strange to say, was nowhere to be seen. Something else stood in its place — a shiny, black affair with a generous supply of oven doors and altogether such a comfortable, homelike look about it, as if it would say, "I'm going to make sunshine in this house!"

"Oh, Joel," cried his mother, turning around on him with very black hands. "You *haven't* told!"

"No," said Joel, "but she's hearin' the noise, Polly is."

"Hush!" said Ben to one of the men.

"We can't put it up without some noise," the man replied, "but we'll be as still as we can."

"Isn't it a big one, ma?" asked Joel in the loudest of stage whispers that Polly on the other side of the door couldn't have failed to hear if Phronsie hadn't laughed just then.

"Go back, Joe, do," said Ben. "Play tag — *anything*," he implored. "We'll be through in a few minutes."

"It takes forever!" said Joel, disappearing within the bedroom door. Luckily for the secret, Phronsie just then ran a pin sticking up on the arm of the old chair into her finger, and Polly, while comforting her, forgot to question Joel. And then the mother came in, and though she had ill-concealed hilarity in her voice, she kept chattering and bustling around with Polly's supper to such an extent that there was no chance for a word to be got in.

Next morning it seemed as if the little brown house would turn inside out with joy.

"Oh, mammy!" cried Polly, jumping into her arms the first thing as Dr. Fisher untied the bandage, "My eyes are *new!* Just the same as if I'd just got 'em! Don't they *look* different?" she asked earnestly, running to the cracked glass to see for herself.

"No," said Ben, "I hope not; the same brown ones, Polly."

"Well," said Polly, hugging first one and then another, "everybody looks different through them, anyway."

"Oh," cried Joel, "come out into the kitchen, Polly. It's a great deal better out there."

"May I?" asked Polly, who was in such a twitter looking at everything that she didn't know which way to turn.

"Yes," said the doctor, smiling at her.

"Well, then," sang Polly, "come, mammy, we'll go first. Isn't it just lovely — oh, *mammy!*" And Polly turned so very pale and looked as if she were going to tumble right over that Mrs. Pepper grasped her arm in dismay.

"What is it?" she asked, pointing to the corner, while all the children stood round in the greatest excitement.

"Why," cried Phronsie, "it's a *stove* — don't you know, Polly?"

But Polly gave one plunge across the room, and before anybody could think, she was down on her knees with her arms flung right around the big, black thing, and laughing and crying over it, all in the same breath!

And then they all took hold of hands and danced around it like wild little things, while Dr. Fisher stole out silently, and Mrs. Pepper laughed till she wiped her eyes to see them go.

"We aren't ever goin' to have any more burned bread," sang Polly, all out of breath.

"Nor your back isn't goin' to break anymore," panted Ben with a very red face.

"Hooray!" screamed Joel and David, to fill any pause that might occur, while Phronsie gurgled and laughed at everything just as it came along. And then they all danced and capered again — all but Polly, who was down before the precious stove examining and exploring into ovens and everything that belonged to it.

"Oh, ma," she announced, coming up to Mrs. Pepper, who had been obliged to fly to her sewing again, and exhibiting a very crocky face and a pair of extremely smutty hands, "it's most all ovens, and it's just splendid!"

"I know it," answered her mother, delighted in the joy of her child. "My! How black you are, Polly!"

"Oh, I wish," cried Polly, as the thought struck her, "that Dr. Fisher could see it! Where did he go to, ma?"

"I guess Dr. Fisher has seen it before," said Mrs. Pepper, and then she began to laugh. "You haven't ever asked where the stove came from, Polly."

And to be sure, Polly had been so overwhelmed that if the stove had really dropped from the clouds, it would have been small matter of astonishment to her, as long as it had *come;* that was the main thing!

"Mammy," said Polly, turning around slowly with the stove lifter in her hand, "did Dr. Fisher bring that stove?"

"He didn't exactly *bring* it," answered her mother, "but I guess he knew something about it."

"Oh, he's the splendidest, *goodest* man," cried Polly, "that ever breathed! Did he *really* get us that stove?"

"Yes," said Mrs. Pepper, "he would. I couldn't stop him. I don't know how he found out you wanted one so bad; but he said it must be kept as a surprise when your eyes got well."

"And he saved my eyes!" cried Polly, full of gratitude. "I've got a stove and two new eyes, mammy. Just to think!"

"We ought to be good after all our mercies," said Mrs. Pepper thankfully, looking around on her little group. Joel was engaged in the pleasing occupation of seeing how far he could run his head into the biggest oven, and then pulling it out to exhibit its blackness, thus engrossing the others in a perfect hubbub.

"I'm going to bake my doctor some little cakes," declared Polly when there was comparative quiet.

"Do, Polly," cried Joel, "and then leave one or two over."

"No," said Polly, "we can't have any, because these must be very nice. Mammy, can't I have some white on top, just once?" she pleaded.

"I don't know," dubiously replied Mrs. Pepper. "Eggs are dreadful dear, and — "

"I don't care," said Polly recklessly. "I must just once, for Dr. Fisher."

"I tell you, Polly," said Mrs. Pepper, "what you might do — you might make him some little apple tarts; most everyone likes them, you know."

"Well," said Polly with a sigh, "I s'pose they'll *have* to do; but *sometime,* mammy, I'm going to bake him a big cake, so there!"

A THREATENED BLOW

ONE day a few weeks after, Mrs. Pepper and Polly were busy in the kitchen. Phronsie was out in the "orchard," as the one scraggy apple tree was called by courtesy, singing her rag doll to sleep under its sheltering branches. But "Baby" was cross and wouldn't go to sleep, and Phronsie was on the point of giving up and returning to the house when a strain of music made her pause with dolly in her apron. There she stood with her finger in her mouth, in utter astonishment, wondering where the sweet sounds came from.

"Oh, Phronsie!" screamed Polly from the back door. "Where are — oh, here, come quick! It's the beau-ti-fullest!"

"What is it?" eagerly asked the little one, hopping over the stubby grass, leaving poor, discarded Baby on its snubby nose where it dropped in her hurry.

"Oh, a monkey!" cried Polly. "Do hurry! The sweetest little monkey you ever saw!"

"What is a monkey?" asked Phronsie, scurrying after Polly to the gate where her mother was waiting for them.

"Why, a monkey's — a — monkey," explained Polly.

"I don't know any better'n that. Here he is! Isn't he splendid!" and she lifted Phronsie up to the big post where she could see finely.

"Ooh! Ow!" screamed little Phronsie. "See him, Polly! Just see him!"

A man with an organ was standing in the middle of the road, playing away with all his might, and at the end of a long rope was a lively little monkey in a bright red coat and a smart cocked hat. The little creature pulled off his hat and, with one long jump coming on the fence, he made Phronsie a most magnificent bow. Strange to say, the child wasn't in the least frightened but put out her little fat hand, speaking in gentle tones. "Poor little monkey! Come here, poor little monkey!"

Turning up his little wrinkled face and glancing fearfully at his master, Jocko began to grimace and beg for something to eat. The man pulled the string and struck up a merry tune, and in a minute the monkey spun around and around at such a lively pace and put in so many queer antics that the little audience were fairly convulsed with laughter.

"I can't pay you," said Mrs. Pepper, wiping her eyes, when at last the man pulled up the strap, whistling to Jocko to jump up, "but I'll give you something to eat, and the monkey, too. He shall have something for his pains in amusing my children."

The man looked very cross when she brought him out only brown bread and two cold potatoes.

"Haven't you got nothin' better'n *that*?"

"It's as good as we have," answered Mrs. Pepper.

The man threw down the bread in the road. But Jocko thankfully ate his share, Polly and Phronsie busily feeding him, and then he turned and snapped up the portion his master had left in the dusty road.

Then they moved on, Mrs. Pepper and Polly going back to their work in the kitchen. A little down the road the man struck up another tune. Phronsie, who had started merrily to tell Baby all about it, stopped a minute to hear, and — she didn't go back to the orchard!

About two hours later, Polly said merrily, "I'm going to call Phronsie in, mammy. She must be awfully tired and hungry by this time."

She sang gaily on the way, "I'm coming, Phronsie, coming — why, where — " peeping under the tree.

Baby lay on its face disconsolately on the ground, and the orchard was empty! Phronsie was gone!

"It's no use," said Ben to the distracted household and such of the neighbors as the news had brought hurriedly to the scene, "to look anymore around here, but somebody must go toward Hingham. He'd be likely to go that way."

"No one could tell where he *would* go," cried Polly, wringing her hands.

"But he'd change, Ben, if he thought folks would think he'd gone there," said Mrs. Pepper.

"We must go *all* roads," said Ben firmly. "One must take the stage to Boxville, and I'll take Deacon Brown's wagon on the Hingham road, and somebody else must go to Toad Hollow."

"I'll go in the stage," screamed Joel, who could scarcely see out of his eyes, he had cried so. "I'll find — find her — I know."

"Be spry, then, Joe, and catch it at the corner!"

Everybody soon knew that little Phronsie Pepper had

gone off with "a cross organ man and an awful monkey!" And in the course of an hour dozens of people were out on the hot, dusty roads in search.

"What's the matter?" asked a testy old gentleman in the stage, of Joel, who, in his anxiety to see both sides of the road at once, bobbed the old gentleman in the face so often as the stage lurched that at last he knocked his hat over his eyes.

"My sister's gone off with a monkey," explained Joel, bobbing over to the other side, as he thought he caught sight of something pink that he felt sure *must* be Phronsie's apron. "Stop! stop! There she is!" he roared, and the driver, who had his instructions and was fully in sympathy, pulled up so suddenly that the old gentleman flew over into the opposite seat.

"Where?"

But when they got up to it, Joel saw that it was only a bit of pink calico flapping on a clothesline; so he climbed back and away they rumbled again.

The others were having the same luck. No trace could be found of the child. To Ben, who took the Hingham road, the minutes seemed like hours.

"I *won't* go back," he muttered, "until I take her. I *can't* see mother's face!"

But the ten miles were nearly traversed; almost the last hope was gone. Into every thicket and lurking place by the roadside had he peered — but no Phronsie! Deacon Brown's horse began to lag.

"*Go on!*" said Ben hoarsely. "Oh, dear Lord, *make* me find her!"

The hot sun poured down on the boy's face, and he had no cap. What cared he for that? On and on he went.

Suddenly the horse stopped. Ben doubled up the reins to give him a cut, when *"Whoa!"* he roared so loud that the horse in very astonishment gave a lurch that nearly flung him headlong. But he was over the wheel in a twinkling and up with a bound to a small thicket of scrubby bushes on a high hill by the roadside. Here lay a little bundle on the ground, and close by it a big, black dog; and over the whole, standing guard, was a boy a little bigger than Ben, with honest gray eyes. And the bundle was Phronsie!

"Don't wake her up," said the boy warningly as Ben, with a hungry look in his eyes, leaped up the hill. "She's tired to death!"

"She's my sister!" cried Ben. *"Our Phronsie!"*

"I know it," said the boy kindly, "but I wouldn't wake her up yet if I were you. I'll tell you all about it," and he took Ben's hand, which was as cold as ice.

SAFE

"It's all right, Prince," the boy added encouragingly to the big dog, who, lifting his noble head, had turned two big eyes steadily on Ben. "He's all right! Lie down again!"

Then, flinging himself down on the grass, he told Ben how he came to rescue Phronsie.

"Prince and I were out for a stroll," said he. "I live over in Hingham," pointing to the pretty little town just a short distance before them in the hollow. "That is" — laughing — "I do this summer. Well, we were out strolling along about a mile below here on the crossroad, and all of a sudden, just as if they sprung right up out of the ground, I saw a man with an organ, and a monkey, and a little girl, coming along the road. She was crying, and as soon as Prince saw that, he gave a growl, and then the man saw us, and he looked so mean and cringing, I knew there must be something wrong, and I inquired of him what he was doing with that little girl, and then she looked up and begged so with her eyes, and all of a sudden broke away from him and ran toward me screaming 'I want Polly!' Well, the man sprang after her, then I tell you" — here the boy forgot his caution about waking Phronsie — "we went for him, Prince and I! Prince is a noble fellow" — here the dog's ears twitched very perceptibly — "and he kept at that man. Oh! How he bit him! Till he had to run for fear the monkey would get killed."

"Was Phronsie frightened?" asked Ben. "She's never seen strangers."

"Not a bit," said the boy cheerily. "She just clung to me like everything. I only wish she was my sister," he added impulsively.

"What were you going to do with her if I hadn't come along?" asked Ben.

"Well, I got out on the main road," said the boy, "because I thought anybody who had lost her would probably come through this way. But if somebody hadn't come, I was going to carry her in to Hingham, and the father and I'd had to contrive some way to do."

"Well," said Ben as the boy finished and fastened his bright eyes on him, "somebody did come along. And now I must get her home about as fast as I can for poor mammy — and Polly!"

"Yes," said the boy, "I'll help you lift her. Perhaps she won't wake up."

The big dog moved away a step or two but still kept his eye on Phronsie.

"There," said the boy brightly as they laid the child on the wagon seat. "Now, when you get in you can hold her head; that's it," he added, seeing them both fixed to his satisfaction. But still Ben lingered.

"Thank you," he tried to say.

"I know," laughed the boy. "Only it's Prince instead of me." And he pulled forward the big black creature, who had followed faithfully down the hill to see the last of it. "To the front, sir, there! We're coming to see you," he continued, "if you will let us. Where do you live?"

"Do come," said Ben, lighting up, for he was just feeling he couldn't bear to look his last on the merry, honest face. "Anybody'll tell you where Mrs. Pepper lives."

"Is she a Pepper?" asked the boy, laughing and pointing to the unconscious little heap in the wagon. "And are you a Pepper?"

"Yes," said Ben, laughing too. "There are five of us besides mother."

"Jolly! That's something like! Good-bye! Come on, Prince!"

Then away home to mother! Phronsie never woke up or turned over once till she was put, a little pink sleepy heap, into her mother's arms. Joel was there, crying bitterly at his forlorn search. The testy old gentleman in the seat opposite had relented and ordered the coach about and brought him home in an outburst of grief when all hope was gone. And one after another they had all come back, disheartened, to the distracted mother. Polly alone clung to hope.

"Ben *will* bring her, mammy; I *know* God will let him," she whispered.

But when Ben did bring her, Polly, for the second time in her life, tumbled over with a gasp into old Mrs. Bascom's lap.

Home and mother! Little Phronsie slept all that night

straight through. The neighbors came in softly and with awestruck visages stole into the bedroom to look at the child. And as they crept out again, thoughts of their own little ones tugging at their hearts, the tears would drop unheeded.

NEW FRIENDS

UP the stairs of the hotel, two steps at a time, ran a boy with a big black dog at his heels. "Come on, Prince; soft, now," as they neared a door at the end of the corridor.

It opened into a corner room overlooking "the Park," as the small open space in front of the hotel was called. Within the room there was sunshine and comfort, it being the most luxurious one in the house, which the proprietor had placed at the disposal of this most exacting guest. He didn't look very happy, however — the gentleman who sat in an easy chair by the window; a large, handsome old gentleman whose whole bearing showed plainly that personal comfort had always been his and was, therefore, neither a matter of surprise nor thankfulness.

"Where have you been?" he asked, turning around to greet the boy who came in, followed by Prince.

"Oh, such a long story, father!" he cried, flushed, his eyes sparkling as he flung back the dark hair from his forehead. "You can't even guess!"

"Never mind now," said the old gentleman testily. "Your stories are always long. The paper hasn't come —

strange, indeed, that one must needs be so annoyed! Do ring that bell again."

So the bell was pulled, and a porter popped in his head.

"What is it, sir?"

"The *paper*," said the old gentleman irritably. "Hasn't it come yet?"

"No, sir," said the man, and then he repeated, " 'Taint in yet, please, sir."

"Very well, you said so once; that's all," waving his hand. Then as the door closed, he said to his son, "That pays one for coming to such an out-of-the-way country place as this, away from papers. I never will do it again."

As the old gentleman, against the advice of many friends who knew his dependence on externals, had *determined* to come to this very place, the boy was not much startled at the decisive words. He stood very quietly, however, until his father finished. Then he said, "It's too bad, father! Supposing I tell you my story. Perhaps you'll enjoy hearing it while you wait — it's really quite newspaperish."

"Well, you might as well tell it now, I suppose," said the old gentleman. "But it is a great shame about the paper! To advertise that morning papers are to be obtained — it's a swindle, Jasper! A complete swindle!" And the old gentleman looked so very irate that the boy exerted himself to soothe him.

"I know," he said. "But they can't help the trains being late."

"They shouldn't *have* the trains late," said his father unreasonably. "There's no necessity for all this prating about 'trains late.' I'm convinced it's because they forgot to send down for the papers till they were all sold."

"I don't believe that's it, father," said the boy, trying to change the subject. "But you don't know how splendid Prince has been, nor — "

"And then *such* a breakfast!" continued the old gentleman. "My liver certainly will be in a dreadful state if these things continue!" And he got up and, going to the corner of the room, opened his medicine chest, and taking a box of pills therefrom, he swallowed two, which done, he came back with a somewhat easier expression to his favorite chair.

"He was just *splendid*, father," began the boy. "He went for him, I tell you!"

"I hope, Jasper, your dog has not been doing anything violent," said the old gentleman. "I must caution you — he'll get you into trouble someday, and then there'll be a heavy bill to pay. He grows more irritable every day."

"*Irritable!*" cried the boy, flinging his arms around the dog's neck, who was looking up at the old gentleman in high disdain. "He's done the most splendid thing you ever saw! Why, he saved a little girl, father, from a cross old organ man, and he drove that man — oh, you ought to have seen him run!"

And now that it was over, Jasper put back his head and laughed long and loud as he remembered the rapid transit of the musical pair.

"Well, how do you know she wasn't the man's daughter?" asked his father, determined to find fault some way. "You haven't any business to go around the country setting your dog on people. I shall have an awful bill to pay some day, Jasper, an awful bill!" he continued, getting up and commencing to pace up and down the floor in extreme irritation.

"Father," cried the boy, half laughing, half vexed, springing to his side and keeping step with him, "we found her brother. He came along when we were by the side of the road. We couldn't go any further, for the poor little thing was all tired out. And don't you think they live over in Badgertown, and — "

"Well," said the old gentleman, pausing in his walk and taking out his watch to wonder if that paper would ever come, "she had probably followed the organ man, so it served her right after all."

"Well, but, father," and the boy's dark eyes glowed, "she was such a cunning little thing! She wasn't more than four years old, and she had such a pretty little yellow head, and she said so funny — 'I want Polly.' "

"Did she?" said the old gentleman, getting interested in spite of himself. "What then?"

"Why, then, sir," said Jasper, delighted at his success in diverting his thoughts, "Prince and I waited — and waited. And I was just going to bring her here to ask you what we should do, when — "

"Dear me!" said the old gentleman, instinctively starting back as if he actually saw the forlorn little damsel. "You needn't ever bring such people here, Jasper! I don't know what to do with them, I'm sure!"

"Well," said the boy, laughing, "we didn't have to, did we, Prince?" stroking the big head of the dog, who was slowly following the two as they paced up and down, but keeping carefully on the side of his master. "For just as we really didn't know what to do, don't you think there was a big wagon came along, drawn by the ricketiest old horse, and a boy in the wagon looking both sides of the road and into every bush, just as wild as he could be, and before I could think, hardly, he spied us, and if he didn't jump! I thought he'd broken his leg — "

"And I suppose he just abused you for what you had done," observed the old gentleman petulantly. "That's about all the gratitude there is in *this* world."

"He didn't seem to see *me* at all," said the boy. "I thought he'd eat the little girl up."

"Ought to have looked out for her better, then," grumbled the old gentleman, determined to find fault with somebody.

"And he's a splendid fellow, I just know," cried Jasper, waxing enthusiastic. "And his name is Pepper."

"Pepper!" repeated his father. "No nice family ever had the name of *Pepper!*"

"Well, I don't care," and Jasper's laugh was loud and merry. "*He's* nice anyway, *I know,* and the little thing's nice; and I'm going to see them — can't I, father?"

"Dear me!" said his father. "How can you, Jasper? You do have the strangest tastes I ever saw!"

"It's dreadful dull here," pleaded the boy, touching the right string. "You know that yourself, father, and I don't know any boys around here. And Prince and I are *so* lonely on our walks — do permit me, father!"

The old gentleman, who really cared very little about it, turned away, muttering, "Well, I'm sure I don't care; go where you like," when a knock was heard at the door, and the paper was handed in, which broke up the conversation and restored good humor.

The next day but one, Ben was out by the woodpile, trying to break up some kindlings for Polly, who was washing up the dishes and otherwise preparing for the delights of baking day.

"Hulloa!" said a voice he thought he knew.

He turned around to see the merry-faced boy and the big black dog, who immediately began to wag his tail as if willing to recognize him.

"You see, I thought you'd *never* look round," said the boy with a laugh. "How's the little girl?"

"Oh! You have come, really," cried Ben, springing over the woodpile with a beaming face. "Polly!"

But Polly was already by the door, with dish cloth in hand.

"This is my sister, Polly," began Ben, and then stopped, not knowing the boy's name.

"I'm Jasper King," said the boy, stepping upon the flat stone by Polly's side, and taking off his cap, he put out his hand. "And this is Prince," he added.

Polly put her hand in his and received a hearty shake, and then she sprang over the big stone, dish cloth and all, and just flung her arms around the dog's neck.

"Oh, you splendid fellow, you!" said she. "Don't you know we all think you're as good as gold?"

The dog submitted to the astonishing proceeding as if he liked it, while Jasper, delighted with Polly's appreciation, beamed down on them and struck up friendship with her on the instant.

"Now I must call Phronsie," said Polly, getting up, her face as red as a rose.

"Is her name Phronsie?" asked the boy with interest.

"No, it's Sophronia," said Polly, "but we call her Phronsie."

"What a very funny name," said Jasper, "Sophronia is, for such a little thing. And yours is Polly, is it not?" he asked, turning around suddenly on her.

"Yes," said Polly. "No, not truly Polly; it's Mary, my real name is, but I've always been Polly."

"I like Polly best, too," declared Jasper. "It sounds so nice."

"And his name is Ben," said Polly.

"Ebenezer, you mean," said Ben, correcting her.

"Well, we call him Ben," said Polly. "It don't ever seem as if there was any Ebenezer about it."

"I should think not," laughed Jasper.

"Well, I must get Phronsie," again said Polly, running back into the bedroom, where that small damsel was busily engaged in washing Baby in the basin of water that she had with extreme difficulty succeeded in getting down on the floor. She had then, by means of a handful of soft soap, taken from Polly's soap bowl during the dish washing, and a bit of old cotton, plastered both herself and Baby to a comfortable degree of stickiness.

"Phronsie," said Polly. "Dear me! What are you doing? The big dog's out there, you know, that scared the naughty organ man, and the boy" — but before the words were half out, Phronsie had slipped from under her hands and, to Polly's extreme dismay, clattered out into the kitchen.

"Here she is!" cried Jasper, meeting her at the door. The little soapy hands were grasped, and kissing her —

"Ugh!" he said as the soft soap plentifully spread on her face met his mouth.

"Oh, Phronsie! You shouldn't," cried Polly, and then they all burst out into a peal of laughter at Jasper's funny grimaces.

"She's been washing Baby," explained Polly, wiping her eyes and looking at Phronsie, who was hanging over Prince in extreme affection. Evidently Prince still regarded her as his especial property.

"Have you got a baby?" asked Jasper. "I thought *she* was the baby," pointing to Phronsie.

"Oh, I mean her littlest dolly; she always calls her Baby," said Polly. "Come, Phronsie, and have *your* face washed, and a clean apron on."

When Phronsie could be fairly persuaded that Prince would not run away during her absence, she allowed herself to be taken off, and soon reappeared, her own dainty little self. Ben, in the meantime, had been initiating Jasper into the mysteries of cutting the wood, the toolhouse, and all the surroundings of the little brown house. They had received a reinforcement in the advent of Joel and David, who stared delightedly at Phronsie's protector, made friends with the dog, and altogether had had such a thoroughly good time that Phronsie, coming back, clapped her hands in glee to hear them.

"I wish mammy was home," said Polly, polishing up the last cup carefully.

"Let me put it up," said Jasper, taking it from her. "It goes up here, don't it, with the rest?" reaching up to the upper shelf of the old cupboard.

"Yes," said Polly.

"Oh, I should think you'd have real good times!" said the boy enviously. "I haven't a single sister or brother."

"Haven't you?" said Polly, looking at him in extreme pity. "Yes, we do have real fun," she added, answering his questioning look. "The house is just brimful sometimes, even if we are poor."

"We aren't poor," said Joel, who never could bear to be pitied. Then, with a very proud air, he said in a grand way, "At any rate, we aren't going to be, long, for something's coming!"

"What *do* you mean, Joey?" asked Ben, while the rest looked equally amazed.

"Our ships," said Joel confidently, as if they were right before their eyes, at which they all screamed.

"See Polly's stove!" cried Phronsie, wishing to entertain in her turn. "Here 'tis," running up to it, and pointing with her fat little finger.

"Yes, I see," cried Jasper, pretending to be greatly surprised. "It's new, isn't it?"

"Yes," said the child. "It's very all new; four yesterdays ago!"

And then Polly stopped in, sweeping up, and related, with many additions and explanations from the others, the history of the stove, and good Dr. Fisher (upon whom they all dilated at great length), and the dreadful measles, and everything. And Jasper sympathized and rejoiced with them to their hearts' content, and altogether got so very homelike, that they all felt as if they had known him for a year. Ben neglected his work a little, but then visitors didn't come every day to the Peppers. So while Polly worked away at her bread, which she was "going to make like biscuits," she said, the audience gathered in the little old kitchen was in the merriest mood and enjoyed everything to the fullest extent.

"Do put in another stick, Bensie dear," said Polly. "This bread won't be fit for anything!"

"Isn't this fun, though!" cried Jasper, running up to try the oven. "I wish I could ever bake," and he looked longingly at the little brown biscuits waiting their turn out on the table.

"You come out someday," said Polly sociably, "and we'll all try baking. Mammy'd like to have you, I know," feeling sure that nothing would be too much for Mrs. Pepper to do for the protector of little Phronsie.

"I will!" cried Jasper, perfectly delighted. "You can't think how awfully dull it is out in Hingham!"

"Don't you *live* there?" asked Polly with a gasp, almost dropping a tin full of little brown lumps of dough she was carrying to the oven.

"*Live there!*" cried Jasper, and then he burst out into a merry laugh. "No *indeed!* I hope not! Why, we're only spending the summer there, father and I, in the hotel."

"Where's your mother?" asked Joel, squeezing in between Jasper and his audience. And then they all felt instinctively that a very wrong question had been asked.

"I haven't any mother," said the boy in a low voice.

They all stood quite still for a moment. Then Polly said, "I wish you'd come out sometime, and you may bake — or anything else," she added, and there was a kinder ring to her voice than ever.

No mother! Polly for her life couldn't imagine how anybody *could* feel without a mother, but the very words alone smote her heart. And there was nothing she wouldn't have done to give pleasure to one who had done so much for them.

"I wish you could see *our* mother," she said gently. "Why, here she comes now! Oh, mamsie, dear," she cried. "Do, Joe, run and take her bundle."

Mrs. Pepper stopped a minute to kiss Phronsie — her baby was dearer than ever to her now. Then her eye fell on Jasper, who stood respectfully waiting and watching her with great interest.

"Is this," she asked, taking it all in at the first glance — the boy with the honest eyes, as Ben had described him, and the big, black dog — "is this the boy who saved my little girl?"

"Oh, ma'am," cried Jasper, "*I* didn't do much; 'twas Prince."

"I guess you never'll know how much you *did* do," said Mrs. Pepper. Then, looking with a long, keen gaze into the boy's eyes that met her own so frankly and kindly, "I'll trust him," she said to herself. "A boy with those eyes can't help but be good."

"Her eyes are just the same as Polly's," thought Jasper. "Just such laughing ones, only Polly's were brown," and he liked her on the spot.

And then, somehow, the hubbub ceased. Polly went on with her work, and the others separated, and Mrs. Pepper and Jasper had a long talk. When the mother's eyes fell on Phronsie playing around on the floor, she gave the boy a grateful smile that he thought was beautiful.

"Well, I declare," said Jasper at last, looking up at the

old clock in the corner by the side of the cupboard. "I'm afraid I'll miss the stage, and then father never'll let me come again. Come, Prince."

"Oh, don't go," cried Phronsie, wailing. "Let doggie stay! Oh, *make* him stay, mammy!"

"I can't, Phronsie," said Mrs. Pepper, smiling, "if he thinks he ought to go."

"I'll come again," said Jasper eagerly, "if I may, ma'am." He looked up at Mrs. Pepper as he stood cap in hand, waiting for the answer.

"I'm sure we should be glad, if your father'll be willing," she added, thinking, proudly, "My children are an honor to anybody, I'm sure," as she glanced around on the bright little group she could call her own. "But be sure, Jasper," and she laid her hand on his arm as she looked down into his eyes, "that your father *is* willing, that's all."

"Oh, yes, ma'am," said the boy. "But he will be, I guess, if he feels well."

"Then come on Thursday," said Polly. "And can't we bake something then, mammy?"

"I'm sure I don't care," laughed Mrs. Pepper, "but you won't find much but brown flour and meal to bake with."

"Well, we can pretend," said Polly. "And we can cut the cakes with the heart shape, and they'll do for anything."

"Oh, I'll come," laughed Jasper, ready for such lovely fun in the old kitchen. "Look out for me on Thursday, Ben!"

So Jasper and Prince took their leave, all the children accompanying them to the gate. And then after seeing him fairly started on a smart run to catch the stage, Prince scampering at his heels, they all began to sing his praises and to wish for Thursday to come.

But Jasper didn't come! Thursday came and went, a beautiful, bright, sunny day, but with no signs of the merry boy whom all had begun to love, nor of the big black dog. The children had made all the needful preparations with much ostentation and bustle and were in a state of excited happiness, ready for any gale. But the last hope had to be given up as the old clock ticked away hour after hour. And at last Polly had to put Phronsie to bed, who wouldn't stop crying enough to get her supper at the dreadful disappointment.

"He *couldn't* come, I know," said both Ben and Polly, standing staunchly up for their new friend. But Joel and David felt that he had broken his word.

"He promised," said Joel vindictively.

"I don't believe his father'd let him," said Polly, wiping away a sly tear. "I know Jasper'd come if he could."

Mrs. Pepper wisely kept her own counsel, simply giving them a kindly caution. "Don't you go to judging him, children, till you know."

"Well, he *promised*," said Joel as a settler.

"Aren't you ashamed, Joe," said his mother, "to talk about anyone whose back is turned? Wait till he tells you the reason himself."

Joel hung his head and then began to tease David in the corner to make up for his disappointment.

The next morning Ben had to go to the store after some more meal. As he was going out rather dismally, the storekeeper, who was also postmaster, called out, "Oh, halloa, there!"

"What is it?" asked Ben, turning back, thinking perhaps Mr. Atkins hadn't given him the right change.

"Here," said Mr. Atkins, stepping up to the post office department, quite smart with its array of boxes and official notices, where Ben had always lingered, wishing there might be *sometime* a letter for him — or some of them. "You've got a sister Polly, haven't you?"

"Yes," said Ben, wondering what was coming next.

"Well, she's got a letter," said the postmaster, holding up a nice big envelope looking just like those that Ben had so many times wished for.

That magic piece of white paper danced before the boy's eyes for a minute. Then he said, "It can't be for her, Mr. Atkins. Why, she's *never* had one."

"Well, she's got one now, sure enough," said Mr. Atkins. "Here 'tis, plain enough," and he read what he had no need to study much as it had already passed examination by his own and his wife's faithful eyes. " 'Miss Polly Pepper, near the Turnpike, Badgertown' — that's her, isn't it?" he added, laying it down before Ben's eyes. "Must be a first time for everything, you know, my boy!" And he laughed long over his own joke. "So take it and run along home." For Ben still stood looking at it and not offering to stir.

"If you say so," said the boy, as if Mr. Atkins had given him something out of his own pocket. "But I'm afraid 'tisn't for Polly." Then, buttoning up the precious letter in his jacket, he spun along home as never before.

"Polly! Polly!" he screamed. "Where is she, mother?"

"I don't know," said Mrs. Pepper, coming out of the bedroom. "Dear me! Is anybody hurt, Ben?"

"I don't know," said Ben, in a state to believe anything, "but Polly's got a letter."

"Polly got a letter!" cried Mrs. Pepper. "What do you mean, Ben?"

"I don't know," repeated the boy, still holding out the precious letter. "But Mr. Atkins gave it to me. Where *is* Polly?"

"I know where she is," said Joel. "She's upstairs." And he flew out in a twinkling and just as soon reappeared with Polly scampering after him in the wildest excitement.

And then the kitchen was in an uproar as the precious missive was put into Polly's hand, and they all gathered around her, wondering and examining, till Ben thought he would go wild with the delay.

"I wonder where it did come from," said Polly in the greatest anxiety, examining again the address.

"Where does the postmark say?" asked Mrs. Pepper, looking over her shoulder.

"It's all rubbed out," said Polly, peering at it. "You can't see anything."

"Do *open* it," said Ben, "and then you'll find out."

"But p'raps 'tisn't for me," said Polly timidly.

"Well, Mr. Atkins says 'tis," said Ben impatiently. "Here, I'll open it for you, Polly."

"No, let her open it for herself, Ben," protested his mother.

"But she *won't*," said Ben. "Do *tear* it open, Polly."

"No, I'm goin' to get a knife," she said.

"I'll get one," cried Joel, running up to the table drawer. "Here's one Polly."

"Oh, dear," groaned Ben. "You never'll get it open at this rate!"

But at last it was cut, and they all, holding their breath, gazed awestruck while Polly drew out the mysterious missive.

"What *does* it say?" gasped Mrs. Pepper.

" 'Dear Miss Polly,' " began both Ben and Polly in a breath.

"Let Polly read," said Joel, who couldn't hear in the confusion.

"Well, go on, Polly," said Ben. *"Hurry!"*

" 'Dear Miss Polly, I was *so* sorry I couldn't come on Thursday — ' "

"Oh, it's Jasper! It's Jasper!" cried all the children in a breath.

"I told you so!" cried Ben and Polly, perfectly delighted to find their friend vindicated fully. *"There,* Joey Pepper!"

"Well, I don't care," cried Joe, nothing daunted. "He *didn't* come, anyway. Do go on, Polly."

" 'I was *so* sorry I couldn't come,' " began Polly.

"You read that," said Joel.

"I know it," said Polly, "but it's just lovely: 'on Thursday; but my father was sick, and I couldn't leave him. If you don't mind, I'll come again — I mean I'll come some other day, if it's just as convenient for you, for I do *so want* the baking, and the nice time. I forgot to say that I had a cold, to,' " (here Jasper had evidently had a struggle in his mind whether there should be two *o*'s or one, and he had at last decided it, by crossing out one) " 'but my father is willing I should come when I get well. Give my love to all, and especially remember me respectfully to your mother. Your friend, Jasper Elyot King.'

"Oh, *lovely, lovely!*" cried Polly, flying around with the letter in her hand. "So he is coming!"

Ben was just as wild as she was, for no one knew but Polly just how the new friend had stepped into his heart. Phronsie went to sleep happy, hugging Baby.

"And don't you think, Baby dear," she whispered sleepily, and Polly heard her say as she was tucking her in, "that Jasper is *really* comin'; really — and the big, be-you-ti-ful doggie, too!"

PHRONSIE PAYS A DEBT
OF GRATITUDE

"AND now I tell you," said Polly the next day, "let's make Jasper something; can't we, ma?"

"Oh, *do! Do!*" cried all the other children. "*Let's.* But what'll it be, Polly?"

"I don't know about this," interrupted Mrs. Pepper. "I don't see how you could get anything to him if you could make it."

"Oh, we could, mamsie," said Polly eagerly, running up to her. "For Ben knows, and he says we can do it."

"Oh, well, if Ben and you have had your heads together, I suppose it's all right," laughed Mrs. Pepper, "but I don't see how you can do it."

"Well, we can, mother, truly," put in Ben. "I'll tell you how, and you'll say it'll be splendid. You see, Deacon Blodgett's goin' over to Hingham tomorrow — I heard him tell Miss Blodgett so. And he goes right past the hotel. And we can do it up real nice — and it'll please Jasper so — do, mammy!"

"And it's real dull there, Jasper says," put in Polly persuasively. "And just think, mammy, no brothers and sisters!" And Polly looked around on the others.

After that there was no need to say anything more; her mother would have consented to almost any plan then.

"Well, go on, children," she said. "You may do it. I don't see but what you can get 'em there well enough, but I'm sure I don't know what you can *make*."

"Can't we," said Polly — and she knelt down by her mother's side and put her face in between the sewing in Mrs. Pepper's lap, and the eyes bent kindly down on her — "make some little cakes, real cakes, I mean? Now, don't say no, mammy!" she said, alarmed, for she saw a "no" slowly coming in the eyes above her as Mrs. Pepper began to shake her head.

"But we haven't any white flour, Polly," began her mother.

"I know," said Polly. "But we'll make 'em of brown. It'll do, if you'll give us some raisins — you know there's *some* in the bowl, mammy."

"I was saving them for a nest egg," said Mrs. Pepper, meaning at some future time to indulge in another plum pudding that the children so loved.

"Well, do give 'em to us," cried Polly. "Do, ma!"

"I want 'em for a plum pudding sometime," said Mrs. Pepper.

"*Ow!*" and Joel with a howl sprang up from the floor where he had been trying to make a cart for Baby out of an old box, and joined Mrs. Pepper and Polly. "No, don't give 'em away, ma!" he screamed. "Let's have our plum pudding. Now, Polly Pepper, you're a-goin' to bake up all our raisins in nasty little cakes — and — "

"*Joey!*" commanded Mrs. Pepper. "*Hush!* What word did you say!"

"Well," blubbered Joel, wiping his tears away with his grimy little hand, "Polly's — a-goin' — to give — "

"I should rather you'd *never* have a plum pudding than to say such words," said Mrs. Pepper sternly, taking up her work again. "And besides, do you think what Jasper has done for you?" And her face grew very white around the lips.

"Well, he can have plum puddings," said Joel, whimpering, "forever an' ever, if he wants them — and — and — "

"Well, Joey," said Polly, "there, don't feel bad," and she put her arms around him and tried to wipe away the tears that still rolled down his cheeks. "We won't give 'em if you don't want us to. But Jasper's sick, and there isn't anything for him to do, and" — here she whispered slyly up into his ear — "don't you remember how you liked folks to send *you* things when you had the measles?"

"Yes, I know," said Joel, beginning to smile through his tears. "Wasn't it fun, Polly?"

"I guess *'twas*," laughed Polly back again, pleased at the return of sunshine. "Well, Jasper'll be just as pleased as you were, 'cause we love him and want to do somethin' for him, he was so good to Phronsie."

"I will, Polly, I will," cried Joel, completely won over. "Do let's make 'em for him, and put 'em in thick — oh, thick as you can." And, determined to do nothing by halves, Joel ran generously for the precious bowl of raisins, and after setting it on the table, began to help Polly in all needful preparations.

Mrs. Pepper smiled away to herself to see happiness restored to the little group. And soon a pleasant hum and bustle went on around the baking table, the center of attraction.

"Now," said Phronsie, coming up to the table and standing on tiptoe to see Polly measure out the flour, "I'm a-goin' to bake something for my sick man, I *am*."

"Oh, no, Phronsie, you can't," began Polly.

"Hey?" asked Joel, with a dab of flour on the tip of his chubby nose, gained by too much peering into Polly's flour bag. "What did she say, Polly?" watching her shake the clouds of flour in the sieve.

"She said she was goin' to bake something for Jasper," said Polly. "There," as she whisked in the flour, "now that's done."

"No, I didn't say Japser," said Phronsie. "I didn't *say* Japser," she repeated emphatically.

"Why, what did you say, pet?" asked Polly, astonished, while little Davie repeated, "What did you say, Phronsie?"

"I said my sick *man*," said Phronsie, shaking her yellow head. "Poor sick man."

"Who *does* she mean?" said Polly in despair, stopping a moment her violent stirring that threatened to overturn the whole cake bowl.

"I guess she means Prince," said Joel. "Can't I stir, Polly?"

"Oh, no," said Polly. "Only one person must stir a cake."

"Why?" asked Joel. "Why, Polly?"

"Oh, I don't know," said Polly. " 'Cause 'tis so; never mind now, Joel. *Do* you mean Prince, Phronsie?"

"*No*, I don't mean Princey," said the child decisively. "I mean my sick *man*."

120

"It's Jasper's father, I guess she means," said Mrs. Pepper over in the corner. "But what in the world!"

"Yes, yes," cried Phronsie, perfectly delighted at being at last understood, and hopping on one toe. "My sick man."

"I *shall* give up!" said Polly, tumbling over in a chair with the cake spoon in her hand, from which a small sticky lump fell on her apron, which Joel immediately pounced upon and devoured. "What do you want to bake, Phronsie?" she gasped, holding the spoon sticking up straight and staring at the child.

"A gingerbread boy," said the child promptly. "He'd like that best, poor, sick man!" and she commenced to climb up to active preparations.

A LETTER TO JASPER

"Mamsie, what *shall* we do?" implored Polly of her mother.

"I don't know," said her mother. "However did that get into her head, do you suppose?"

"I am sure I can't tell," said Polly, jumping up and beginning to stir briskly to make up for lost time. "P'r'aps she heard us talking about Jasper's having to take care of his sick father, and how hard it must be to be sick away from home."

"Yes," said Phronsie, "but he'll be glad to see my gingerbread boy, I guess, poor, sick man."

"Oh, Phronsie," cried Polly, in great distress. "You aren't ever going to make a 'gingerbread boy' today! See, we'll put in a cunning little cake for Mr. King, full of raisins, Phronsie. Won't that be lovely!" and Polly began to fill a little scalloped tin with some of the cake mixture.

"N-no," said the child, eyeing it suspiciously. "That isn't like a gingerbread boy, Polly. He'll like that best."

"Mamsie," said Polly. "We *can't* let her make a dreadful, horrid gingerbread boy to send Mr. King! He never'll let Jasper come here again."

"Oh, let her," cried Joel. "She can bake it, and Dave an' I'll eat it." And he picked up a raisin that had fallen under the table and began crunching it with great gusto.

"That wouldn't be fair," said Polly gloomily. "Do get her off from it, mammy."

"Phronsie," said Mrs. Pepper, going up back of the child, who sat patiently in her high chair waiting for Polly to let her begin, "hadn't you rather wait and give your gingerbread boy to Jasper for his father, when he comes?"

"Oh, no, no," cried Phronsie, twisting in her chair in great apprehension. "I want to send it now, I *do*."

"Well, Polly," said her mother, laughing, "after all it's best, I think, to let her. It can't do any harm, anyway. And instead of Mr. King's not letting Jasper come, if he's a sensible man, that won't make any difference; and if he isn't, why, then there'd sure to be something come up sometime to make trouble."

"Well," said Polly, "I suppose she's got to. And perhaps" — as a consoling idea struck her — "perhaps she'll want to eat it up herself when it's done. Here, Phronsie," giving her a handful of the cake mixture, which she stiffened to the right thickness, "there, you can call that a gingerbread boy. See, won't it make a beautiful one!"

"You needn't think," said Mrs. Pepper, seeing Phronsie's delighted face and laughing as she went back to her work, "but what that gingerbread boy'll go."

When the little cakes were done, eight of them, and set upon the table for exhibition, they one and all protested that they never saw so fine a lot. Polly was delighted with the praise they received and her mother's commendation that she was "growing a better cook every day." "How glad Jasper'll be, won't he, mamsie?" said she.

The children walked around and around the table, admiring and pointing out the chief points of attraction as they appeared before their discriminating eyes.

"I should choose that one," said Joel, pointing at one which was particularly plummy, with a raisin standing up on one end with a festive air as if to say, "There's lot's of us inside, you better believe!"

"I wouldn't," said Davie. "*I'd* have that — that's cracked so pretty."

"So 'tis," said Mrs. Pepper. "They're all as light as a feather, Polly."

"But my gingerbread boy," cried Phronsie, running eagerly along with a particularly ugly-looking specimen of a cake figure in her hand, "is the be-yew-tifullest, isn't it, Polly?"

"Oh, dear," groaned Polly. "It looks just awfully, don't it, Ben!"

"Hoh, hoh!" laughed Joel in derision. "His leg is crooked, see Phronsie — you better let Davie an' me have it."

"No, *no*," screamed the child in terror. "That's my sick man's gingerbread boy, it *is!*"

"Joe, put it down," said Ben. "Yes, Phronsie, you shall have it; there, it's all safe." And he put it carefully into Phronsie's apron, when she breathed easier.

"And he hasn't but one eye," still laughed Joel, while little Davie giggled too.

"He did have two," said Polly, "but she punched the other in with her thumb. Don't, boys," she said, aside.

"You'll make her feel bad. Do stop laughing. Now, how'll we send the things?"

"Put 'em in a basket," said Ben. "That's nicest."

"But we haven't got any basket," said Polly, "except the potato basket, and they'd be lost in that."

"Can't we take your work basket, mamsie?" asked Ben. "They'd look so nice in that."

"Oh," said Mrs. Pepper, "that wouldn't do; I couldn't spare it. And besides, it's all broken at the side, Ben. That don't look nice."

"Oh, dear," said Polly, sitting down on one of the hard wooden chairs to think. "I *do* wish we had things nice to send to sick people." And her forehead puckered up in a little hard knot.

"We'll have to do 'em up in a paper, Polly," said Ben. "There isn't any other way. They'll look nice in anything, 'cause they *are* nice," he added comfortingly.

"If we only had some flowers," said Polly. "That would set 'em off."

"You're always a-thinkin' of flowers, Polly," said Ben. "I guess the cakes'll have to go without 'em."

"I suppose they will," said Polly, stifling a little sigh. "Where's the paper?"

"I've got a nice piece upstairs," said Ben. "Just right. I'll get it."

"Put my gingerbread boy on top," cried Phronsie, handing him up.

So Polly packed the little cakes neatly in two rows, and laid the gingerbread boy in a fascinating attitude across the top.

"He looks as if he'd been struck by lightning!" said

Ben, viewing him critically as he came in the door with the paper.

"Be still," said Polly, trying not to laugh. "That's because he baked so funny; it made his feet stick out."

"Children," said Mrs. Pepper, "how'll Jasper know where the cakes come from?"

"Why, he'll know it's us," said Polly, "of course, 'cause it'll make him think of the baking we're going to have when he gets well."

"Well, but you don't say so," said Mrs. Pepper, smiling. " 'Tisn't polite to send it this way."

"Whatever'll we do, mammy!" said all four children in dismay, while Phronsie simply stared. "Can't we send 'em at all?"

"Why, yes," said their mother. "I hope so, I'm sure, after you've got 'em baked. But you might answer Jasper's letter, I should think, and tell him about 'em, and the gingerbread boy."

"Oh, dear," said Polly, ready to fly. "I *couldn't,* mamsie. I *never* wrote a letter."

"Well, you never had one before, did you?" said her mother, composedly biting her thread. "Never say you can't, Polly, 'cause you don't know what you can do till you've tried."

"You write, Ben," said Polly imploringly.

"No," said Ben, "I think the nicest way is for all to say somethin' then 'twont be hard for any of us."

"Where's the paper," queried Polly, "coming from, I wonder!"

"Joel," said Mrs. Pepper, "run to the bureau in the bedroom, and open the top drawer, and get a green box there."

So Joel, quite important at the errand, departed, and presently put the designated box into his mother's hand.

"There, now I'm going to give you this." And she took out a small sheet of paper slightly yellowed by age, but being gilt-edged, it looked very magnificent to the five pairs of eyes directed to it.

"Now, Ben, you get the ink bottle and the pen, and then go to work."

So Ben reached down from the upper shelf in the cupboard the ink bottle, and a pen in a black wooden pen holder.

"Oh, mamsie," cried Polly, "that's where Phronsie bit it off when she was a baby, isn't it?" holding up the stubby end where the little ball had disappeared.

"Yes," said Mrs. Pepper, "and now you're going to write about her gingerbread boy with it. Well, time goes, to be sure." And she bent over her work again, harder than ever. Poor woman! If she could only scrape together enough money to get her children into school — that was the earnest wish of her heart. She *must* do it soon, for Ben was twelve years old. But with all her strivings and scrimpings she could only manage to put bread into their mouths, and live from day to day. "I know I ought to be thankful for that," she said to herself, not taking time even to cry over her troubles. "But, oh, the learning! They *must* have that!"

"Now," said Polly, "how'll we do it, Ben?" as they ranged themselves around the table, on which reposed the cakes. "You begin."

"How *do* folks begin a letter?" asked Ben, in despair, of his mother.

"How did Jasper begin his?" asked Mrs. Pepper back again.

"Oh," cried Polly, running into the bedroom to get the precious missive. " 'Dear Miss Polly' — that's what it says."

"Well," said Mrs. Pepper, "then you'd better say 'Dear Mr. Jasper' — or you might say, 'Dear Mr. King.' "

"Oh, dear!" cried Polly. "That would be the father, then. S'pose he should think we wrote to *him!*" And Polly looked horror-stricken to the last degree.

"There, there 'tis," said Ben. " 'Dear Mr. Jasper' — now what'll we say?"

"Why, say about the cakes," replied Polly.

"And the gingerbread boy," cried Phronsie. "Oh, tell about him, Polly, *do.*"

"Yes, yes, Phronsie," said Polly, "we will. Why, tell him how we wish he could have come, and that we baked him some cakes, and that we *do* so want him to come just as soon as he can."

"All right," said Ben. So he went to work laboriously, only his hard breathing showing what a hard task it was, as the stiff old pen scratched up and down the paper.

"There, that's done," he cried at length in great satisfaction, holding it up for inspection.

"Oh, I do wish," cried Polly in intense admiration, "I could write so nice and so fast as you can, Ben."

"Read it, Polly," said Mrs. Pepper in pride.

So Polly began: " 'Dear Mr. Jasper, We were all dreadfully sorry that you didn't come and so we baked you some cakes.' You didn't say anything about his being sick, Ben."

"I forgot it," said Ben, "but I put it in farther down — you'll see if you read on."

" 'Baked you some cakes — that is, Polly did, for this is Ben that's writing.' "

"You needn't said that, Ben," said Polly, dissatisfied. "We all baked 'em, I'm sure. 'And just as soon as you get well we do want you to come over and have the baking. We're real sorry you're sick — boneset's good for colds.' "

"Oh, Ben!" said Mrs. Pepper. "I guess his father knows what to give him."

"And, oh! The bitter stuff!" cried Polly with a wry face.

"Well, it's hard work to write," said Ben, yawning. "I'd rather chop wood."

"I wish I knew how," exclaimed Joel longingly.

"Just you try every day; Ben'll teach you, Joe," said his mother eagerly. "And then I'll let you write."

"I will!" cried Joe. "Then, Dave, you'll see how I'll write — I tell you!"

"And I'm goin' to — ma, can't I?" said Davie, unwilling to be outdone.

"Yes, you may, be sure," said Mrs. Pepper, delighted. "That'll make a man of you fast."

"Oh, boys," said Polly, lifting a very red face, "you joggle the table so I can't do anything."

"I wasn't jogglin'," said Joel. "The old thing tipped. Look!" he whispered to Davie. "See Polly — she's writing crooked."

So while the others hung around her and looked over her shoulder while they made their various comments, Polly finished her part and also held it up for inspection.

"Let us see," said Ben, taking it up.

"It's after 'boneset's good for colds,' " said Polly, puckering up her face again at the thought.

" 'We most of us knew you were sick — I'm Polly now — because you didn't come; and we liked your letter telling us so — ' "

"Oh, Polly! We weren't glad to hear he was sick!" cried Ben in horror.

"I didn't say so!" cried Polly, starting up. "Why, Ben Pepper, I *never* said so!" and she looked ready to cry.

"It sounds something like it, don't it, mammy?" said Ben, unwilling to give her pain, but appealing to Mrs. Pepper.

"Polly didn't mean it," said her mother consolingly. "But if I were you, I'd say something to explain it."

"I can't put anything in now," said poor Polly. "There isn't any room nor any more paper either. What *shall* I do! I told you, Ben, I couldn't write." And Polly looked helplessly from one to the other for comfort.

"Yes, you can," said Ben. "There, now, I'll show you: write it fine, Polly — you write so big — little bits of letters, like these."

So Polly took the pen again with a sigh. "Now he won't think so, I guess," she said, much relieved, as Ben began to read again.

"I'll begin yours again," Ben said. " 'We most of us knew you were sick because you didn't come, and we liked your letter telling us so because we'd all felt so badly, and Phronsie cried herself to sleep.' (That's good, I'm sure.) 'The gingerbread boy is for your father — please excuse it, but Phronsie would make it for him because he is sick. There isn't any more to write, and

130

besides, I can't write good, and Ben's tired. From all of us.'"

"Why, how's he to know?" cried Ben. "That won't do to sign it."

"Well, let's say from Ben and Polly, then," said Polly. "Only all the others want to be in the letter."

"Well, they can't write," said Ben.

"We might sign their names for 'em," suggested Polly.

"Here's mine," said Ben, putting under the "From all of us" a big, bold "Ben."

"And here's mine," echoed Polly, setting a slightly crooked "Polly" by its side.

"Now, Joe, you better let Ben hold your hand," said Polly warningly. But Joel, declaring he could write, had already begun, so there was no hope for it; and a big drop of ink falling from the pen, he spattered the *J* so that no one could tell what it was. The children looked at each other in despair.

"Can we ever get it out, mammy?" said Polly, running to Mrs. Pepper with it.

"I don't know," said her mother. "How could you try it, Joe?"

"I didn't mean to," said Joel, looking very downcast and ashamed. "The ugly old pen did it!"

"Well," said Polly, "it's got to go. We can't help it." But she looked so sorrowful over it that half the pleasure was gone for Ben, for Polly wanted everything just right, and was very particular about things.

"Now, Dave." Ben held his hand, and "David" went down next to "Joel."

But when it was Phronsie's turn, she protested that Polly and no one else must hold her hand.

"It's a dreadful hard name to write Phronsie is," said Polly as she guided Phronsie's fat little hand that clung faithfully to the stubby old pen. "There, it's over now," she cried, "and I'm thankful! I wouldn't write another for anything!"

"Read it all over now, Ben," cried Mrs. Pepper. "And don't speak, children, till he gets through."

"Don't it sound elegant!" said Polly, clasping her hands, when he had finished. "I didn't think we ever could do it so nice, did you, Ben?"

"No, indeed, I didn't," replied Ben, in a highly ecstatic frame of mind. "Now — oh! What'll we do for an envelope?" he asked in dismay.

"You'll have to do without that," said Mrs. Pepper, "for there isn't any in the house. But see here, children," she added as she saw the sorry faces before her, "you just fold up the letter and put it inside the parcel. That'll be just as good."

"Oh, dear," said Polly. "But it would have been splendid the other way, mammy — just like other folks!"

"You must make believe this is like other folks," said Mrs. Pepper cheerily, "when you can't do any other way."

"Yes," said Ben, "that's so, Polly. Tie 'em up quick's you can, and I'll take 'em over to Deacon Blodgett's, for he's goin' to start early in the morning."

So after another last look all around, Polly put the cakes in the paper and tied it with four or five strong knots, to avoid all danger of its undoing.

"He'll never untie it, Polly," said Ben. "That's just like a girl's knots!"

"Why didn't you tie it, then?" said Polly. "I'm sure it's

as good as a boy's knots, and they always muss up a parcel so." And she gave a loving, approving little pat to the top of the package, which despite its multitude of knots, was certainly very neat indeed.

"Now," said Ben, grasping the pen again, "here goes for the direction."

"Deary, yes!" said Polly. "I forgot all about that; I thought 'twas done."

"How'd you s'pose he'd get it?" asked Ben, coolly beginning the *M*.

"I don't know," replied Polly, looking over his shoulder. "S'pose anybody else *had* eaten 'em up, Ben!" And she turned pale at the very thought.

"There," said Ben at last, after a good many flourishes. "Now *'tis* done! You can't think of another thing to do to it, Polly!"

"Mamsie, see!" cried Polly, running with it to Mrs. Pepper. "Isn't that fine! 'Mr. Jasper E. King, at the Hotel Hingham.'"

"Yes," said Mrs. Pepper admiringly, to the content of all the children. "I should think it was!"

"Let me take it in my hand," screamed Joel, reaching eagerly up for the tempting brown parcel.

"Be careful then, Joe," said Polly, with an important air.

So Joel took a comfortable feel, and then Davie must have the same privilege. At last it was off, and with intense satisfaction the children watched Ben disappear with it down the long hill to Deacon Blodgett's.

The next day Ben came running in from his work at the deacon's.

"Oh, Polly, you had 'em!" he screamed, all out of breath. "You had 'em!"

"Had what?" asked Polly in astonishment. "Oh, Bensie, what *do* you mean?"

"Your flowers," he panted. "You sent some flowers to Jasper."

"Flowers to Jasper!" repeated Polly, afraid Ben had gone out of his wits.

"Yes," said Ben. "I'll begin at the beginning. You see, Polly, when I went down this morning, Betsey was to set me to work. Deacon Blodgett and Mrs. Blodgett had started early, you know. And while I was a-cleanin' up the woodshed, as she told me, all of a sudden she said, as she stood in the door looking on, 'Oh, Ben, Miz Blodgett took some posies along with your parcel.' *'What?'* said I. I didn't know as I'd heard straight. *'Posies,* I said,' says Betsey. 'Beautiful ones they were, too, the best in the garding. I heard her tell Mr. Blodgett it would be a pity if that sick boy couldn't have some flowers, and she knew the Pepper children were crazy about 'em, so she twisted 'em in the string around the parcel, and there they stood up and looked *fine,* I tell you, as they drove away.' So, Polly!"

"Bensie Pepper!" cried Polly, taking hold of his jacket and spinning him around. "I told you so! I *told* you so!"

"I know you did," said Ben as she gave him a parting whirl. "An' I wish you'd say so about other things, Polly, if you can get 'em so easy."

JOLLY DAYS

"Oh, Ben," cried Jasper, overtaking him by a smart run as he was turning in at the little brown gate one morning three days after. "Do wait."

"Halloa!" cried Ben, turning around and setting down his load — a bag of salt and a basket of potatoes — and viewing Jasper and Prince with great satisfaction.

"Yes, here I am," said Jasper. "And how I've run. That fellow on the stage was awful slow in getting here — oh, you're so good," he said, and his eyes, brimful of gladness, beamed on Ben. "The cakes were just prime, and 'twas great fun to get your letter."

"Did you like it?" asked Ben, the color up all over his brown face.

"*Like* it!" cried Jasper. "Why 'twas just splendid. And the cakes were royal! Isn't Polly smart, though, to bake like that!" he added admiringly.

"I guess she *is*," said Ben, drawing himself up to his very tallest dimensions. "She knows how to do everything, Jasper King!"

"I should think she did," responded the boy quickly. "I wish she was my sister," he finished longingly.

"Well, I don't," quickly replied Ben, "for then she wouldn't be mine; and I couldn't think of being without Polly! Was your father angry about — about — the gingerbread boy?" he asked timidly, trembling for an answer.

"Oh, dear, " cried Jasper, tumbling over on the grass. "Don't, *don't!* I shan't be good for anything if you make me laugh! Oh! Wasn't it funny!" And he rolled over and over, shaking with glee.

"Yes," said Ben, immensely relieved to find that no offense had been taken. "But she would send it; Polly tried not to have her, and she almost cried when Phronsie was so determined, 'cause she said your father never'd let you come again — "

" 'Twas just lovely in Phronsie," said the boy, sitting up and wiping his eyes, "but oh, it was *so* funny! You *ought* to have seen my father, Ben Pepper."

"Oh, then he *was* angry," cried Ben.

"No indeed he wasn't!" said Jasper. "Don't you think it! Do you know it did him lots of good, for he'd been feeling real badly that morning. He hadn't eaten any breakfast, and when he saw that gingerbread boy" — here Jasper rolled over again with a peal of laughter — "and heard the message, he just put back his head, and he laughed. Why, I never heard him laugh as he did then! The room shook all over. And he ate a big dinner, and all that afternoon he felt as good as could be. But he says he's coming to see the little girl that baked it for him before we go home."

Ben nearly tumbled over by the side of Jasper at these words. *"Coming to see us!"* he gasped.

"Yes," said Jasper, who had scarcely got over his own

astonishment about it, for if the roof had suddenly whisked off onto the church steeple, he couldn't have been more amazed than when he heard his father say cheerily, "Well, Jasper, my boy, I guess I shall have to drive over and see your little girl, since she's been polite enough to bake me this," pointing to the wild-looking gingerbread boy.

"Come in and tell 'em about it," cried Ben radiantly, picking up his potatoes and salt. "It's all right, Polly!" he said in a jubilant voice. "For here's Jasper, and he'll tell you so himself."

"Hush!" said Jasper warningly. "Don't let Phronsie hear. Well, here's my pet now," and after bobbing lovingly to the others, with eyes beaming over with fun, he caught up with the little girl, who was screaming, "Oh, here's Jasper! And my be-yew-ti-ful doggie!"

"Now, Phronsie," he cried, "give me a kiss. You haven't any soft soap today, have you? No; that's a good, nice one! Now, your gingerbread boy was just splendid!"

"Did he *eat* it?" asked the child in grave delight.

"Well — no — he hasn't eaten it yet," said Jasper, smiling on the others. "He's keeping it to look at, Phronsie."

"I should think so!" groaned Polly.

"Never mind, Polly," Ben whispered. "Jasper's been a-tellin' me about it; his father liked it — he did truly."

"Oh!" said Polly. "I'm *so* glad!"

"He had eyes," said Phronsie, going back to the charms of the gingerbread boy.

"I know it," said Jasper admiringly. "So he did."

"Rather deep sunk, one of 'em was," muttered Ben.

"And I'll bake you one, Jasper," said the child as he put her down. "I will very truly — someday."

"Will you," smiled Jasper. "Well, then." And there was a whispered conference with Phronsie that somehow sent that damsel into a blissful state of delight. And then while Phronsie monopolized Prince, Jasper told them all about the reception of the parcel — how very dull and forlorn he was feeling that morning, Prince and he shut up indoors, and how his father had had a miserable night and had eaten scarcely any breakfast, and just at this juncture there came a knock at the door. "And," said Jasper, "your parcel walked in, all dressed up in flowers!"

"They weren't our flowers," said Polly honestly. "Mrs. Blodgett put 'em on."

"Well, she couldn't have if you hadn't sent the parcel," said Jasper in a tone of conviction.

Then he launched out into a description of how they opened the package, Prince looking on and begging for one of the cakes.

"Oh, didn't you give him one?" cried Polly at this. "Good old Prince!"

"Yes I did," said Jasper. "The biggest one of all."

"The one, I guess," interrupted Joel, "with the big raisin on top."

Polly spoke up quickly to save any more remarks on Joel's part. "Now tell us about your father and the gingerbread boy."

So Jasper broke out with a merry laugh into this part of the story and soon had them all in such a gale of merriment that Phronsie stopped playing out on the doorstep with Prince and came in to see what the matter was.

"Never mind," said Polly, trying to get her breath, just as Jasper was relating how Mr. King set up the gingerbread boy on his writing table before him while he leaned back in his chair for a hearty laugh.

"And to make it funnier still," said Jasper, "don't you think, a little pen wiper he has, made like a cap, hanging on the pen rack above him, tumbled off just at this very identical minute right on the head of the gingerbread boy, and there it stuck!"

"*Oh!*" they all screamed. "If we could only have seen it."

"What was it?" asked Phronsie, pulling Polly's sleeve to make her hear.

So Jasper took her in his lap, and told how funny the gingerbread boy looked with a cap on, and Phronsie clapped her hands, and laughed with the rest, till the little old kitchen rang and rang again.

And then they had the baking! And Polly tied one of her mother's ample aprons on Jasper, as Mrs. Pepper had left directions if he should come while she was away. And he developed such a taste for cookery, and had so many splendid improvements on the Peppers' simple ideas, that the children thought it the most fortunate thing in the world that he came; and one and all voted him a most charming companion.

"You could cook a Thanksgiving dinner in this stove just as easy as not," said Jasper, putting into the oven something on a little cracked plate that *would* have been a pie if there were any center, but lacking that necessary accompaniment, probably was a shortcake. "Just as easy as not," he repeated with emphasis, slamming the door to give point to his remarks.

"No, you couldn't either," said Ben at the table with equal decision. "Not a bit of it, Jasper King!"

"Why, Ben Pepper?" asked Jasper. "That oven's big enough! I should like to know why not?"

" 'Cause there isn't anything to cook," said Ben coolly, cutting out a piece of dough for a jumble. "We don't keep Thanksgiving."

"Not keep Thanksgiving!" said Jasper, standing quite still. *"Never had a Thanksgiving!* Well, I declare," and then he stopped again.

"Yes," answered Ben. "We had one once; 'twas last year — but that wasn't much."

"Well, then," said Jasper, leaning over the table, "I'll tell you what I should think you'd do — try Christmas."

"Oh, that's always worse," said Polly, setting down her rolling pin to think, which immediately rolled away by itself off the table.

"We never had a Christmas," said little Davie reflectively. "What are they like, Jasper?"

Jasper sat quite still and didn't reply to this question for a moment or two.

To be among children who didn't like Thanksgiving, and who "never had seen a Christmas," and "didn't know what it was like" was a new revelation to him.

"They hang up stockings," said Polly softly.

How many, many times she had begged her mother to try it for the younger ones; but there was never anything to put in them, and the winters were cold and hard, and the strictest economy only carried them through.

"Oh!" said little Phronsie in horror. "Are their feet in 'em, Polly?"

"No, dear," said Polly, while Jasper, instead of laughing, only stared. Something requiring a deal of thought was passing through the boy's mind just then. "They *shall* have a Christmas!" he muttered. "I know father'll let me." But he kept his thoughts to himself and, becoming his own gay, kindly self, he explained and told to Phronsie and the others so many stories of past Christmasses he had enjoyed that the interest over the baking soon dwindled away — until a horrible smell of something burning brought them all to their senses.

"Oh! The house is burning?" cried Polly. "Oh, get a pail of water!"

" 'Tisn't either," said Jasper, snuffing wisely. "Oh! I know — I forgot all about it — I do beg your pardon." And running to the stove, he knelt down and drew out of the oven a black, odorous mass, which with a crestfallen air he brought to Polly.

"I'm no end sorry I made such a mess of it," he said. "I meant it for you."

" 'Tisn't any matter," said Polly kindly.

"And now do you go on," cried Joel and David both in the same breath, "all about the tree, you know."

"Yes, yes," said the others. "If you're not tired, Jasper."

"Oh, no," cried their accommodating friend, "I love to tell about it. Only wait — let's help Polly clear up first."

So after all traces of the frolic had been tidied up and made nice for the mother's return, they took seats in a circle and Jasper regaled them with story and reminiscence till they felt as if fairyland were nothing to it!

"How did you ever live through it, Jasper King," said Polly, drawing the first long breath she had dared to indulge in. "Such an *elegant* time!"

Jasper laughed. "I hope I'll live through plenty more of them," he said merrily. "We're going to sister Marian's again, father and I; we always spend our Christmas there, you know, and she's to have all the cousins, and I don't know how many more, and a tree. But the best of all, there's going to be a German carol sung by choirboys — I shall like that best of all."

"What are choirboys?" asked Polly, who was intensely fond of music.

"In some of the churches," explained Jasper, "the choir is all boys; and they do chant and sing anthems perfectly beautifully, Polly!"

"Do you play on the piano, and sing?" asked Polly, looking at him in awe.

"Yes," said the boy simply. "I've played ever since I was a little fellow no bigger'n Phronsie."

"Oh, Jasper!" cried Polly, clasping her hands, her cheeks all aflame. "Do you mean to say you do *really and truly play on the piano?*"

"Why, yes," said the boy, looking into her flashing eyes.

"Polly's always crazy about music," explained Ben. "She'll drum on the table, and anywhere, to make believe it's a piano."

"There's Dr. Fisher going by," said Joel, who, now that they had gotten on the subject of music, began to find prickles running up and down his legs from sitting so still. "I wish he'd stop."

"Is he the one that cured your measles — and Polly's eyes?" asked Jasper, running to the window. "I want to see him."

"Well, there he is," cried Ben, as the doctor put his head out of the gig and bowed and smiled to the little group in the window.

"He's just lovely," cried Polly. "Oh! I wish you knew him."

"If father's sick again," said Jasper, "we'll have him — he looks nice, anyway — for father don't like the doctor over in Hingham. Do you know, perhaps we'll come again next summer. Wouldn't that be nice!"

"Oh!" cried the children rapturously. "Do come, Jasper, *do!*"

"Well, maybe," said Jasper. "If father likes it and sister Marian and her family will come with us; they do some summers. You'd like little Dick, I know," turning to Phronsie. "And I guess all of you'd like all of them," he added, looking at the group of interested listeners. "They wanted to come this year awfully; they said — 'Oh, grandpapa, do let us go with you and Jappy, and — '"

"*What!*" said the children.

"Oh," said Jasper with a laugh, "they call me Jappy — it's easier to say than Jasper; ever so many people do for short. You may if you want to," he said, looking around on them all.

"How funny!" laughed Polly. "But I don't know as it is any worse than Polly or Ben."

"Or Phronsie," said Jappy. "Don't *you* like Jappy?" he said, bringing his head down to her level as she sat on the little stool at his feet, content in listening to the merry chat.

"Is that the same as Japser?" she asked gravely.

"Yes, the very same," he said.

When they parted, Jappy and the little Peppers were sworn friends. And the boy, happy in his good times in the cheery little home, felt the hours long between the visits that his father, when he saw the change that they wrought in his son, willingly allowed him to make.

"Oh, dear!" said Mrs. Pepper one day in the last of September, as a carriage drawn by a pair of very handsome horses stopped at their door. "Here comes Mr. King, I do believe. We never looked worse'n we do today!"

"I don't care," said Polly, flying out of the bedroom. "Jappy's with him, mamma, and it'll be nice, I guess. At any rate, Phronsie's clean as a pink," she thought to herself, looking at the little maiden, busy with Baby, to whom she was teaching deportment in the corner. But there was no time to fix up, for a tall, portly gentleman, leaning on his heavy gold cane, was walking up from the little brown gate to the big flat stone that served as a step. Jasper and Prince followed decorously.

"Is this little Miss Pepper? he asked pompously of Polly, who answered his rap on the door. Now, whether she was little "Miss Pepper" she never had stopped to consider.

"I don't know, sir; I'm Polly." And then she blushed bright as a rose, and the laughing brown eyes looked beyond to Jasper, who stood on the walk and smiled encouragingly.

"Is your mother in?" asked the old gentleman, who was so tall he could scarcely enter the low door. And then Mrs. Pepper came forward, and Jasper introduced her, and the old gentleman bowed and sat down in the seat Polly placed for him. And Mrs. Pepper thanked him with a heart overflowing with gratitude, through lips that would tremble even then, for all that Jasper had done for them. And the old gentleman said, "Humph!" but he looked at his son, and something shone in his eye just for a moment.

Phronsie had retreated with Baby in her arms behind the door on the new arrival. But seeing everything progressing finely, and overcome by her extreme desire to see Jappy and Prince, she began by peeping out with big eyes to observe how things were going on. Just then the old gentleman happened to say, "Well, where is my little girl that baked me a cake so kindly?"

Then Phronsie, forgetting all else but her "poor, sick man," who also was Jasper's father, rushed out from behind the door, and coming up to the stately old gentleman in the chair, she looked up pityingly and said, shaking her yellow head, "Poor, sick man, was my boy good?"

After that there was no more gravity and ceremony. In a moment, Phronsie was perched upon old Mr. King's knee and playing with his watch, while the others, freed from all restraint, were chattering and laughing happily, till some of the cheeriness overflowed and warmed the heart of the old gentleman.

"We go tomorrow," he said, rising and looking at his watch. "Why, is it possible that we have been here an hour! There, my little girl, will you give me a kiss?" And he bent his handsome old head down to the childish face upturned to his confidingly.

"Don't go," said the child as she put up her little lips in grave confidence. "I do like you — I *do!*"

"Oh, Phronsie," began Mrs. Pepper.

"Don't reprove her, madam," said the old gentleman, who liked it immensely. "Yes, we go tomorrow," he said, looking around on the group, to whom this was a blow they little expected. They had surely thought Jasper was to stay a week longer.

"I received a telegram this morning that I must be in the city on Thursday. And besides, madam," he said, addressing Mrs. Pepper, "I think the climate is bad for me now, as it induces rheumatism. The hotel is also getting unpleasant. There are many annoyances that I cannot put up with; so that altogether I do not regret it."

Mrs. Pepper, not knowing exactly what to say to this, wisely said nothing. Meantime, Jappy and the little Peppers were having a sorry time over in the corner by themselves.

"Well, I'll write," cried Jasper, not liking to look at Polly just then, as he was sure he shouldn't want anyone to look at him if he felt like crying. "And you must answer 'em all."

"Oh, we will! We will!" they cried. "And, Jappy, do come next summer," said Joel.

"If father'll only say yes, we will, I tell you!" he responded eagerly.

"Come, my boy," said his father the third time, and Jasper knew by the tone that there must be no delay.

Mr. King had been nervously putting his hand in his pocket during the last few moments that the children were together. But when he glanced at Mrs. Pepper's eyes, something made him draw it out again hastily, as empty as he put it in. "No, 'twouldn't do," he said to himself. "She isn't the kind of woman to whom one could offer money."

The children crowded back their tears and hastily said

their last good-bye, some of them hanging on to Prince till the last moment.

And then the carriage door shut with a bang, Jasper giving them a bright parting smile, and they were gone.

And the Peppers went into their little brown house and shut the door.

GETTING A CHRISTMAS
FOR THE LITTLE ONES

AND so October came and went. The little Peppers were very lonely after Jasper had gone. Even Mrs. Pepper caught herself looking up one day when the wind blew the door open suddenly, half expecting to see the merry whole-souled boy and the faithful dog come scampering in.

But the letters came, and that was a comfort; and it was fun to answer them. The first one spoke of Jasper's being under a private tutor, with his cousins; then they were less frequent, and they knew he was studying hard. Full of anticipations of Christmas himself, he urged the little Peppers to try for one. And the life and spirit of the letter was so catching that Polly and Ben found their souls fired within them to try at least to get for the little ones a taste of Christmastide.

"Now, mammy," they said at last one day in the latter part of October, when the crisp, fresh air filled their little healthy bodies with springing vitality that must bubble over and rush into something, "we don't want a Thanksgiving, truly we don't. But may we try for a

Christmas — just a *little* one." They added, timidly, "For the children?" Ben and Polly always called the three younger ones of the flock the children.

To their utter surprise, Mrs. Pepper looked mildly assenting, and presently she said, "Well, I don't see why you can't try; 'twon't do any harm, I'm sure."

You see, Mrs. Pepper had received a letter from Jasper, which at present she didn't feel called upon to say anything about.

"Now," said Polly, drawing a long breath as she and Ben stole away into a corner to talk over and lay plans, "what does it mean?"

"Never mind," said Ben. "As long as she's given us leave, I don't *care* what it is."

"I neither," said Polly, with the delicious feeling as if the whole world were before them to choose. "It'll be just *gorgeous*, Ben!"

"What's that?" asked Ben, who was not as much given to long words as Polly, who dearly loved to be fine in language as well as other things.

"Oh, it's something Jappy said one day; and I asked him, and he says it's fine, and lovely, and all that," answered Polly, delighted that she knew something she could really tell Ben.

"Then why not *say* fine?" commented Ben practically with a little upward lift of his nose.

"Oh, I don't know, I'm sure," laughed Polly. "Let's think what'll we do for Christmas — how many weeks are there, anyway, Ben?" And she began to count on her fingers.

"That's no way," said Ben, "I'm going to get the almanac."

So he went to the old clock, where, hanging up by its side, was a Farmer's Almanac.

"Now, we'll know," he said, coming back to their corner. So with heads together they consulted and counted up till they found that eight weeks and three days remained in which to get ready.

"Dear me!" said Polly. "It's most a year, isn't it, Ben?"

" 'Twon't be much time for us," said Ben, who thought of the many hours to be devoted to hard work that would run away with the time. "We'd better begin right away, Polly."

"Well, all right," said Polly, who could scarcely keep her fingers still as she thought of the many things she should so love to do if she could. "But first, Ben, what let's do?"

"Would you rather hang up their stockings?" asked Ben, as if he had unlimited means at his disposal. "Or have a tree?"

"Why," said Polly, with wide-open eyes at the two magnificent ideas, "we haven't got anything to put *in* the stockings when we hang 'em, Ben."

"That's just it," said Ben. "Now, wouldn't it be better to have a tree, Polly? I can get that easy in the woods, you know."

"Well," interrupted Polly eagerly, "we haven't got anything to hang on that, either, Ben. You know Jappy said folks hang all sorts of presents on the branches. So I don't see," she continued impatiently, "as that's any good. We can't do anything, Ben Pepper, so there! There isn't anything to do anything with." And with a flounce Polly sat down on the old wooden stool and, folding her hands, looked at Ben in a most despairing way.

"I know," said Ben, "we haven't got much."

"We haven't got anything," said Polly, still looking at him.

"Why, we've got a tree," replied Ben, hopefully.

"Well, what's a tree?" retorted Polly scornfully. "Anybody can go out and look at a tree outdoors."

"Well, now, I tell you, Polly," said Ben, sitting down on the floor beside her and speaking very slowly and decisively, "we've got to do something 'cause we've begun; and we might make a tree real pretty."

"How?" asked Polly, ashamed of her ill humor but not in the least seeing how anything could be made of a tree. "How, Ben Pepper?"

"Well," said Ben pleasantly, "we'd set it up in the corner — "

"Oh, no, not in the corner," cried Polly, whose spirits began to rise a little as she saw Ben so hopeful. "Put it in the middle of the room, *do!*"

"I don't care where you put it," said Ben, smiling, happy that Polly's usual cheerful energy had returned, "but I thought — 'twill be a little one, you know, and I thought 'twould look better in the corner."

"What else?" asked Polly, eager to see how Ben would dress the tree.

"Well," said Ben, "you know the Henderson boys gave me a lot of corn last week."

"I don't see as that helps much," said Polly, still incredulous. "Do you mean hang the cobs on the branches, Ben? That would be just dreadful!"

"I should think likely," laughed Ben. "No, indeed, Polly Pepper! But if we should pop a lot — oh, a bushel — and then we should string 'em, we could wind

151

it all in and out among the branches, and — ”

“Why, wouldn’t that be pretty?” cried Polly. “Real pretty. And we can do that, I’m sure.”

“Yes,” continued Ben. “And then, don’t you know, there’s some little candle ends in that box in the Provision Room — maybe mammy’d give us them.”

“I don’t believe but she would,” cried Polly. “ ’Twould be just like Jappy’s if she would! Let’s ask her now — this very same minute!”

And they scampered hurriedly to Mrs. Pepper, who to their extreme astonishment, after all, said yes, and smiled encouragingly on the plan.

“Isn’t mammy good?” said Polly with loving gratitude as they seated themselves again.

“Now we’re all right,” exclaimed Ben. “And I tell you we can make the tree look perfectly *splendid*, Polly Pepper!”

“And I’ll tell you another thing, Ben,” Polly said. “Oh! Something elegant! You must get ever so many hickory nuts. And you know those bits of bright paper I’ve got in the bureau drawer? Well, we can paste them onto the nuts and hang ’em on for the balls Jappy tells of.”

“Polly,” cried Ben, “it’ll be such a tree as never was, won’t it?”

“Yes. But dear me,” cried Polly, springing up, “the children are coming! Wasn’t it good grandma wanted ’em to come over this afternoon, so’s we could talk! Now *hush!*” as the door opened to admit the noisy little troop.

“If you think of any new plan,” whispered Ben behind his hand, while Mrs. Pepper engaged their attention, “you’ll have to come out into the woodshed to talk after this.”

"I know it," whispered Polly back again. "Oh! We've got just heaps of things to think of, Bensie!"

Such a contriving and racking of brains as Polly and Ben set up after this! They would bob over at each other and smile with significant gesture as a new idea would strike one of them, in the most mysterious way that, if observed, would drive the others wild. And then, frightened lest in some hilarious moment the secret should pop out, the two conspirators would betake themselves to the woodshed as before agreed on. But Joel, finding this out, followed them one day — or, as Polly said, tagged — so that was no good.

"Let's go behind the woodpile," she said to Ben in desperation. "He can't hear there, if we whisper real soft."

"Yes, he will," said Ben, who knew Joel's hearing faculties much better. "We'll have to wait till they're a-bed."

So after that, when nightfall first began to make its appearance, Polly would hint mildly about bedtime.

"You hustle us so!" said Joel after he had been sent off to bed for two or three nights unusually early.

"Oh, Joey, it's good for you to get to bed," said Polly coaxingly. "It'll make you grow, you know, real fast."

"Well, I don't grow a-bed," grumbled Joel, who thought something was in the wind. "You and Ben are going to talk, I know, and wink your eyes, as soon as we're gone."

"Well, go along, Joe, that's a good boy," said Polly, laughing, "and you'll know someday."

"What'll you give me?" asked Joel, seeing a bargain, his foot on the lowest stair leading to the loft. "Say, Polly?"

"Oh, I haven't got much to give," she said cheerily. "But I'll tell you what, Joey, I'll tell you a story every day that you go to bed."

"Will you?" cried Joe, hopping back into the room. "Begin now, Polly, begin now!"

"Why, you haven't been to bed yet," said Polly, "so I can't till tomorrow."

"Yes, I have. You've made us go for three — no, I guess fourteen nights," said Joel indignantly.

"Well, you were *made* to go," laughed Polly. "I said if you'd go good, you know. So run along, Joe, and I'll tell you a nice one tomorrow."

"It's got to be long," shouted Joel when he saw he could get no more, making good time up to the loft.

To say that Polly, in the following days, was Master Joel's slave, was stating the case lightly. However, she thought by her storytelling she got off easily, as each evening saw the boys drag their unwilling feet bedward, and leave Ben and herself in peace to plan and work undisturbed. There they would sit by the little old table, around the one tallow candle, while Mrs. Pepper sewed away busily, looking up to smile or to give some bits of advice; keeping her own secret meanwhile, which made her blood leap fast, as the happy thoughts nestled in her heart of her little ones and their coming glee. And Polly made the loveliest of paper dolls for Phronsie out of the rest of the bits of bright paper; and Ben made windmills and whistles for the boys; and a funny little carved basket with a handle, for Phronsie, out of a hickory nut shell; and a new pink calico dress for Seraphina peered out from the top drawer of the old bureau in the bedroom whenever anyone opened it, for Mrs. Pepper kindly let the children lock up their treasures there as fast as completed.

"I'll make Seraphina a bonnet," said Mrs. Pepper, "for there's that old bonnet string in the bag, you know, Polly. That'll make it beautiful."

"Oh, do, mother," cried Polly. "She's been wanting a new one awfully."

"And I'm going to knit some mittens for Joel and David," continued Mrs. Pepper, " 'cause I can get the yarn cheap now. I saw some down at the store yesterday I could have at half price."

"I don't believe anybody'll have as good a Christmas as we shall," cried Polly, pasting on a bit of trimming to the gayest doll's dress. "No, not even Jappy."

An odd little smile played around Mrs. Pepper's mouth but she said not a word, and so the fun and the work went on.

The tree was to be set up in the Provision Room; that was finally decided, as Mrs. Pepper showed the children how utterly useless it would be to try having it in the kitchen.

"I'll find the key, children," she said. "I think I know where 'tis, and then we can keep them out."

"Well, but it looks so — " said Polly, demurring at the prospect.

"Oh, no, Polly," said her mother. "At any rate it's *clean*."

"Polly," said Ben, "we can put evergreen around, you know."

"So we can," said Polly brightly. "Oh, Ben, you do think of the *best* things. We couldn't have had *them* in the kitchen."

"And don't let's hang the presents on the tree," continued Ben. "Let's have the children hang up their stockings. They want to, awfully, for I heard David tell Joel this morning before we got up — they thought I was asleep, but I wasn't — that he did so wish they could, but, says he, 'Don't tell mammy, 'cause that'll make her feel bad.' "

"The little dears!" said Mrs. Pepper impulsively. "They shall have their stockings, too."

"And we'll make the tree pretty enough," said Polly enthusiastically. "We shan't want the presents to hang on; we've got so many things. And then we'll have hickory nuts to eat; and perhaps mammy'll let us make some molasses candy the day before," she said with a sly look at her mother.

"You may," said Mrs. Pepper, smiling.

"Oh, goody!" they both cried, hugging each other ecstatically.

"And we'll have a frolic in the Provision Room afterwards," finished Polly. "Oh! Ooh!"

And so the weeks flew by — one, two, three, four, five, six, seven, eight! Till only the three days remained, and to think the fun that Polly and Ben had had already!

"It's better'n a Christmas," they told their mother, "to get ready for it!"

"It's too bad you can't hang up *your* stockings," said Mrs. Pepper, looking keenly at their flushed faces and bright eyes. "You've never hung 'em up."

"That isn't any matter, mamsie," they both said cheerily. "It's a great deal better to have the children have a nice time. Oh, won't it be elegant! P'r'aps we'll have ours next year!"

For two days before, the house was turned upside down for Joel to find the biggest stocking he could. But, on Polly telling him it must be his own, he stopped his search, and bringing down his well-worn one, hung it by the corner of the chimney to be ready.

"You put yours up the other side, Dave," he advised.

"There isn't any nail," cried David, investigating.

"I'll drive one," said Joel, so he ran out to the tool house, as one corner of the woodshed was called, and brought in the hammer and one or two nails.

"Phronsie's a-goin' in the middle," he said, with a nail in his mouth.

"Yes, I'm a-goin' to hang up my stockin'," cried the child, hopping from one toe to the other.

"Run get it, Phronsie," said Joel, "and I'll hang it up for you."

"Why, it's two days before Christmas yet," said Polly, laughing. "How they'll look hanging there so long."

"I don't care," said Joel, giving a last thumb to the nail. "We're a-goin' to be ready. Oh, dear! I wish 'twas tonight!"

"Can't Seraphina hang up her stocking?" asked Phronsie, coming up to Polly's side. "And Baby, too?"

"Oh, let her have part of yours," said Polly. "That'll be best — Seraphina and Baby and you have one stocking together."

"Oh, yes," cried Phronsie, easily pleased. "That'll be best."

So for the next two days they were almost distracted,

the youngest ones asking countless questions about Santa Claus and how he possibly could get down the chimney, Joel running his head up as far as he dared to see if it was big enough.

"I guess he can," he said, coming back in a sooty state, looking very much excited and delighted.

"Will he be black like Joey?" asked Phronsie, pointing to his grimy face.

"No," said Polly. "He don't ever get black."

"Why?" they all asked. And then, over and over, they wanted the delightful mystery explained.

"We never'll get through this day," said Polly in despair as the last one arrived. "I wish 'twas tonight, for we're all ready."

"Santy's coming! Santy's coming!" sang Phronsie as the bright afternoon sunlight went down over the fresh, crisp snow, "for it's night now."

"Yes, Santa is coming!" sang Polly. And "Santa Claus is a-coming" rang back and forth through the old kitchen till it seemed as if the three little old stockings would hop down and join in the dance going on so merrily.

"I'm glad mine is red," said Phronsie at last, stopping in the wild jig and going up to see if it was all safe, " 'cause then Santy'll know it's mine, won't he, Polly?"

"Yes, dear," cried Polly, catching her up. "Oh, Phronsie! You *are* going to have a Christmas!"

"Well, I wish," said Joel, "I had my name on mine! I know Dave'll get some of my things."

"Oh, no, Joe," said Mrs. Pepper. "Santa Claus is smart; he'll know yours is in the left-hand corner."

"Will he?" asked Joel, still a little fearful.

"Oh, yes, indeed," said Mrs. Pepper confidently. "I never knew him to make a mistake."

"Now," said Ben, when they had all made a pretense of eating supper, for there was such an excitement prevailing that no one sat still long enough to eat much. "You must every one fly off to bed as quick as ever can be."

"Will Santa Claus come faster then?" asked Joel.

"Yes," said Ben, "just twice as fast."

"I'm going, then," said Joel, "but I ain't going to sleep, 'cause I mean to hear him come over the roof. Then I'm going to get up, for I do so want a squint at the reindeer!"

"I am, too," cried Davie excitedly. "Oh, do come, Joe!" and he began to mount the stairs.

"Good night," said Phronsie, going up to the center of the chimneypiece, where the little red stocking dangled limpsily. "Lift me up, Polly, do."

"What you want to do?" asked Polly, running and giving her a jump. "What you goin' to do, Phronsie?"

"I want to kiss it good night," said the child, with eyes big with anticipation and happiness, hugging the well-worn toe of the little old stocking affectionately. "I wish I had something to give Santa, Polly, I *do*," she cried, as she held her fast in her arms.

"Never mind, pet," said Polly, nearly smothering her with kisses. "If you're a good girl, Phronsie, that pleases Santa the most of anything."

"Does it?" cried Phronsie, delighted beyond measure, as Polly carried her into the bedroom. "Then I'll be good always, I *will!*"

CHRISTMAS BELLS!

IN the middle of the night Polly woke up with a start.

"What in the world!" she said, and she bobbed up her head and looked over at her mother, who was still peacefully sleeping, and was just going to lie down again when a second noise out in the kitchen made her pause and lean on her elbow to listen. At this moment she thought she heard a faint whisper, and springing out of bed, she ran to Phronsie's crib. It was empty. As quick as a flash she sped out into the kitchen. There, in front of the chimney, were two figures. One was Joel, and the other, unmistakably, was Phronsie!

"What are you doing?" gasped Polly, holding on to a chair.

The two little nightgowns turned round at this.

"Why, I thought it was morning," said Joel, "and I wanted my stocking. Oh!" — as he felt the toe, which was generously stuffed — "give it to me, Polly Pepper, and I'll run right back to bed again!"

"Dear me!" said Polly. "And you, too, Phronsie! Why, it's the middle of the night! Did I ever!" And she had to pinch her mouth together tight to keep from bursting out into a loud laugh. "Oh, dear, I shall laugh! Don't look so scared, Phronsie, there won't anything hurt you." For Phronsie, who, on hearing Joel fumbling around the precious stockings, had been quite willing to hop out of bed and join him, had now, on Polly's saying the dire words "in the middle of the night," scuttled over to her protecting side like a frightened rabbit.

"It never'll be morning," said Joel, taking up first one cold toe and then the other. "You *might* let us have 'em now, Polly, *do!*"

"No," said Polly sobering down. "You can't have yours till Davie wakes up, too. Scamper off to bed, Joey, dear, and forget all about 'em, and it'll be morning before you know it."

"Oh, I'd rather go to bed," said Phronsie, trying to tuck up her feet in the little flannel nightgown, which was rather short, "but I don't know the way back, Polly. Take me, Polly, do," and she put up her arms to be carried.

"Oh, *I* ain't a-goin' back alone, either," whimpered Joel, coming up to Polly, too.

"Why, you came down alone, didn't you?" whispered Polly with a little laugh.

"Yes, but I thought 'twas morning," said Joel, his teeth chattering with something beside the cold.

"Well, you must think of the morning that's coming," said Polly cheerily. "I'll tell you — you wait till I put Phronsie into the crib, and then I'll come back and go halfway up the stairs with you."

"I won't never come down till it's morn' again," said Joel, bouncing along the stairs, when Polly was ready to go with him, at a great rate.

"Better not," laughed Polly softly. "Be careful and not wake Davie nor Ben."

"I'm *in*," announced Joel in a loud whisper, and Polly could hear him snuggle down among the warm bed-clothes. "Call us when 'tis mornin', Polly."

"Yes," said Polly, "I will. Go to sleep."

Phronsie had forgotten stockings and everything else on Polly's return and was fast asleep in the old crib. The result of it was that the children slept over, when morning did really come, and Polly had to keep her promise, and go to the foot of the stairs and call —

"*Merry Christmas!* Oh, Ben! And Joel! And Davie!"

"Oh! — oh! — oo-h!" And then the sounds that answered her, as with smothered whoops of expectation they one and all flew into their clothes!

Quick as a flash Joel and Davie were down and dancing around the chimney.

"Mammy! Mammy!" screamed Phronsie, hugging her stocking, which Ben lifted her up to unhook from the big nail. "Santy did *come*, he *did!*" And then she spun around in the middle of the floor, not stopping to look in it.

"Well, open it, Phronsie," called Davie, deep in the exploring of his own. "Oh! Isn't that a splendid windmill, Joe?"

"Yes," said that individual, who, having found a big piece of molasses candy, was so engaged in enjoying a huge bite that, regardless alike of his other gifts or of the smearing his face was getting, he gave himself wholly up to its delights.

"Oh, Joey," cried Polly laughingly. "Molasses candy for breakfast!"

162

"That's *prime!*" cried Joel, swallowing the last morsel. "Now I'm going to see what's this — oh, Dave, see here! See here!" he cried in intense excitementt, pulling out a nice little parcel which, unrolled, proved to be a bright pair of stout mittens. "See if you've got some — look quick!"

"Yes, I have," said David, picking up a parcel about as big. "No, that's molasses candy."

"Just the same as I had," said Joel. "Do look for the mittens. P'r'aps Santa Claus thought you had some — oh, dear!"

"Here they are!" screamed Davie. "I *have* got some, Joe, just exactly like yours! See, Joe!"

"Goody!" said Joel, immensely relieved, for now he could quite enjoy his to see a pair on Davie's hands, also. "Look at Phron," he cried. "She hasn't got only half of her things out!"

To tell the truth, Phronsie was so bewildered by her riches that she sat on the floor with the little red stocking in her lap, laughing and cooing to herself amid the few things she had drawn out. When she came to Seraphina's bonnet, she was quite overcome. She turned it over and over and smoothed out the little white feather that had once adorned one of Grandma Bascom's chickens, until the two boys with their stockings and the others sitting around in a group on the floor watching them laughed in glee to see her enjoyment.

"Oh, dear," said Joel at last, shaking his stocking. "I've got all there is. I wish there were forty Christmases coming!"

"I haven't!" screamed Davie. "There's something in the toe."

"It's an apple, I guess," said Joel. "Turn it up, Dave."

" 'Tisn't an apple," exclaimed Davie. " 'Tisn't round. It's long and thin; here 'tis." And he pulled out a splendid long whistle on which he blew a blast long and terrible, and Joel immediately following, all quiet was broken up, and the wildest hilarity reigned.

"I don't know as you'll want any breakfast," at last said Mrs. Pepper, when she had got Phronsie a little sobered down.

"I do, I do!" cried Joel.

"Dear me! After your candy?" said Polly.

"That's all gone," said Joel, tooting around the table on his whistle. "What are we going to have for breakfast?"

"Same as ever," said his mother. "It can't be Christmas all the time."

"I wish 'twas," said little Davie, "forever and ever!"

"Forever an' ever," echoed little Phronsie, flying up, her cheeks like two pinks, and Serpahina in her arms with her bonnet on upside down.

"Dear, dear," said Polly, pinching Ben to keep still as they tumbled down the little rickety steps to the Provision Room after breakfast. The children, content in their treasures, were holding high carnival in the kitchen. "Suppose they *should* find it out now — I declare I should feel most awfully. Isn't it *elegant?*" she asked in a subdued whisper, going all around and around the tree, magnificent in its dress of bright red and yellow balls, white festoons, and little candle ends all ready for lighting. "Oh, Ben, did you lock the door?"

"Yes," he said. "That's a mouse," he added as a little rustling noise made Polly stop where she stood back of the tree and prick up her ears in great distress of mind. " 'Tis elegant," he said, turning around in admiration and taking in the tree, which, as Polly said, was quite "gorgeous," and the evergreen branches twisted up on the beams and rafters, and all the other festive arrangements. "Even Jappy's isn't better, I don't believe!"

"I wish Jappy was here," said Polly with a small sigh.

"Well, he isn't," said Ben. "Come, we must go back into the kitchen or all the children will be out here. Look your last, Polly; 'twon't do to come again till it's time to light up."

"Mammy says she'd rather do the lighting up," said Polly.

"Had she?" said Ben, in surprise. "Oh, I suppose she's afraid we'll set somethin' afire. Well, then, we shan't come in till we *have* it."

"I can't bear to go," said Polly, turning reluctantly away. "It's most beautiful. Oh, Ben," and she faced him for the five-hundredth time with the question "Is your Santa Claus dress all safe?"

"Yes," said Ben. "I'll warrant they won't find that in one hurry! Such a time as we've had to make it!"

"I know it," laughed Polly. "Don't that cotton wool look just like bits of fur, Ben?"

"Yes," said Ben. "And when the flour's shaken over me, it'll be Santa himself."

"We've got to put back the hair into mamsie's cushion the first thing tomorrow," whispered Polly anxiously, "and we mustn't forget it, Bensie."

"I want to keep the wig awfully," said Ben. "You did make that just magnificent, Polly!"

"If you could see yourself," giggled Polly. "Did you

put it *in* the straw bed? And are you sure you pulled the ticking over it smooth?"

"Yes, *sir*," replied Ben. "Sure's my name's Ben Pepper! If you'll only keep them from seeing me when I'm in it till we're ready — that's all I ask."

"Well," said Polly, a little relieved, "but I hope Joe won't look."

"Come on! They're a-comin'!" whispered Ben. "Quick!"

"Polly!" rang a voice dangerously near — so near that Polly, speeding over the stairs to intercept it, nearly fell on her nose.

"Where you been?" asked one.

"Let's have a concert," put in Ben. Polly was so out of breath that she couldn't speak. "Come, now, each take a whistle, and we'll march round and round and see which can make the biggest noise."

In the rattle and laughter which this procession made, all mystery was forgotten and the two conspirators began to breathe freer.

Five o'clock! The small ones of the Pepper flock, being pretty well tired out with noise and excitement, all gathered around Polly and Ben and clamored for a story.

"Do, Polly, do," begged Joel. "It's Christmas, and 'twon't come again for a year."

"I can't," said Polly, in such a twitter that she could hardly stand still, and for the first time in her life refusing. "I can't think of a thing."

"I will, then," said Ben. "We must do something," he whispered to Polly.

"Tell it good," said Joel, settling himself.

So for an hour the small tyrants kept their entertainers well employed.

"Isn't it growing awful dark?" said Davie, rousing himself at last as Ben paused to take breath.

Polly pinched Ben.

"Mammy's a-goin' to let us know," he whispered in reply. "We must keep on a little longer."

"Don't stop," said Joel, lifting his head where he sat on the floor. "What you whisperin' for, Polly?"

"I'm not," said Polly, glad to think she hadn't spoken.

"Well, do go on, Ben," said Joel, lying down again.

"Polly'll have to finish it," said Ben. "I've got to go upstairs now."

So Polly launched out into such an extravagant story that they all, perforce, *had* to listen.

All this time Mrs. Pepper had been pretty busy in *her* way. And now she came into the kitchen and set down her candle on the table. "Children," she said. Everybody turned and looked at her, her tone was so strange. And when they saw her dark eyes shining with such a new light, little Davie skipped right out into the middle of the room. "What's the matter, mammy?"

"You may all come into the Provision Room," said she.

"What for?" shouted Joel in amazement, while the others jumped to their feet and stood staring.

Polly flew around like a general, arranging her forces. "Let's march there," said she. "Phronsie, you take hold of Davie's hand and go first."

"I'm goin' first," announced Joel, squeezing up past Polly.

"No, you mustn't, Joe," said Polly decidedly. "Phronsie and David are the youngest."

"They're *always* the youngest," said Joel, falling back with Polly to the rear.

"*Forward* march!" sang Polly. "Follow mamsie!"

Down the stairs they went with military step and into the Provision Room. And then, with one wild look the little battalion broke ranks, and tumbling one over the other in decidedly unmilitary style, presented a very queer appearance.

And Captain Polly was the queerest of all, for she just gave one gaze at the tree and then sat right down on the floor and said, *"Oh! Oh!"*

Mrs. Pepper was flying around delightedly and saying, "Please to come right in," and "How do you do?"

And before anybody knew it, there were the laughing faces of Mrs. Henderson and the parson himself, Dr. Fisher and old Grandma Bascom; while the two Henderson boys, unwilling to be defrauded of any of the fun, were squeezing themselves in between everybody else and coming up to Polly every third minute and saying, "There, aren't you surprised?"

"It's Fairyland!" cried little Davie, out of his wits with joy. "Oh! Aren't we in Fairyland, ma?"

The whole room was in one buzz of chatter and fun, and everybody beamed on everybody else, and nobody knew what they said, till Mrs. Pepper called, *"Hush!* Santa Claus is coming!"

A rattle at the little old window made everybody look there just as a great snow-white head popped up over the sill.

"Oh!" screamed Joel. " *'Tis Santy!"*

"He's a-comin' in!" cried Davie in chorus, which sent Phronsie flying to Polly. In jumped a little old man, quite spry for his years; with a jolly, red face and a pack on his back, and flew into their midst, prepared to do his duty. But what should he do, instead of making his speech, "this jolly Old Saint" — but first fly up to Mrs. Pepper and say, *"Oh, mammy, how did you do it?"*

"It's Ben!" screamed Phronsie. But the little Old Saint didn't hear, for he and Polly took hold of hands and pranced around that tree while everybody laughed till they cried to see them go!

And then it all came out!

"Order!" said Parson Henderson in his deepest tones, and then he put into Santa Claus's hands a letter, which he requested him to read. And the jolly Old Saint, although he was very old, didn't need any spectacles, but piped out in Ben's loudest tones.

"Dear Friends — A Merry Christmas to you all! And that you'll have a good time, and enjoy it all as much as I've enjoyed my good times at your house, is the wish of your friend,

Jasper Elyot King."

"Hurray for Jappy!" cried Santa Claus, pulling his beard. And "Hurray for Jasper!" went all around the room, and this ended in three good cheers, Phronsie coming in too late with her little crow, which was just as well, however!

"Do your duty now, Santa Claus!" commanded Dr. Fisher as master of ceremonies, and everything was as still as a mouse!

And the first thing she knew, a lovely brass cage, with a dear little bird with two astonished black eyes, dropped down into Polly's hands. The card on it said, *"For Miss Polly Pepper, to give her music every day in the year."*

"Mammy," said Polly. And then she did the queerest thing of the whole! She just burst into tears! "I never thought I should have a bird for *my very own!"*

"Hulloa!" said Santa Claus. "I've got something myself!"

"Santa Claus's clothes are too old," laughed Dr. Fisher, holding up a stout, warm suit that a boy about as big as Ben would delight in.

And then that wonderful tree just rained down all manner of lovely fruit. Gifts came flying thick and fast till the air seemed full, and each one was greeted with a shout of glee as it was put into the hands of its owner. A shawl flew down on Mrs. Pepper's shoulders; and a workbasket tumbled on Polly's head; and tops and balls and fishing poles sent Joel and David into a corner with howls of delight!

But the climax was reached when a large wax doll in a very gay pink silk dress was put into Phronsie's hands, and Dr. Fisher, stooping down, read in loud tones, *"For Phronsie, from one who enjoyed her gingerbread boy."*

After that, nobody had anything to say! Books jumped down unnoticed, and gay boxes of candy. Only Polly peeped into one of her books, and saw in Jappy's plain hand, *"I hope we'll both read this next summer."* And turning over to the title page, she saw *A Complete Manual of Cookery.*

"The best is to come," said Mrs. Henderson in her gentle way. When there was a lull in the gale, she took

170

Polly's hand and led her to a little stand of flowers in the corner concealed by a sheet — pinks and geraniums, heliotropes and roses, blooming away and nodding their pretty heads at the happy sight. Polly had her flowers.

"Why didn't we know?" cried the children at last, when everybody was trying on their hoods and getting their hats to leave the festive scene. "How *could* you keep it secret, mammy?"

"They all went to Mrs. Henderson's," said Mrs. Pepper. "Jasper wrote me, and asked where to send 'em, and Mrs. Henderson was so kind as to say that they might come there. And we brought 'em over last evening, when you were all abed. I couldn't have done it," she said, bowing to the parson and his wife, "if 'twasn't for their kindness — never in all this world!"

"And I'm sure," said the minister, looking around on the bright group, "if we can help along a bit of happiness like this, it is a blessed thing!"

And here Joel had the last word. "You said 'twan't goin' to be Christmas always, mammy. I say," looking around on the overflow of treasures and the happy faces, "it'll be just *forever!*"

EDUCATION AHEAD

AFTER that they couldn't thank Jasper enough! They tried to, lovingly, and an elaborate letter of thanks, headed by Mrs. Pepper, was drawn up and sent with a box of the results of Polly's diligent study of Jasper's book. Polly stripped off recklessly her choicest buds and blossoms from the gay little stand of flowers in the corner that had already begun to blossom, and tucked them into every little nook in the box that could possibly hold a posy. But as for thanking him enough!

"We can't do it, mammy," said Polly, looking around on all the happy faces, and then up at Cherry, who was singing in the window, and who immediately swelled up his little throat and poured out such a merry burst of song that she had to wait for him to finish. "No, not if we tried a thousand years!"

"I'm a-goin'," said Joel, who was busy as a bee with his new tools that the tree had shaken down for him, "to make Jappy the splendidest box *you* ever saw, Polly! I guess that'll thank him!"

"Do," cried Polly. "He'd be so pleased, Joey."

"And I," said Phronsie, over in the corner with her

172

children, "I'm goin' to see my poor, sick man sometime, Polly, I *am!*"

"Oh, dear!" cried Polly, whirling around and looking at her mother in dismay. "She'll be goin' tomorrow! Oh, no, Phronsie, you can't. He lives miles and miles away — oh, ever so far!"

"Does he live as far as the moon?" asked little Phronsie, carefully laying Seraphina down and looking up at Polly anxiously.

"Oh, I don't know," said Polly, giving Cherry a piece of bread and laughing to see how cunning he looked. "Oh, no, of course not, but it's an *awful* long ways, Phronsie."

"I don't care," said Phronsie determinedly, giving the new doll a loving little pat. "I'm goin' sometime, Polly, to thank my poor, sick man, yes I am!"

"You'll see him next summer, Phronsie," sang Polly, skipping around the kitchen, "and Jappy's sister Marian, the lovely lady, and all the boys. Won't that be nice?" And Polly stopped to pat the yellow head bending in motherly attentions over her array of dolls.

"Ye-es," said Phronsie slowly. "The whole of 'em, Polly?"

"Yes, indeed!" said Polly gaily. "The whole of 'em, Phronsie!"

"Hooray!" shouted the two boys, while Phronsie only gave a long sigh and clasped her hands.

"Better not be looking for summer," said Mrs. Pepper, "until you do your duty by the winter; *then* you can enjoy it," and she took a fresh needleful of thread.

"Mamsie's right," said Ben, smiling over at her. And he threw down his book and jumped for his cap. "Now for a good chop!" he cried, and, snatching a kiss from Phronsie, he rushed out of the door to his work, whistling as he went.

"Warn't Mr. Henderson good, ma," asked Polly, watching his retreating figure, "to give Ben learning?"

"Yes, he was," replied Mrs. Pepper enthusiastically. "*We've* got a parson, if anybody has in *this* world!"

"And Ben's learning," said Polly, swelling with pride as she sat down by her mother and began to sew rapidly, "so that he'll be a big man right off! Oh, dear," as a thought made her needle pause a minute in its quick flying in and out.

"What is it, Polly?" Mrs. Pepper looked keenly at the troubled face and downcast eyes.

"Why," began Polly, and then she finished very slowly, "I shan't know anything, and Ben'll be ashamed of me."

"Yes, you will!" cried Mrs. Pepper energetically. "You keep on trying, and the Lord'll send some way. Don't you go to bothering your head about it now, Polly — it'll come when it's time."

"Will it?" asked Polly doubtfully, taking up her needle again.

"Yes, indeed!" cried Mrs. Pepper briskly. "Come fly at your sewing; that's *your* learning now."

"So 'tis," said Polly with a little laugh. "Now let's see which'll get their seam done first, mamsie?"

And now letters flew thick and fast from the city to the little brown house and back again, warming Jasper's heart and filling the tedious months of that winter with more of jollity and fun than the lad ever enjoyed before. And never was fun and jollity more needed than now, for Mr. King, having nothing to do, and each year finding himself less inclined to exercise any thoughtful energy for others, began to look at life something in the light of a serious bore, and accordingly made it decidedly disagreeable for all around him, and particularly for Jasper, who was his constant companion. But the boy was looking forward to summer, and so held on bravely.

"I do verily believe, Polly," he wrote, "that Badgertown'll see the gayest times it ever knew! Sister Marian wants to go, so that's all right. Now, hurrah for a good time — it's surely coming!"

But alas! For Jasper! As spring advanced, his father took a decided aversion to Hingham, Badgertown, and all other places that could be mentioned in that vicinity.

"It's a wretched climate," he asserted over and over, "and the foundation of all my ill feelings this winter was laid, I'm convinced, in Hingham last summer."

No use to urge the contrary; and all Jasper's pleadings were equally vain. At last sister Marian, who was kindhearted to a fault, sorry to see her brother's dismay and disappointment, said one day, "Why not have one of the children come here? I should like it very much. Do invite Ben."

"I don't want Ben," said Jasper gloomily. "I want Polly." He added this in much the same tone as Phronsie's when she had rushed up to him the day she was lost, declaring, "I want Polly!"

"Very well, then," said sister Marian, laughing. "I'm sure I didn't mean to dictate which one. Let it *be* Polly, then. Yes, I should prefer Polly myself, I think, as we've enough boys now," smiling to think of her own brood of wide-awake youngsters.

"If you only will, father, I'll try to be *ever* so good!" said Jasper, turning suddenly to his father.

"Jasper needs some change," said sister Marian kindly. "He really has grown very pale and thin."

"Hey!" said Mr. King sharply, looking at him over his eyeglasses. "The boy's well enough; well enough!" But he twisted uneasily in his chair all the same. At last he flung down his paper, twitched his fingers through his hair two or three times, and then burst out, "Well, why don't you send for her? I'm sure I don't care. I'll write myself, and I had better do it now. Tell Thomas to be ready to take it right down; it must get into this mail."

When Mr. King had made up his mind to do anything, everybody else must immediately give up their individual plans and stand out of the way for him to execute his at just that particular moment! Accordingly Thomas was dragged from his work to post the letter, while the old gentleman occupied the time in pulling out his watch every third second until the slightly out of breath Thomas reported on his return that the letter did get in. Then Mr. King settled down satisfied, and everything went on smoothly as before.

But Polly didn't come! A grateful, appreciative letter, expressed in Mrs. Pepper's own stiff way, plainly showed the determination of that good woman not to accept what was such a favor to her child.

In vain Mr. King stormed, and fretted, and begged, offering every advantage possible — Polly should have the best foundation for a musical education that the city could afford; also lessons in the schoolroom under the boys' private tutor — it was all of no avail. In vain sister Marian sent a gentle appeal, fully showing her heart was

176

in it. Nothing broke down Mrs. Pepper's resolve, until, at last, the old gentleman wrote one day that Jasper, being in such failing health, really depended on Polly to cheer him up. That removed the last straw that made it "putting one's self under an obligation," which, to Mrs. Pepper's independent soul, had seemed insurmountable.

And now it was decided that Polly was *really* to go! And pretty soon all Badgertown knew that Polly Pepper was going to the big city. And there wasn't a man, woman, or child but what greatly rejoiced that a sunny time was coming to one of the chicks in the little brown house. With many warm words and some substantial gifts, kind friends helped forward the outing. Only one person doubted that this delightful chance should be grasped at once, and that one was Polly herself!

"I *can't*," she said, and stood quite pale and still when the Hendersons advised her mother's approval, and even Grandma Bascom said, "Go." "I can't go and leave mammy to do all the work."

"But don't you see, Polly," said Mrs. Henderson, drawing her to her side, "that you will help your mother twice as much as you possibly could here, by getting a good education? Think what your music will be; only think, Polly!"

Polly drew a long breath at this and turned away.

"Oh, Polly!" cried Ben, though his voice choked. "If you give this up, there never'll be another chance," and the boy put his arm around her and whispered something in her ear.

"I know," said Polly quietly, and then she burst out, "Oh, but I can't! 'Tisn't right."

177

"Polly," said Mrs. Pepper, and never in all their lives had the children seen such a look in mamsie's eyes as met them then. "It does seem as if my heart would be broken if you didn't go!" And then she burst out crying, right before them all!

"Oh, mammy," cried Polly, breaking away from everybody and flinging herself into her arms. "I'll go if you think I ought to. But it's too good! Don't cry — *don't*, mammy, dear." And Polly stroked the careworn face lovingly and patted the smooth hair that was still so black.

"And, Polly," said Mrs. Pepper, smiling through her tears, "just think what a comfort you'll be to me, and us all," she added, taking in the children who were crowding around Polly as the center of attraction. "Why, you'll be the making of us," she added hopefully.

"I'll do *something*," said Polly, her brown eyes kindling, "or I shan't be worthy of you, mammy."

"Oh, you'll do it," said Mrs. Pepper confidently, "now that you're going."

But when Polly stepped into the stage, with her little hair trunk strapped on behind, containing her one brown merino that Mrs. Henderson had made over for her out of one of her own, and her two new ginghams, her courage failed again, and she astonished everybody, and nearly upset a mild-faced old lady who was in the corner placidly eating doughnuts, by springing out and rushing up through the little brown gate, past all the family drawn up to see her off. She flew over the old flat door stone and into the bedroom, where she flung herself down between the old bed and Phronsie's crib in a sudden torrent of tears. "I *can't* go!" she sobbed. "Oh, I *can't!*"

"Why, Polly!" cried Mrs. Pepper, hurrying in, followed by Joel and the rest of the troops at his heels. "What are you thinking of!"

"Think of by and by, Polly," put in Ben, patting her on the back with an unsteady hand, while Joel varied the proceedings by running back and forth, screaming at the top of his lungs, "The stage's going! Your trunk'll be taken!"

"Dear me!" ejaculated Mrs. Pepper. "Do stop it, somebody! There, Polly, come now! Do as mother says!"

"I'll try again," said poor Polly, choking back her sobs and getting on her feet.

Then Polly's tears were wiped away, her hat straightened, after which she was kissed all round again by the whole family, Phronsie waiting for the last two, and then was helped again into the stage. The bags and parcels, and box for Jappy, which, as it wouldn't go into the trunk, Joel had insisted Polly should carry in hand, were again piled around her, and Mr. Tisbett mounted to his seat and, with a crack of the whip, bore her safely off this time.

The doughnut lady, viewing poor Polly with extreme sympathy, immediately forced upon her acceptance three of the largest and sugariest.

" 'Twill do you good," she said, falling to, herself, on another with good zeal. "I always eat 'em, and then there ain't any room for homesickness!"

And away, and away, and away they rumbled and jumbled to the cars.

Here Mr. Tisbett put Polly and her numerous bundles under the care of the conductor, with manifold charges and explicit directions to see her safely into Mr. King's own hands. He left her sitting straight up among her parcels, her sturdy little figure drawn up to its full height and the clear brown eyes regaining a little of their dancing light. For although a dreadful feeling tugged at her heart as she thought of the little brown house she was fast flying away from, there was something else — our Polly had begun to realize that now she was going to help mother.

And now they neared the big city, and everybody began to bustle around and get ready to jump out, and the minute the train stopped, the crowd poured out from the cars, making way for the crowd pouring in, for this was a through train.

"All *aboard!*" sang the conductor. "Oh, my senses!" he said, springing to Polly, "I forgot you — *here!*"

But as quick as a flash he was pushed aside and a bright, boyish figure dashed up.

"Oh, Polly!" he said in such a ringing voice! And in another second, Polly and her bag, and the bundle of cakes and apples that Grandma Bascom had put up for her and Joel's box were one and all bundled out upon the platform, and the train whizzed on, and there Mr. King was fuming up and down, berating the departing conductor and speaking his mind in regard to all the railroad officials he could think of. He pulled himself up long enough to give Polly a hearty welcome, and then away again he flew in righteous indignation, while Jasper rushed off into the baggage room with Polly's check.

However, every now and then, turning to look down into the little rosy face beside him, the old gentleman would burst forth, "Bless me, child! I'm glad you're here, Polly! How could the fellow forget when — "

180

"Oh, well, you know," said Polly, with a happy little wriggle under her brown coat, "I'm here now."

"So you are! So you are!" laughed the old gentleman suddenly. "Where can Jasper be so long?"

"They're all in the carriage," answered the boy, skipping back. "Now, father! Now, Polly!"

He was fairly bubbling over with joy, and Mr. King forgot his dudgeon and joined in the general glee, which soon became so great that travelers gave many a glance at the merry trio who bundled away to Thomas and the waiting grays.

"You're sure you've got the right check?" asked Mr. King nervously, getting into a handsome coach lined with dark green satin and settling down among its ample cushions with a sigh of relief.

"Oh, yes," laughed Jasper. "Polly didn't have anyone else's check, I guess!"

Over through the heart of the city, down narrow, noisy business streets, out into wide avenues with handsome, stately mansions on either side — they flew along.

"Oh," said Polly, and then she stopped, and blushed very hard.

"What is it, my dear?" asked Mr. King kindly.

Polly couldn't speak at first, but when Jasper stopped his merry chat and begged to know what it was, she turned on him and burst out, "You *live* here?"

"Why, yes," laughed the boy. "Why not?"

"*Oh!*" said Polly again, her cheeks as red as two roses. "It's *so lovely!*"

And then the carriage turned in at a brown stone gateway and, winding up among some fine old trees, stopped before a large, stately residence that in Polly's eyes seemed like one of the castles of Ben's famous stories. And then Mr. King got out and gallantly escorted Polly out and up the steps, while Jasper followed with Polly's bag, which he couldn't be persuaded to resign to Thomas. A stiff waiter held the door open — and then the rest was only a pleasant, confused jumble of kind welcoming words, smiling faces, with a background of high spacious walls, bright pictures, and soft elegant hangings, everything and all inextricably mixed, till Polly herself seemed floating — away — away, fast to the Fairyland of her dreams. Now Mr. King was handing her around, like a precious parcel, from one to the other — now Jasper was bobbing in and out everywhere, introducing her on all sides, and then Prince was jumping up and trying to lick her face every minute. But best of all was it when a lovely face looked down into hers and Jasper's sister bent to kiss her.

"I am *very* glad to have you here, little Polly." The words were simple, but Polly, lifting up her clear brown eyes, looked straight into the heart of the speaker, and from that moment never ceased to love her.

"It was a good inspiration," thought Mrs. Whitney to herself. "This little girl is going to be a comfort, I know." And then she set herself to conduct successfully her three boys into friendliness and good fellowship with Polly, for each of them was following his own sweet will in the capacity of host, and besides staring at her with all his might, was determined to do the whole of the entertaining, a state of things which might become unpleasant. However, Polly stood it like a veteran.

"This little girl must be very tired," said Mrs. Whitney

at last with a bright smile. "Besides, I am going to have her to myself now."

"Oh, no, no," cried little Dick in alarm. "Why, she's just come — we want to see her."

"For shame, Dick!" said Percy, the eldest, a boy of ten years, who took every opportunity to reprove Dick in public. "She's come a great ways, so she ought to rest, you know."

"You wanted her to come out to the greenhouse yourself, you know you did," put in Van, the next to Percy, who never would be reproved or patronized. "Only she wouldn't go."

"You'll come down to dinner," said Percy politely, ignoring Van. "Then you won't be tired, perhaps."

"Oh, I'm not very tired now," said Polly brightly, with a merry little laugh. "Only I've never been in the cars before, and — "

"Never been in the cars before!" exclaimed Van, crowding up, while Percy made a big rough *O* with his mouth, and little Dick's eyes stretched to their widest extent.

"No," said Polly simply. "Never in all my life."

"Come, dear," said sister Marian, rising quickly and taking Polly's hand, while Jasper, showing unmistakable symptoms of pitching into all the three boys, followed with the bag.

Up the broad oak staircase they went, Polly holding on to Mrs. Whitney's soft hand, as if for dear life, and Jasper tripping up two steps at a time in front of them. They turned after reaching the top, down a hall soft to the foot and brightly lighted.

"Now, Polly," said sister Marian, "I'm going to have

you here, right next to my dressing room. This is your nest, little bird, and I hope you'll be very happy in it."

And here Mrs. Whitney turned up the gas, and then, just because she couldn't help it, gathered Polly up in her arms without another word. Jasper set down the bag on a chair and came and stood by his sister's side, looking down at her as she stroked the brown wavy hair on her bosom.

"It's *so* nice to have Polly here, sister," he said, and he put his hand on Mrs. Whitney's neck and then, with the other hand, took hold of both of Polly's chubby ones, who looked up and smiled. And in that smile the little brown house seemed to hop right out and bring back in a flash all the nice times those eight happy weeks had brought him.

"Oh, 'twas so perfectly splendid, sister Marian," he cried, flinging himself down on the floor by her chair.

"You don't know *what* good times we had, does she, Polly?" And then he launched out into a perfect shower of "Don't you remember this?" or "Oh, Polly! You surely haven't forgotten that!" Mrs. Whitney good-naturedly entering into it and enjoying it all with them until, warned by the lateness of the hour, she laughingly reminded Jasper of dinner and dismissed him to prepare for it.

When the three boys saw Polly coming in again, they welcomed her with a cordial shout, for one and all, after careful measurement of her, had succumbed entirely to Polly, and each was unwilling that the others should get ahead of him in her regard.

"This is your seat, Polly," said sister Marian, touching the chair next to her own.

184

"Thereupon a small fight ensued between the little Whitneys, while Jasper looked decidedly discomfited.

"Let Polly sit next to me," said Van, as if a seat next to him was of all things most to be desired.

"Oh, no, I want her," said little Dick.

"Pshaw, Dick! You're too young," put in Percy. "You'd spill the bread and butter over her."

"I wouldn't either," said little Dick indignantly, beginning to crawl into his seat. "I don't spill bread and butter now, Percy; you know."

"See here," said Jasper decidedly, "she's coming up here by father and me — that is, sister Marian," he finished more politely, "if you're willing."

All this while Polly had stood quietly watching the group, the big, handsome table, the bright lights, and the well-trained servants with a curious feeling at her heart — what were the little-brown-house-people doing?

"Polly shall decide it," said sister Marian, laughing. "Now, where will you sit, dear?" she added, looking down on the little quiet figure beside her.

"Oh, by Jappy, please," said Polly quickly, as if there *could* be no doubt. "And kind Mr. King," she added, smiling at him.

"That's right, that's right, my dear," cried the old gentleman, pleased beyond measure at her honest choice. And he pulled out her chair and waited upon her into it so handsomely that Polly was happy at once, while Jasper, with a proud toss of his dark, wavy hair, marched up delightedly and took the chair on her other side.

And now in two or three minutes it seemed as if Polly had always been there. It was the most natural thing in the world that sister Marian should smile down the table at the bright-faced narrator, who answered all their numerous questions and entertained them all with accounts of Ben's skill, of Phronsie's cunning ways, of the boys who made fun for all, and above everything else of the dear mother whom they all longed to help, and of all the sayings and doings in the little brown house. No wonder that the little boys forgot to eat and for once never thought of the attractions of the table. And, as they left the table at last, little Dick rushed impulsively up to Polly and, flinging himself into her arms, declared, "I love you! And you're my sister!" Nothing more was needed to make Polly feel at home.

"Yes," said Mrs. Whitney, and nodded to herself in the saying. "It was a good thing. And a comfort, I believe, has come to this house this day!"

BRAVE WORK
AND THE REWARD

AND on the very first morrow came Polly's music teacher!

The big drawing room, with its shaded light and draped furniture, with its thick soft carpet, on which no footfall could be heard, with all its beauty and loveliness on every side, was nothing to Polly's eyes; only the room that contained the piano!

That was all she saw! And when the teacher came, he was simply the Fairy (an ugly little one, it is true, but still a most powerful being) who was to unlock its mysteries and conduct her into Fairyland itself. He was a homely little Frenchman with a long, curved nose and an enormous black mustache, magnificently waxed, who bowed elaborately and called her "Mademoiselle Peppaire"; but he had music in his soul, and Polly couldn't reverence him too much.

And now the big piano gave out new sounds; sounds that told of a strong purpose and steady patience. Every note was struck for mother and the home brood. Monsieur Tourtelotte, after watching her keenly out of his little black eyes, would nod to himself like a mandarin, and the nod would be followed by showers of extra politeness at his appreciation of her patient energy and attention.

Every chance she could get, Polly would steal away into the drawing room from Jappy and the three boys and all the attractions they could offer, and laboriously work away over and over at the tedious scales and exercises that were to be stepping-stones to so much that was glorious beyond. Never had she sat still for so long a time in her active little life. And now, with her arms at just such an angle, with the stiff, chubby fingers kept under training and restraint — well, Polly realized, years after, that only her love of the little brown house could *ever* have kept her from flying up and spinning around in perfect despair.

"She likes it!" said Percy in absolute astonishment one day, when Polly had refused to go out driving with all the other children in the park, and had gone resolutely, instead, into the drawing room and shut the door. "She likes those hateful old exercises and she don't like anything else."

"Much you know about it," said Jappy. "She's perfectly aching to go now, Percy Whitney!"

"Well, why don't she, then?" said Percy, opening his eyes to their widest extent.

" 'Cause," said Jasper, stopping on his way to the door to look him full in the face, "she's commenced to learn to play, and there won't *anything* stop her."

"I'm going to try," said Percy gleefully. "I know lots of ways I can do to try, anyway."

"See here, now," said Jasper, turning back. "You let her alone! Do you hear?" he added, and there must have been something in his eye to command attention, for Percy instantly signified his intention not to tease this young music student in the least.

"Come on, then, old fellow," and Jasper swung his cap on his head. "Thomas will be like forty bears if we keep him waiting much longer."

And Polly kept at it steadily day after day, getting through with the lessons in the schoolroom as quickly as possible to rush to her music, until presently the little Frenchman waxed enthusiastic to the degree that, as day after day progressed and swelled into weeks, and each lesson came to an end, he would skip away on the tips of his toes, his nose in the air and the waxed ends of his mustache fairly trembling with delight.

"Ah, such patience as Mademoiselle Pep-paire has! I know no other such little Americane!"

"I think," said Jasper one evening after dinner, when all the children were assembled as usual in their favorite place on the big rug in front of the fire in the library, Prince in the middle of the group, his head on his paws, watching everything in infinite satisfaction, "that Polly's getting on in music as I never saw anyone do, and that's a fact!"

"*I* mean to begin," said Van ambitiously, sitting up straight and staring at the glowing coals. "I guess I will tomorrow," which announcement was received with a perfect shout, Van's taste being anything rather than of a musical nature.

"If you do," said Jappy, when the merriment had a

little subsided, "I shall go out of the house at every lesson. There won't anyone stay in it, Van."

"I can bang all I want to, then," said Van, noways disturbed by the reflection, and pulling one of Prince's long ears. "You think you're so big, Jappy, just because you're thirteen."

"He's only three ahead of me, Van," bristled Percy, who never could forgive Jappy for being his uncle, much less the still greater sin of having been born three years earlier than himself.

"Three's just as bad as four," said Van.

"Let's tell stories," began Polly, who never could remember such goings-on in the little brown house. "We must each tell one," she added with the greatest enthusiasm, "and see which will be the biggest and the best."

"Oh, no," said Van, who perfectly reveled in Polly's stories and who now forgot his trials in the prospect of one. "You tell, Polly — you tell alone."

"Yes, do, Polly," said Jasper. "We'd rather."

So Polly launched out into one of her gayest and finest, and soon they were in such a peal of laughter, and had reached such heights of enjoyment, that Mr. King popped his head in at the door and then came in and took a seat in a big rocking chair in the corner to hear the fun go on.

"Oh, dear," said Van, leaning back with a long sigh and wiping his flushed face as Polly wound up with a triumphant flourish. "How ever do you think of such things, Polly Pepper?"

"That isn't anything," said Jappy, bringing his handsome face out into the strong light. "Why, it's just nothing to what she has told time and again in the little brown

190

house in Badgertown." And then he caught sight of Polly's face, which turned a little pale in the firelight as he spoke, and the brown eyes had such a pathetic droop in them that it went to the boy's very heart.

Was Polly homesick? And so soon!

POLLY IS COMFORTED

Yᴇs, it must be confessed. Polly was homesick. All her imaginations of her mother's hard work, increased by her absence, loomed up before her, till she was almost ready to fly home without a minute's warning. At night, when no one knew it, the tears would come racing over the poor, forlorn little face and would not be squeezed back. It got to be noticed finally, and one and all redoubled their exertions to make everything twice as pleasant as ever!

The only place, except in front of the grand piano, where Polly approached a state of comparative happiness was in the greenhouse.

Here she would stay, comforted and soothed among the lovely plants and rich exotics, rejoicing the heart of Old Turner the gardener, who since Polly's first rapturous entrance had taken her into his good graces for all time.

Every chance she could steal after practice hours were over, and after the clamorous demands of the boys upon her time were fully satisfied, was seized to fly on the wings of the wind to the flowers.

But even with the music and flowers, the dancing light in the eyes went down a little, and Polly, growing more silent and pale, moved around with a little droop to the small figure that had only been wont to fly through the wide halls and spacious rooms with gay and springing step.

"Polly don't like us," at last said Van one day in despair.

"Then, dear," said Mrs. Whitney, "you must be kinder to her than ever. Think what it would be for one of you to be away from home even among friends."

"I'd like it first-rate to be away from Percy," said Van reflectively. "I wouldn't come back in three — no, six weeks."

"My son," said his mamma, "just stop and think how badly you would feel if you really couldn't see Percy."

"Well," said Van, and he showed signs of relenting a little at that, "but Percy is perfectly awful, mamma, you don't know. And he feels so smart too," he added vindictively.

"Well," said Mrs. Whitney softly, "let's think what we can do for Polly. It makes me feel very badly to see her sad little face."

"I don't know," said Van, running over in his mind all the possible ways he could think of for entertaining anybody. "Unless she'd like my new book of travels — or my velocipede," he added.

"I'm afraid those wouldn't quite answer the purpose," said his mamma, smiling. "Especially the last; yet we must think of something."

But just here Mr. King thought it about time to take matters into *his* hands. So, with a great many chucklings and shruggings when no one was by, he had departed after breakfast one day, simply saying he shouldn't be back to lunch.

Polly sat in the drawing room, near the edge of the twilight, practicing away bravely. Somehow, of all the days when the home feeling was the strongest, this day it seemed as if she could bear it no longer. If she could only see Phronsie for just one moment! "I shall *have* to give up!" she moaned. "I *can't* bear it!" and over went her head on the music rack.

"Where is she?" said a voice over in front of the piano, in the gathering dusk — unmistakably Mr. King's.

"Oh, she's always at the piano," said Van's. "She must be there now, somewhere," and then somebody laughed. Then came in the loudest of whispers from little Dick. "Oh, Jappy, what'll she say?"

"Hush!" said one of the other boys. "Do be still, Dick!"

Polly sat up very straight and whisked off the tears quickly. Up came Mr. King with an enormous bundle in his arms, and he marched up to the piano, puffing with his exertions.

"Here, Polly, hold your arms," he had only strength to gasp. And then he broke out into a loud burst of merriment, in which all the troop joined, until the big room echoed with the sound.

At this, the bundle opened suddenly, and — out popped Phronsie!

"Here I am! I'm here, Polly!"

But Polly couldn't speak. And if Jasper hadn't caught her just in time, she would have tumbled over backward from the stool, Phronsie and all!

"Aren't you glad I've come, Polly?" asked Phronsie, with her little face close to Polly's own.

194

That brought Polly to. "Oh, *Phronsie!*" she cried, and strained her to her heart while the boys crowded around and plied her with sudden questions.

"Now you'll stay," cried Van. "Stay, Polly, won't you?"

"Weren't you awfully surprised?" cried Percy. "Say, Polly, *awfully?*"

"Is her name Phronsie?" put in Dick, unwilling to be left out and not thinking of anything else to ask.

"Boys," whispered their mother warningly, "she *can't* answer you. Just look at her face."

And to be sure, our Polly's face was a study to behold. All its old sunniness was as nothing to the joy that now transfigured it.

"Oh!" she cried, coming out of her rapture a little and springing over to Mr. King with Phronsie still in her arms. "Oh, you are the *dearest* and *best* Mr. King I ever saw! But how *did you make mammy let her come?*"

"Isn't he splendid!" cried Jasper in intense pride, swelling up. "Father knew how to do it."

But Polly's arms were around the old gentleman's neck, so she didn't hear. "There, there," he said soothingly, patting her brown, fuzzy head. Something was going down the old gentleman's neck that wet his collar and made him whisper very tenderly in her ear. "Don't give way now, Polly; Phronsie'll see you."

"I know," gasped Polly, controlling her sobs. "I won't — only — I *can't* thank you!"

"Phronsie," said Jasper quickly, "what do you suppose Prince said the other day?"

"What?" asked Phronsie in intense interest, slipping down out of Polly's arms and crowding up close to Jasper's side. "What did he, Jasper?"

"Oh-ho, how funny!" laughed Van, while little Dick burst right out, "*Jasper!*"

"Be still," said Jappy warningly, while Phronsie stood surveying them all with grave eyes.

"Well, I asked him, 'Don't you want to see Phronsie Pepper, Prince?' And do you know, he just stood right upon his hind legs, Phronsie, and said: '*Bark!* Yes, *bark! Bark!*' "

"Did he *really*, Jasper?" cried Phronsie, delighted beyond measure and clasping her hands in rapture. "All alone by himself?"

"Yes, all alone by himself," asserted Jasper vehemently and winking furiously to the others to stop their laughing. "He did now, truly, Phronsie."

"Then mustn't I go and see him *now*, Japser? Yes, pretty soon *now?*"

"So you must," cried Jasper, enchanted at his success in amusing. "And I'll go with you."

"Oh, no," cried Phronsie, shaking her yellow head. "Oh, no, Jasper; I must go by my very own self."

"There, Jap, you've caught it," laughed Percy, while the others screamed at the sight of Jasper's face.

"Oh, Phronsie!" cried Polly, turning around at the last words. "How *could* you!"

"Don't mind it, Polly," whispered Jasper. " 'Twasn't her fault."

"Phronsie," said Mrs. Whitney smilingly, stooping over the child, "would you like to see a little pussy I have for you?"

But the chubby face didn't look up brightly, as usual: and the next moment, without a bit of warning, Phronsie sprang past them all, even Polly, and flung herself into

Mr. King's arms in a perfect torrent of sobs. "Oh! Let's *go back!*" was all they heard!

"Dear me!" ejaculated the old gentleman in the utmost amazement. "And such a time as I've had to get her here, too!" he added, staring around on the astonished group, none of whom had a word to say.

But Polly stood like a statue! All Jasper's frantic efforts at comfort utterly failed. To think that Phronsie had left her for *any*one — even good Mr. King! The room seemed to buzz and everything to turn upside down. And just then she heard another cry — "Oh, I *want* Polly, I *do!*"

With a bound Polly was at Mr. King's side, with her face on his coat, close to the little tearstained one. The fat little arms unclasped their hold and transferred themselves willingly to Polly's neck, and Phronsie hugged up comfortingly to Polly's heart, who poured into her ear all the loving words she had so longed to say.

Just then there was a great rush and a scuffling noise, and something rushed up to Phronsie. *"Oh!"* And then the next minute she had her arms around Prince's neck, too, who was jumping all over her and trying as hard as he could to express his overwhelming delight.

"She's the cunningest little thing I ever saw," said Mrs. Whitney enthusiastically afterward, aside to Mr. King. "Such lovely yellow hair, and such exquisite brown eyes — the combination is very striking. How did her mother ever let her go?" she asked impulsively. "I didn't believe you *could* persuade her, father."

"I didn't have any fears, if I worked it rightly," said the old gentleman complacently. "I wasn't coming without her, Marian, if it could possibly be managed. The truth is that Phronsie had been pining for Polly to such an extent that there was no other way but for her to *have* Polly; and her mother was just on the point, although it almost killed her, of sending for Polly — as if we should have let her go!" he cried in high dudgeon; just as if he owned the whole of the Peppers and could dispose of them all to suit his fancy! "So you see, I was just in time; in the very nick of time, in fact!"

"So her mother was willing?" asked his daughter curiously.

"Oh, she couldn't help it," cried Mr. King, beginning to walk up and down the floor and beaming as he recalled his successful strategy. "There wasn't the smallest use in thinking of anything else. I told her 'twould just stop Polly from ever being a musician if she broke off now — and so 'twould, you know yourself, Marian, for we should never get the child here again if we let her go now. And I talked — well, I had to talk *some*, but, well — the upshot is, I *did* get her, and I *did* bring her — and here she is!" And the old gentleman was so delighted with his success that he had to burst out into a series of short, happy bits of laughter that occupied quite a space of time. At last he came out of them and wiped his face vigorously.

"And to think how fond the little girl is of you, father!" said Mrs. Whitney, who hadn't yet gotten over her extreme surprise at the old gentleman's complete subjection to the little Peppers: he whom all children had by instinct always approached so carefully, and whom everyone found it necessary to conciliate!

"Well, she's a nice child," he said. "A *very* nice child. And," straightening himself up to his fullest height and looking so very handsome that his daughter could not conceal her admiration, "I shall always take care of Phronsie Pepper, Marian!"

"So I hope," said Mrs. Whitney. "And, father, I do believe they'll repay you, for I do think there's good blood there. These children have a look about them that shows them worthy to be trusted."

"So they have, so they have," assented Mr. King, and then the conversation dropped.

PHRONSIE

PHRONSIE was toiling up and down the long oak staircase the next morning, slowly going from one step to the other, drawing each little fat foot into place laboriously but with a pleased expression on her face that only gave some small idea of the rapture within. Up and down she had been going for a long time, perfectly fascinated, seeming to care for nothing else in the world but to work her way up to the top of the long flight, only to turn and come down again. She had been going on so for some time till at last Polly, who was afraid she would tire herself all out, sat down at the foot and begged and implored the little girl, who had nearly reached the top, to stop and rest.

"You'll be tired to death, Phronsie!" she said, looking up at the small figure on its toilsome journey. "Why, you must have gone up a million times! Do sit down, pet. We're all going out riding, Phronsie, this afternoon, and you can't go if you're all tired out."

"I won't be tired, Polly," said Phronsie, turning around and looking at her. "*Do* let me go just once more!"

"Well," said Polly, who never could refuse her anything, "just *once*, Phronsie, and then you must stop."

So Phronsie kept on her way rejoicing, while Polly still sat on the lowest stair and drummed impatiently on the stair above her, waiting for her to get through.

Jappy came through the hall and found them thus.

"Hulloa, Polly!" he said, stopping suddenly. "What's the matter?"

"Oh, Phronsie's been going so," said Polly, looking up at the little figure above them, which had nearly reached the top in delight, "that I can't stop her. She has really, Jappy, almost all the morning. You can't think how crazy she is over it."

"Is that so?" said Jasper with a little laugh. "Hulloa, Phronsie, is it nice?" and he tossed a kiss to the little girl and then sat down by Polly.

"Oh," said Phronsie, turning to come down, "it's the be-yew-tiflest place I ever saw, Japser! The very be-yew-tiflest!"

"I wish she could have her picture painted," whispered Jasper enthusiastically. "Look at her now, Polly, quick!"

"Yes," said Polly, "isn't she sweet!"

"*Sweet!*" said Jasper. "I should think she *was!*"

The sunlight through an oriel window fell on the childish face and figure, glinting the yellow hair and lighting up the radiant face, that yet had a tender, loving glance for the two who waited for her below. One little foot was poised, just in the act of stepping down to the next lower stair, and the fat hand grasped the polished railing, expressive of just enough caution to make it truly childish. In after years Jasper never thought of Phronsie without bringing up this picture on that April morning, when Polly and he sat at the foot of the stairs and looked up and saw it.

"Where's Jap?" called one of the boys, and then there was a clatter out into the hall.

"What are you doing?" and Van came to a full stop of amazement and stared at them.

"Resting," said Jappy concisely. "What do you want, Van?"

"I want you," said Van. "We can't do anything without you, Jappy; you know that."

"Very well," said Jasper, getting up. "Come on, Polly, we must go."

"And Phronsie," said Van anxiously, looking up to Phronsie, who had nearly reached them by this time. "We want her, too."

"Of course," said Polly, running up and meeting her to give her a hug. "*I* don't go unless she does."

"Where are we going, Polly?" asked Phronsie, looking back longingly to her beloved stairs as she was borne off.

"To the greenhouse, chick!" said Jasper. "To help Turner; and it'll be good fun, won't it, Polly?"

"What is a greenhouse?" asked the child wonderingly. "All green, Japser?"

"Oh, dear me," said Van, doubling up, "*do* you suppose she thinks it's painted green?"

"It's green inside, Phronsie dear," said Jasper, kindly, "and that's the best of all."

When Phronsie was really let loose in the greenhouse, she thought it decidedly best of all, and she went into nearly as much of a rapture as Polly did on her first visit to it.

In a few moments she was cooing and jumping among the plants, while old Turner, staid and particular as he was, laughed to see her go.

"She's your sister, Miss Mary, ain't she?" at last he asked as Phronsie bent lovingly over a little pot of heath and just touched one little leaf carefully with her finger.

"Yes," said Polly, "but she don't look like me."

"She *is* like you," said Turner respectfully, "if she don't look like you. And the flowers know it, too," he added, "and they'll love to see her coming, just as they do you."

For Polly had won the old gardener's heart completely by her passionate love for flowers, and nearly every morning a little nosegay, fresh and beautiful, came up to the house for "Miss Mary."

And now nobody liked to think of the time, or to look back to it, when Phronsie hadn't been in the house. When the little feet went pattering through halls and over stairs, it seemed to bring sunshine and happiness into everyone's heart just to hear the sounds. Polly and the boys in the schoolroom would look up from their books and nod away brightly to each other, and then fall to faster than ever on their lessons, to get through the quicker to be with her again.

One thing Phronsie always insisted on, and kept to it pertinaciously, and that was to go into the drawing room with Polly when she went to practice, and there, with one of her numerous family of dolls, to sit down quietly in some corner and wait till she got through.

Day after day she did it, until Polly, who was worried

to think how tedious it must be for her, would look around and say, "Oh, childie, do run out and play."

"I want to stay," Phronsie would beg in an injured tone. "Please let me, Polly."

So Polly would jump and give her a kiss, and then, delighted to know that she was there, would go at her practicing with twice the vigor and enthusiasm.

But Phronsie's chief occupation, at least when she wasn't with Polly, was the entertainment and amusement of Mr. King and never was she very long absent from his side, which so pleased the old gentleman that he could scarcely contain himself as, with a gravity befitting the importance of her office, she would follow him around in a happy contented way that took with him immensely. And nowadays no one ever saw the old gentleman going out of a morning, when Jasper was busy with his lessons, without Phronsie by his side, and many people turned to see the portly figure with the handsome head bent to catch the prattle of a little sunny-haired child, who trotted along, clasping his hand confidingly. And nearly all of them stopped to gaze the second time before they could convince themselves that it was really that queer, stiff old Mr. King of whom they had heard so much.

And now the accumulation of dolls in the house became something alarming, for Mr. King, observing Phronsie's devotion to her family, thought there couldn't possibly be too many of them. So he scarcely ever went out without bringing home one at least to add to them, until Phronsie had such a remarkable collection as would have driven almost any other child nearly crazy with delight. She, however, regarded them something in the light of a grave responsibility, to be taken care of tenderly, to be watched over carefully as to just the right kind of bringing up, and to have small morals and manners taught in just the right way.

Phronsie was playing in the corner of Mrs. Whitney's little boudoir, engaged in sending out invitations for an elaborate tea party to be given by one of the dolls, when Polly rushed in with consternation in her tones and dismay written all over her face.

"What is it, dear?" asked Mrs. Whitney, looking up from her embroidery.

"Why," said Polly, "how *could* I! I don't see — but I've forgotten to write to mamsie today; it's Wednesday, you know, and there's Monsieur coming." And poor Polly looked out in despair to see the lively little music teacher advancing toward the house at an alarming rate of speed.

"That is because you were helping Van so long last evening over his lessons," said Mrs. Whitney. "I am so sorry."

"Oh, no," cried Polly honestly. "I had plenty of time — but I forgot 'twas mamsie's day. What *will* she do!"

"You will have to let it go now till the afternoon, dear; there's no other way. It can go in the early morning mail."

"Oh, dear," sighed Polly. "I suppose I must." And she went down to meet Monsieur with a very distressed little heart.

Phronsie laid down the note of invitation she was scribbling, and stopped to think; and a moment or two after, at a summons from a caller, Mrs. Whitney left the room.

"I know I ought to," said Phronsie to herself and the

dolls. "Yes, I know I had; mamsie will feel, oh! so bad, when she don't get Polly's letter; and I know the way, I do, truly."

She got up and went to the window, where she thought a minute. And then, coming back, she took her little stubby pencil, and bending over a small bit of paper, she commenced to trace with laborious efforts and much hard breathing some very queer hieroglyphics that to her seemed to be admirable, as at last she held them up with great satisfaction.

"Good-bye," she said then, getting up and bowing to the dolls who sat among the interrupted invitations. "I won't be gone but a little bit of one minute." And she went out determinedly and shut the door.

Nobody saw the little figure going down the carriage drive, so of course nobody could stop her. When Phronsie got to the gateway, she looked up and down the street carefully, either way.

"Yes," she said at last, "it was down here. I'm *very* sure, I went with grandpa," and immediately turned down the wrong way, and went on and on, grasping carefully her small and by this time rather soiled bit of paper.

At last she reached the business streets, and although she didn't come to the post office, she comforted herself by the thought, "It must be coming soon. I guess it's round this corner."

She kept turning corner after corner until, at last, a little anxious feeling began to tug at her heart, and she began to think, "I wish I *could* see Polly."

And now she had all she could do to get out of the way of the crowds of people who were pouring up and down the thoroughfare. Everybody jostled against her and gave her a push. "Oh, dear!" thought Phronsie. "There's *such* a many big people!" And then there was no time for anything else but to stumble in and out, to keep from being crushed completely beneath their feet. At last an old huckster woman, in passing along, knocked off her bonnet with the end of her big basket, which flew around and struck Phronsie's head. Not stopping to look into the piteous brown eyes, she strode on without a word. Phronsie turned in perfect despair to go down a street that looked as if there might be room enough for her in it. Thoroughly frightened, she plunged over the crossing to reach it.

"Look out!" cried a ringing voice. *"Stop!"*

"The little girl'll be killed!" said others with bated breath as a powerful pair of horses whose driver could not pull them up in time dashed along just in front of her! With one cry Phronsie sprang between their feet and reached the opposite curbstone in safety!

The plunge brought her up against a knot of gentlemen who were standing talking on the corner.

"What's this!" asked one, whose back being next to the street hadn't seen the commotion, as the small object dashed into their midst and fell up against him.

"Didn't you see that narrow escape?" asked a second, whose face had paled in witnessing it. "This little girl was nearly killed a moment ago — careless driving enough!" And he put out his hand to catch the child.

"Bless me!" cried a third, whirling around suddenly. "Bless me! You don't say so! Why — "

With a small cry, but gladsome and distinct in its utterance, Phronsie gave one look. "Oh, *grandpa!*" was all she could say.

"Oh! *Where* — " Mr. King couldn't possibly have uttered another word, for then his breath gave out entirely as he caught the small figure.

"I went to the post office," said the child, clinging to him in delight, her tangled hair waving over the little white face, into which a faint pink color was quickly coming back. "Only it wouldn't come; and I walked and walked — where is it, grandpa?" And Phronsie gazed up anxiously into the old gentleman's face.

"She went to the post office!" turning around on the others fiercely, as if they had contradicted him. "Why, my child, what were you going to do?"

"Mamsie's letter," said Phronsie, holding up for inspection the precious bit, which by this time was decidedly forlorn. "Polly couldn't write, and mamsie'd feel *so* bad not to get one — she would really," said the child, shaking her head very soberly, "for Polly said so."

"And you've been — oh! I can't *think* of it," said Mr. King, tenderly taking her up on his shoulder. "Well, we must get home now, or I don't know *what* Polly will do!" And without stopping to say a word to his friends, he hailed a passing carriage and, putting Phronsie in, he commanded the driver to get them as quickly as possible to their destination.

In a few moments they were home. Mr. King pushed into the house with his burden. "Don't anybody know," he burst out, puffing up the stairs and scolding furiously at every step, "enough to take better care of this child, than to have such goings-on!"

"What is the matter, father?" asked Mrs. Whitney, coming up the stairs after him. "What has happened out of the way?"

"Out of the way!" roared the old gentleman irascibly. "Well, if you want Phronsie racing off to the post office by herself, and nearly getting killed, poor child! Yes, Marian, I say nearly killed!" he continued.

"What *do* you mean?" gasped Mrs. Whitney.

"Why, where have you been?" asked the old gentleman, who wouldn't let Phronsie get down out of his arms under any circumstances. So there she lay, poking up her head like a little bird and trying to say she wasn't in the least hurt. "Where's everybody been not to know she'd gone?" he exclaimed. "Where's Polly — and Jasper — and all of 'em?"

"Polly's taking her music lesson," said Mrs. Whitney. "Oh, Phronsie darling!" And she bent over the child in her father's arms and nearly smothered her with kisses.

" 'Twas a naughty horse," said Phronsie, sitting up straight and looking at her, "or I should have found the post office. And I lost my bonnet, too," she added, for the first time realizing her loss, putting her hand to her head. "A bad old woman knocked it off with a basket — and now mamsie won't get her letter!" And she waved the bit, which she still grasped firmly between her thumb and finger, sadly toward Mrs. Whitney.

"Oh, dear," groaned that lady, "how could we talk before her! But who would have thought it! Darling," and she took the little girl from her father's arms, who at last let her go, "don't think of your mamma's letter; we'll tell her how it was." And she sat down in the first chair that she could reach, while Phronsie put her tumbled little head down on the kind shoulder and gave a weary little sigh.

"It was *so* long," she said, "and my shoes hurt," and

she thrust out the dusty little boots that spoke pathetically of the long and unaccustomed tramp.

"Poor little lamb!" said Mr. King, getting down to unbutton them. "What a shame!" he mumbled, pulling off half of the buttons in his frantic endeavors to get them off quickly.

But Phronsie never heard the last of his objurgations, for in a minute she was fast asleep. The tangled hair fell off from the tired little face, the breathing came peaceful and regular, and with her little hand fast clasped in Mrs. Whitney's, she slept on and on.

Polly came flying upstairs two or three at a time and humming a scrap of her last piece that she had just conquered.

"Phronsie," she called with a merry little laugh, "where — "

"Hush!" said Mr. King warningly, and then, just because he couldn't explain there without waking Phronsie up, he took hold of Polly's two shoulders and marched her into the next room, where he carefully closed the door and told her the whole thing, using his own discretion about the very narrow escape she had passed through. He told enough, however, for Polly to see what had been so near them, and she stood there so quietly, alternately paling and flushing as he proceeded, till at last, when he finished, Mr. King was frightened almost to death at the sight of her face.

"Oh, goodness me, Polly!" he said, striding up to her and then fumbling around on the table to find a glass of water. "You are not going to faint, are you? Phronsie's all well now — she isn't hurt in the least, I assure you,

I assure you — where *is* a glass of water! Marian ought to see that there's some here — that stupid Jane!" And in utter bewilderment he was fussing here and there, knocking down so many things in general that the noise soon brought Polly to with a little gasp.

"Oh, don't mind me, dear Mr. King — I'm — all well."

"So you are," said the old gentleman, setting up a toilet bottle that he had knocked over. "So you are. I didn't think you'd go and tumble over, Polly, I really didn't." And he beamed admiringly down on her.

And then Polly crept away to Mrs. Whitney's side, where she threw herself down on the floor to watch the little sleeping figure. Her hand was gathered up into the kind one that held Phronsie's, and there they watched and watched and waited.

"Oh, dear," said Phronsie suddenly, turning over with a little sigh and bobbing up her head to look at Polly. "I'm so hungry! I haven't had anything to eat in ever an' ever so long, Polly!" And she gazed at her with a very injured countenance.

"So you must be," said Mrs. Whitney, kissing the flushed little face. "Polly must ring the bell for Jane to bring this little bird some crumbs."

"Can I have a great many?" asked Phronsie, lifting her eyes, with the dewy look of sleep still lingering in them. "As many as *two* birdies?"

"Yes, dear," said Mrs. Whitney, laughing. "I think as many as *three* little birdies could eat, Phronsie."

"Oh," said Phronsie, and leaned back satisfied, while Polly gave the order, which was presently followed by Jane with a well-filled tray.

"Now," said Jappy, when he heard the account of the adventure, "*I* say that letter ought to go to your mother, Polly."

"Oh," said Polly, "it would scare mamsie most to death, Jappy!"

"Don't tell her the whole," said Jasper quickly. "I didn't mean that — about the horses and all that — but only enough to let her see how Phronsie tried to get it to her."

"And I'm going to write to your brother Joel," said Van, drawing up the library table. "I'll scare *him*, Polly, I guess; he won't tell your mother."

"Your crow tracks'll scare him enough without anything else," said Percy pleasantly, who really could write very nicely, while Polly broke out in an agony, "Oh, no, Van, you mustn't! You mustn't!"

"If Van does," said Jasper decidedly, "it'll be the last time he'll write to the brown house, I can tell him. And besides, he'll go to Coventry." This had the desired effect.

"Let's all write," said Polly.

So a space on the table was cleared, and the children gathered around it, when there was great scratching of pens and clearing of ideas, which presently resulted in a respectable budget of letters, into which Phronsie's was lovingly tucked in the center. And then they all filed out to put it into the letter box in the hall, for Thomas to mail with the rest in the morning.

GETTING READY FOR MAMSIE AND THE BOYS

"AND I'll tell you, Marian, what I am going to do."

Mr. King's voice was pitched on a higher key than usual, and extreme determination was expressed in every line of his face. He had met Mrs. Whitney at the foot of the staircase, dressed for paying visits. "Oh, are you going out?" he said, glancing impatiently at her attire. "And I'd just started to speak to you on a matter of great importance! Of the greatest importance indeed!" he repeated irritably as he stood with one gloved hand resting on the balustrade.

"Oh, it's no matter, father," she replied pleasantly. "If it's really important, I can postpone going for another day, and — "

"*Really important!*" repeated the old gentleman irascibly. "Haven't I just told you it's of the *greatest importance?* There's no time to be lost. And with my state of health, too, it's of the utmost consequence that I shouldn't be troubled. It's very bad for me; I should think you would realize that, Marian."

"I'll tell Thomas to take the carriage directly back," said Mrs. Whitney, stepping to the door. "Or stay, father;

I'll just run up and send the children out for a little drive. The horses ought to be used, too, you know," she said lightly, preparing to run up to carry out the changed plan.

"Never mind that now," said Mr. King abruptly. "I want you to give me your attention *directly*." And walking toward the library door, getting a fresh accession of impatience with every step, he beckoned her to follow.

But his progress was somewhat impeded by little Dick — or, rather, little Dick and Prince, who were standing at the top of the stairs to see Mrs. Whitney off. When he saw his mother retrace her steps, supposing her yielding to the urgent entreaties that he was sending after her to stay at home, the child suddenly changed his good-byes to vociferous howls of delight and speedily began to plunge down the stairs to welcome her.

But the staircase was long, and little Dick was in a hurry, and besides, Prince was in the way. The consequence was, nobody knew just how, that a bumping noise struck into the conversation that made the two below in the hall look up quickly, to see the child and dog come rolling over the stairs at a rapid rate.

"Zounds!" cried the old gentleman. "Here, Thomas, *Thomas!*" But as that individual was waiting patiently outside the door on the carriage box, there was small hope of his being in time to catch the boy, who was already in his mother's arms, not quite clear, by the suddenness of the whole thing, as to how he came there.

"Oh! Oh! Dicky's hurt!" cried somebody up above, followed by everyone within hearing distance, and all came rushing to the spot to ask a thousand questions all in the same minute.

There sat Mrs. Whitney in one of the big carved chairs, with little Dick in her lap, and Prince walking gravely around and around him with the greatest expression of concern on his noble face. Mr. King was storming up and down and calling on everybody to bring a "bowl of water, and some brown paper; and *be quick!*" interpolated with showers of blame on Prince for sitting on the stairs and tripping people up! While Dick meanwhile was laughing and chatting and enjoying the distinction of making so many people run and of otherwise being the object of so much attention!

"I don't think he was sitting on the stairs, father," said Jasper, who, when he saw that Dicky was really unhurt, began to vindicate his dog. "He never does that; do you, sir?" he said, patting the head that was lifted up to him, as if to be defended.

"And I expect we shall all be killed someday, Jasper," said Mr. King, warming with his subject and forgetting all about the brown paper and water which he had ordered, and which was now waiting for him at his elbow, "just by that creature."

"He's the noblest — " began Jasper, throwing his arms around his neck; an example which was immediately followed by the Whitney boys and the two little Peppers. When Dick saw this, he began to struggle to get down to add himself to the number.

"Where's the brown paper?" began Mr. King, seeing this and whirling around suddenly. "Hasn't anybody brought it yet?"

"Here 'tis sir," said Jane, handing him a generous supply.

"Oh, I don't want to," cried little Dick in dismay, seeing

his grandfather advance with an enormous piece of paper, which, previously wet in the bowl of water, was now unpleasantly clammy and wet. "Oh, no, I don't want to be all stuck up with old horrid wet paper!"

"Hush, dear!" said his mamma soothingly. "Grandpapa wants to put it on — there — " as Mr. King dropped it scientifically on his head and then proceeded to paste another one over his left eye.

"And I hope they'll all drop off," cried Dick savagely, shaking his head to facilitate matters. "Yes, I do, every single one of 'em!" he added with an expression that, seen under the brown bits, was anything but benign.

"Was Prince on the stairs, Dick?" asked Jasper, coming up and peering under his several adornments. "Tell us how you fell!"

"No," said little Dick crossly, and giving his head another shake. "He was up in the hall — oh, dear, I want to get down." And he began to stretch his legs and to struggle with so much energy that two or three pieces fell off and landed on the floor, to his intense delight.

"And how did you fall, then?" said Jasper perseveringly. "Can't you remember, Dicky boy?"

"I pushed Princey," said Dick, feeling, with freedom from some of his encumbrances, more disposed for conversation, "and made him go ahead, and then I fell on top of him — that's all."

"I guess Prince has *saved* him, father," cried Jasper, turning around with eyes full of pride and love on the dog, who was trying as hard as he could to tell all the children how much he enjoyed their caresses.

And so it all came about that the consultation so summarily interrupted was never held. For, as Mrs. Whitney was about retiring that evening, Mr. King rapped at her door, on his way to bed.

"Oh," he said, popping in his head in response to her invitation to come in, "it's nothing — only I thought I'd just tell you a word or two about what I've decided to do."

"Do you mean what you wanted to see me about this afternoon?" asked Mrs. Whitney, who hadn't thought of it since. "Do come in, father."

"It's of no consequence," said the old gentleman. "No consequence at all," he repeated, waving his hand emphatically, "because I've made up my mind and arranged all my plans. It's only about the Peppers — "

"The Peppers?" repeated Mrs. Whitney.

"Yes. Well, the fact of it is, I'm going to have them here for a visit — the whole of them, you understand; that's all there is to it. And I shall go down to see about all the arrangements — Jasper and I — day after tomorrow," said the old gentleman, as if he owned the whole Pepper family inclusive and was the only responsible person to be consulted about their movements.

"Will they come?" asked Mrs. Whitney doubtfully.

"Come? Of course," said Mr. King sharply. "There isn't any other way. Or else Mrs. Pepper will be sending for her children — and of course you know, Marian, we couldn't allow *that*. Well, that's all; so good night." And the door closed on his retreating footsteps.

And so Polly and Phronsie soon knew that mamsie and the boys were to be invited! And then the grand house, big as it was, didn't seem large enough to contain them.

"I declare," said Jasper next day, when they had been laughing and planning till they were all as merry as grigs, "if this old dungeon don't begin to seem a little like the little brown house, Polly."

" 'Twon't," answered Polly, hopping around on one toe, followed by Phronsie, "till mamsie and the boys get here, Jasper King!"

"Well, they'll be here soon," said Jappy, pleased at Polly's exultation over it, "for we're going tomorrow to do the inviting."

"And Polly's to write a note to slip into Marian's," said Mr. King, putting his head in at the door. "And if you want your mother to come, child, why, you'd better mention it as strong as you can."

"I'm going to write," said Phronsie, pulling up after a prolonged skip, all out of breath. "I'm going to write and beg mamsie dear. *Then* she'll come, I guess."

"I guess she will," said Mr. King, looking at her. "You go on, Phronsie, and write, and that letter shall go straight in my coat pocket alone by itself."

"Shall it?" asked Phronsie, coming up to him. "And nobody will take it out till you give it to mamsie?"

"No, nobody shall touch it," said the old gentleman, stooping to kiss the upturned face, "till I put it into her own hand."

"Then," said Phronsie in the greatest satisfaction, "I'm going to write this very one minute!" And she marched away to carry her resolve into immediate execution.

Before they got through they had quite a bundle of invitations and pleadings, for each of the three boys insisted on doing his part, so that when they were finally done up in an enormous envelope and put into Mr.

King's hands, he told them with a laugh that there was no use for Jappy and himself to go, as those were strong enough to win almost anybody's consent.

However, the next morning they set off, happy in their hopes and bearing the countless messages, which the children would come up every now and then to intrust to them, declaring that they had forgotten to put them in the letters.

"You'd had to have had an express wagon to carry the letters if you had put them all in," at last cried Jasper. "You've given us a bushel of things to remember."

"And oh! Don't forget to ask Ben to bring Cherry," cried Polly the last minute as they were driving off, although she had put it in her letter at least a dozen times. "And oh, dear! Of course the flowers can't come."

"We've got plenty here," said Jasper. "You would not know what to do with them, Polly."

"Well, I do wish mamsie would give some to kind Mrs. Henderson, then," said Polly, on the steps, clasping her hands anxiously while Jasper told Thomas to wait till he heard the rest of the message. "And to grandma — you know Grandma Bascom; she was so good to us," she said impulsively. "And oh! Don't let her forget to carry some to dear, *dear* Dr. Fisher; and don't forget to give him our love, Jappy; *don't* forget that!" And Polly ran down the steps to the carriage door, where she gazed up imploringly to the boy's face.

"I guess I won't," cried Jasper, "when I think how he saved your eyes, Polly! He's the best fellow I know!" he finished in an impulsive burst.

"And don't let mamsie forget to carry some in to good old Mr. and Mrs. Beebe in town — where Phronsie got

219

her shoes, you know; that is, if mamsie can," she added, remembering how very busy her mother would be.

"I'll carry them myself," said Jasper. "We're going to stay over till the next day, you know."

"Oh!" cried Polly, radiant as a rose. "Will you really, Jappy? You're *so* good!"

"Yes, I will," said Jasper. "Everything you want done, Polly. Anything else?" he asked quickly, as Mr. King, impatient to be off, showed unmistakable symptoms of hurrying up Thomas.

"Oh, no," said Polly. "Only do look at the little brown house, Jasper, as much as you can." And Polly left the rest unfinished. Jasper seemed to understand, however, for he smiled brightly as he said, looking into the brown eyes, "I'll do it all, Polly, every single thing." And then they were off.

Mamsie and the boys! Could Polly ever wait till the next afternoon that would bring the decision?

Long before it was possibly time for the carriage to come back from the depot, Polly, with Phronsie and the three boys, who, improving Jasper's absence, had waited upon her with the grace and persistence of cavaliers of the olden time, were drawn up at the old stone gateway.

"Oh, dear," said Van with an impatient fling. "They *never* will come!"

"Won't they, Polly?" asked Phronsie anxiously and standing quite still.

"Dear me, yes," said Polly with a little laugh. "Van only means they'll be a good while, Phronsie. They're *sure* to come sometime."

"Oh!" said Phronsie, quite relieved, and she commenced her capering again in extreme enjoyment.

"I'm going," said little Dick, "to run down and meet them."

Accordingly off he went, and was immediately followed by Percy, who started with the laudable desire of bringing him back. But finding it so very enjoyable, he stayed himself and frolicked with Dick, till the others, hearing the fun, all took hold of hands and flew off to join them.

"Now," said Polly when they recovered their breath a little, "let's all turn our backs to the road, and the minute we hear the carriage we must whirl round, and the one who sees 'em first can *ask* first, 'Is mamsie coming?' "

"All right," cried the boys.

"Turn round, Dick," said Percy with a little shove, for Dick was staring with all his might right down the road. And so they all flew around till they looked like five statues set up to grace the sidewalk.

"Suppose a big dog *should* come," suggested Van pleasantly, "and snap at our backs!"

At this little Dick gave a small howl and turned around in a fright.

"There isn't any dog coming," said Polly. "What does make you say such awful things, Van?"

"I hear a noise," said Phronsie. And so they all whirled around in expectation. But it proved to be only a market wagon coming at a furious pace down the road, with somebody's belated dinner. So they all had to whirl back again as before. The consequence was that when the carraige *did* come, nobody heard it.

Jasper, looking out, was considerably astonished to see, drawn up in solemn array with their backs to the road, five children, who stood as if completely petrified.

"What in the world!" he began, and called to Thomas to stop, whose energetic *"Whoa!"* reaching the ears of the frozen line, caused it to break ranks and spring into life at an alarming rate.

"Oh, *is* she coming Jappy? *Is* she?" they all screamed together, swarming up to the carriage door and over the wheels.

"Yes," said Jasper, looking at Polly.

At that, Phronsie sat right down on the pavement in an ecstasy.

"Get in here, all of you," said Jasper merrily. "Help Polly in first. For shame, Dick! Don't scramble so."

"Dick always shoves," said Percy, escorting Polly up with quite an air.

"I don't either," said Dick. "You pushed me awful, just a little while ago," he added indignantly.

"Do say *awfully,*" corrected Van, crowding up to get in. "You leave off your *lys* so," he finished critically.

"I don't know anything about any lees," said little Dick, who, usually so good-natured, was now thoroughly out of temper. "I want to get in and go home." And he showed evident symptoms of breaking into a perfect roar.

"There," said Polly, lifting him up, "there he goes! Now — one, two three!" and little Dick was spun in so merrily that the tears changed into a happy laugh.

"Now then, bundle in, all the rest of you," put in Mr. King, who seemed to be in the best of spirits. "That's it; go on, Thomas!"

"When are they coming?" Polly found time to ask in the general jumble.

"In three weeks from tomorrow," said Jasper. "And everything's all right, Polly! And the whole of them, Cherry and all, will be here then!"

"*Oh!*" said Polly.

"Here we are!" cried Van, jumping out almost before the carriage door was open. "Mamma, mamma," he shouted to Mrs. Whitney in the doorway, "the Peppers are coming, and the little brown house too! Everything and everybody!"

"They are!" said Percy, as wild as his brother. "And everything's just splendid! Jappy said so."

"Everything's coming," said little Dick, tumbling up the steps. "And the bird — and — and — "

"And mamsie!" finished Phronsie, impatient to add her part, while Polly didn't say anything, only looked.

Three weeks! "I *can't* wait!" thought Polly at first, in counting over the many hours before the happy day would come. But on Jasper's suggesting that they should all do something to get ready for the visitors, and have a general trimming up with vines and flowers beside, the time passed away much more rapidly than was feared.

Polly chose a new and more difficult piece of music to learn to surprise mamsie. Phronsie had aspired to an elaborate pincushion, that was nearly done, made of bits of worsted and canvas, over whose surface she had wandered according to her own sweet will, in a way charming to behold.

"I don't know what to do," said Van in despair, " 'cause I don't know what she'd like."

"Can't you draw her a little picture?" asked Polly. "She'd like that."

"Does she like pictures?" asked Van with the greatest interest.

"Yes indeed!" said Polly. "I guess you'd think so if you could see her!"

"I know what *I* shall do," with a dignified air said Percy, who couldn't draw and therefore looked down on all Van's attempts with the greatest scorn. "And it won't be any old pictures, either," he added.

"What is it, old fellow?" asked Jasper. "Tell on, now, your grand plan."

"No, I'm not going to tell," said Percy with the greatest secrecy, "until the very day."

"What will *you* do, sir?" asked Jasper, pulling one of Dick's ears, who stood waiting to speak, as if his mind was made up and wouldn't be changed for anyone!

"I shall give Ben one of my kitties — the littlest and the best!" he said with heroic self-sacrifice.

A perfect shout greeted this announcement.

"Fancy Ben going round with one of those awful little things," whispered Jappy to Polly, who shook at the very thought.

"Don't laugh! Oh, it's dreadful to laugh at him, Jappy," she said when she could get voice enough.

"No, I *shan't* tell," said Percy, when the fun had subsided; who, finding that no one teased him to divulge his wonderful plan, kept trying to harrow up their feelings by parading it.

"You *needn't*, then," screamed Van, who was nearly dying to know. "I don't believe it's so very dreadful much, anyway."

"What's yours, Jappy?" asked Polly. "I know yours will be just splendid."

"Oh, no, it isn't," said Jasper, smiling brightly, "but as I didn't know what better I could do, I'm going to get a little stand, and then beg some flowers of Turner to fill it, and — "

"Why, that's *mine!*" screamed Percy in the greatest disappointment. "That's just what *I* was going to do!"

"Hoh, hoh!" shouted Van. "I thought you wouldn't tell, Mr. Percy! Hoh, hoh!"

"Hoh, hoh!" echoed Dick.

"Hush," said Jappy. "Why, Percy, I didn't know as you had thought of that," he said kindly. "Well, then, you do it, and I'll take something else. I don't care, as long as Mrs. Pepper gets 'em."

"I didn't *exactly* mean that," began Percy. "Mine was roots and little flowers growing."

"He means what he gets in the woods," said Polly, explaining. "Don't you, Percy?"

"Yes," said the boy. "And then I was going to put stones and things in among them to make them look pretty."

"And they will," cried Jasper. "Go ahead, Percy. They'll look real pretty, and then Turner will give you some flowers for the stand, I know. I'll ask him tomorrow."

"Will you?" cried Percy. "That'll be fine!"

"Mine is the best," said Van just at this juncture, but it was said a little anxiously, as he saw how things were prospering with Percy. "For my flowers in the picture will always be there, and your old roots and things will die."

"What will yours be, then, Jappy?" asked Polly very soberly. "The stand of flowers would have been just lovely! And you do fix them so nice," she added sorrowfully.

"Oh, I'll find something else," said Jappy cheerfully, who had quite set his heart on giving the flowers. "Let me see — I might carve her a bracket."

"Do!" cried Polly, clapping her hands enthusiastically. "And do carve a little bird, like the one you did on your father's."

"I will," said Jasper. "Just exactly like it. Now, we've got something to do, before we welcome the little brown house people, so let's fly at it, and the time won't seem so long."

And at last the day came when they could all say — tomorrow they'll be here!

Well, the vines were all up, and pots of lovely climbing ferns, and all manner of pretty green things had been arranged and rearranged a dozen times till everything was pronounced perfect, and a big green WELCOME over the library door, made of laurel leaves, by the patient fingers of all the children, stared down into their admiring eyes as much as to say, "I'll do *my* part!"

"Oh, dear," said Phronsie when evening came and the children were, as usual, assembled on the rug before the fire, their tongues running wild with anticipation and excitement. "I don't mean to go to bed at all, Polly; I don't truly."

"Oh, yes, you do," said Polly, laughing. "Then you'll be all fresh and rested to see mammy when she does come."

"Oh, no," said Phronsie, shaking her head soberly and

speaking in an injured tone. "I'm not one bit tired, Polly; not one bit."

"You needn't go yet, Phronsie," said Polly. "You can sit up half an hour yet, if you want to."

"But I don't want to go to bed at all," said the child anxiously. "For then I may be asleep when mamsie comes, Polly."

"She's afraid she won't wake up," said Percy, laughing. "Oh, there'll be oceans of time before they come, Phronsie."

"What *is* oceans?" asked Phronsie, coming up and looking at him doubtfully.

"He means mamsie won't get here till afternoon," said Polly, catching her up and kissing her. "Then I guess you'll be awake, Phronsie, pet."

So Phronsie allowed herself to be persuaded, at the proper time, to be carried off and inducted into her little nightgown. And when Polly went up to bed, she found the little pincushion, with its hieroglyphics, that she had insisted on taking to bed with her, still tightly grasped in the little fat hand.

"She'll roll over and muss it," thought Polly, "and then she'll feel bad in the morning. I guess I'd better lay it on the bureau."

So she drew it carefully away without awaking the little sleeper, and placed it where she knew Phronsie's eyes would rest on it the first thing in the morning.

It was going on toward the middle of the night when Phronsie, whose exciting dreams of mamsie and the boys wouldn't let her rest quietly, woke up, and in the very first flash she thought of her cushion.

"Why, where — " she said in the softest little tones, only half awake. "Why, Polly, where is it?" and she began to feel all around her pillow to see if it had fallen down there.

But Polly's brown head with its crowd of anticipations and busy plans was away off in dreamland, and she breathed on and on, perfectly motionless.

"I guess I better," said Phronsie to herself, now thoroughly awake and sitting up in bed, "not wake her up. Poor Polly's tired. I can find it myself, I know I can."

So she slipped out of bed and, prowling around on the floor, felt all about for the little cushion.

" 'Tisn't here, oh, no, it isn't," she sighed at last, and getting up, she stood still a moment, lost in thought. "Maybe Jane's put it out in the hall," she said as a bright thought struck her. "I can get it there." And out she pattered over the soft carpet to the table at the end of the long hall, where Jane often placed the children's playthings overnight. As she was coming back after her fruitless search, she stopped to peep over the balustrade down the fascinating flight of stairs, now so long and dark. Just then a little faint ray of light shot up from below and met her eyes.

"Why," she said in gentle surprise, "they're all downstairs! I guess they're making something for mamsie — I'm going to see."

So, carefully picking her way over the stairs with her little bare feet, and holding on to the balustrade at every step, she went slowly down, guided by the light, which, as she neared the bottom of the flight, she saw came from the library door.

"Oh, isn't it funny!" And she gave a little happy laugh. "They won't know I'm comin'!" And now the soft little feet went pattering over the thick carpet until she stood just within the door. There she stopped perfectly still.

Two dark figures, big and powerful, were bending over something that Phronsie couldn't see, between the two big windows. A lantern on the floor flung its rays over them as they were busily occupied, and the firelight from the dying coals made the whole stand out distinctly to the gaze of the motionless little figure.

"*Why*, what are you doing with my grandpa's things?"

The soft, clear notes fell like a thunderbolt upon the men. With a start they brought themselves up and stared, only to see a little white-robed figure, with its astonished eyes uplifted with childlike, earnest gaze, as she waited for her answer.

For an instant they were powerless to move and stood as if frozen to the spot, till Phronsie, moving one step forward, piped forth, "Naughty men, to touch my dear grandpa's things!"

With a smothered cry one of them started forward with arm uplifted, but the other sprang like a cat and intercepted the blow.

"Stop!" was all he said. A noise above the stairs — a rushing sound through the hall! Something will save Phronsie, for the household is aroused! The two men sprang through the window, having no time to catch the lantern or their tools, as Polly, followed by one and another, rushed in and surrounded the child.

"What!" gasped Polly, and got no further.

"*Stop, thief!*" roared Mr. King, hurrying over the stairs.

The children, frightened at the strange noises, began

to cry and scream, as they came running through the halls to the spot. Jasper rushed for the menservants.

And there stood Phronsie, surrounded by the pale group.

" 'Twas two naughty men," she said, lifting her little face with the grieved, astonished look still in the big brown eyes, "and they were touching my grandpa's things, Polly!"

"I should think they were," said Jasper, running over among the few scattered tools and the lantern to the windows, where, on the floor, was a large table cover hastily caught up by the corners, into which a vast variety of silver, jewelry, and quantities of costly articles were gathered, ready for flight. "They've broken open your safe, father!" he cried in excitement. "See?"

"And they put up their hand — one man did," went on Phronsie. "And the other said, 'Stop!' Oh, Polly, you hurt me!" she cried as Polly, unable to bear the strain any longer, held her so tightly, she could hardly breathe.

"Go on," said Jasper. "How did they look?"

"All black," said the child, pushing back her wavy hair and looking at him. "Very all black, Japser."

"And their faces, Phronsie?" said Mr. King, getting down on his old knees on the floor beside her. "Bless me! Somebody else ask her. I *can't* talk!"

"How did their faces look, Phronsie, dear?" asked Jasper, taking one of the cold hands in his. "Can't you think?"

"Oh!" said Phronsie, and then she gave a funny little laugh. "Two big holes, Japser, that's all they had!"

"She means they were masked," whispered Jasper.

"What did you get up for?" Mrs. Whitney asked. "Dear

child, what made you get out of bed?"

"Why, my cushion-pin," said Phronsie, looking worried at once. "I couldn't find it, and — "

But just at this, without a bit of warning, Polly tumbled over in a dead faint.

And then it was all confusion again.

And so, on the following afternoon, it turned out that the Peppers, about whose coming there had been so many plans and expectations, just walked in as if they had always lived there. The greater excitement completely swallowed up the less!

WHICH TREATS OF
A GOOD MANY MATTERS

"Pooh!" said Joel a few mornings after the emptying of the little brown house into the big one, when he and Van were rehearsing for the fiftieth time all the points of the eventful night. "Phooh! If I'd been there, they wouldn't have got away, I guess!"

"What would *you* have done?" asked Van, bristling up at this reflection on their courage, and squaring up to him. "What would you have done, Joel Pepper?"

"I'd a-pitched right into 'em — like — everything!" said Joel valiantly. "And a-caught 'em! Yes, every single one of the bunglers!"

"The *what*?" said Van, bursting into a loud laugh.

"The bunglers," said Joel with a red face. "That's what you said they were, anyway," he added positively.

"I said *burglars*," said Van, doubling up with amusement, while Joel stood, a little sturdy figure, regarding him with anything but a sweet countenance.

"Well, anyway, I'd a-caught 'em, so there!" he said, as Van at last showed signs of coming out of his fit of laughter and got up and wiped his eyes.

"How'd you caught 'em?" asked Van, scornfully surveying the square little country figure before him. "You can't hit any."

"Can't?" said Joel, the black eyes flashing volumes, and coming up in front of Van. "You better believe I can, Van Whitney!"

"Come out in the backyard and try, then," said Van hospitably, perfectly delighted at the prospect and flying along toward the door. "Come right out and try."

"All right!" said Joel, following sturdily, equally delighted to show his skill.

"There," said Van, taking off his jacket and flinging it on the grass, while Joel immediately followed suit with his little homespun one. "Now we can begin perfectly splendid! I won't hit hard," he added patronizingly as both boys stood ready.

"Hit as hard as you've a mind to," said Joel. "I'm a-going to."

"Oh, *you* may," said Van politely, "because you're company. All right — now!"

So at it they went. Before very many minutes were over, Van relinquished all ideas of treating his company with extra consideration and was only thinking how he could possibly hold his own with the valiant little country lad. Oh, if he could only be called to his lessons — *anything* that would summon him into the house! Just then a window above their heads was suddenly thrown up, and his mamma's voice in natural surprise and distress called quickly, "Children, what *are* you doing? Oh, Van, how could you!"

Both contestants turned around suddenly. Joel look up steadily. "We're a-hitting, ma'am; he said I couldn't, and so we came out and — "

"Oh, Vanny," said Mrs. Whitney reproachfully. "To treat a little guest in this way!"

"I wanted to," said Joel cheerfully. " 'Twas great fun. Let's begin again, Van!"

"We mustn't," said Van, readily giving up the charming prospect and beginning to edge quickly toward the house. "Mamma wouldn't like it, you know. He hits splendidly, mamma," he added generously, looking up. "He does really."

"And so does Van," cried Joel, his face glowing at the praise. "We'll come out every day," he added, slipping into his jacket and turning enthusiastically back to Van.

"And perhaps he *could* have pitched into the burglars," finished Van, ignoring the invitation and tumbling into his jacket with alarming speed.

"I *know* I could!" cried Joel, scampering after him into the house. "If I'd only a-been here!"

"Where's Ben?" said Van, bounding into the hall and flinging himself down on one of the chairs. "Oh, dear, I'm so hot! Say, Joe, where *do* you s'pose Ben is?"

"I don't know," replied Joel, who didn't even puff.

"I saw him a little while ago with Master Percy," said Jane, who was going through the hall.

"There, now! And they've gone off somewhere," cried Van in extreme irritation, and starting up quickly. "I *know* they have. Which way did they go, Jane? And how long ago?"

"Oh, I don't know," replied Jane carelessly. "Half an hour maybe, and they didn't go nowhere as I see. At least they were talking at the door, and I was going upstairs."

"Right here?" cried Van, and stamping with his foot to point out the exact place. "At *this* door, Jane?"

"Yes, yes," said Jane. "At that very door," and then she went into the dining room to her work.

"Oh, dear me!" cried Van, and flying out on the veranda, he began to peer wildly up and down the drive. "And they've gone to some splendid place, I know, and wouldn't tell us. That's just like Percy!" he added vindictively. "He's *always* stealing away! Don't you see 'em, Joel? Oh, do come out and look!"

" 'Tisn't any use," said Joel coolly, sitting down on the chair Van had just vacated and swinging his feet comfortably. "They're miles away if they've been gone half an hour. *I'm* going upstairs." And he sprang up and energetically pranced to the stairs.

"They aren't up*stairs!*" screamed Van in scorn, bounding into the hall. "Don't go. I know that they've gone down to the museum!"

"The *what?*" exclaimed Joel, nearly at the top, peering over the railing. "What's that you said — what is it?"

"A *museum*," shouted Van, "and it's a perfectly *elegant* place, Joel Pepper, and Percy knows I like to go. And now he's taken Ben off, and he'll show him all the things! And they'll all be old when *I* take him — and — and — oh! I hope the snakes will bite him!" he added, trying to think of something bad enough.

"Do they have snakes there?" asked Joel, staring.

"Yes, they *do*," snapped out Van. "They have *everything!*"

"Well, they shan't bite *Ben!*" cried Joel in terror. "Oh! Do you suppose they *will?*" And he turned right straight around on the stair and looked at Van.

"No," said Van, "they won't bite. What's the matter, Joe?"

"Oh, they *may*," said Joel, his face working, and screwing both his fists into his eyes. At last he burst right out into a torrent of sobs. "Oh, don't let 'em, Van — *don't!*"

"Why, they *can't*," said Van in an emphatic voice, running up the stairs to Joel's side, frightened to death at his tears. Then he began to shake his jacket sleeve violently to bring him back to reason. "Wait, Joe! Oh, do stop! Oh, dear, what *shall* I do! I tell you, they *can't* bite," he screamed as loud as he could into his ear.

"You   said — you — hoped — they — would,"   said Joel's voice in smothered tones.

"Well, they *won't* anyway," said Van decidely. " 'Cause they're all stuffed. So there now!"

"Ain't they alive — nor anythin'?" asked Joel, bringing one black eye into sight from behind his chubby hands.

"No," said Van, "they're just as dead as anything, Joel Pepper — been dead years! And there's old crabs there, too, old dead crabs — and they're just lovely! Oh, *such* a lots of eggs as they've got! And there are shells and bugs and stones — and an *awful* old crocodile, and — "

"Oh, dear!" sighed Joel, perfectly overcome at such a vision and sitting down on the stairs to think. "Well, mamsie'll know where Ben is," he said, springing up. "And then I tell you, Van, we'll just tag 'em!"

"So *she* will," cried Van. "Why didn't we think of that before? I *wanted* to think."

"I did," said Joel. "That was where I was goin'."

Without any more ado they rushed into Mrs. Pepper's big sunny room, there to see, seated at the square table between the two large windows, the two lost ones bending over what seemed to be an object of the greatest importance, for Polly was hanging over Ben's shoulder with intense pride and delight, which she couldn't possibly conceal, and Davie was crowded as near as he could get to Percy's elbow.

Phronsie and little Dick were perched comfortably on the corner of the table, surveying the whole scene in quiet rapture, and Mrs. Pepper, with her big mending basket, was ensconced over by the deep window seat just on the other side of the room, underneath Cherry's cage, and looking up between quick energetic stitches, over at the busy group, with the most placid expression on her face.

"*Oh!* What you doin'?" cried Joel, flying up to them. "Let us see, *do*, Ben!"

"What is it?" exclaimed Van, squeezing in between Percy and Ben.

"Don't — " began Percy. "There, see, you've knocked his elbow and spoilt it!"

"Oh, no, he hasn't," said Ben, putting down his pencil and taking up a piece of rubber. "There, see — it all comes out as good as ever."

"Isn't that just *elegant?*" said Percy in the most pleased tone, and wriggling his toes under the table to express his satisfaction.

"Yes," said Van, craning his neck to get a better view of the picture, now nearly completed. "It's perfectly splendid. How'd you do it, Ben?"

"I don't know," replied Ben with a smile, carefully shading in a few last touches. "It just drew itself."

" 'Tisn't anything to what he *can* do," said Polly, standing up as tall as she could and beaming at Ben. "He used to draw most beautiful at home."

"Better than this?" asked Van with great respect, and taking up the picture, after some demur on Percy's part, and examining it critically. "I don't believe it, Polly."

"Phooh, he did!" exclaimed Joel, looking over his shoulder at a wonderful view of a dog in an extremely excited state of mind running down an interminable hill to bark at a locomotive and train of cars whizzing along a curve in the foreground. "Lots better'n that! Ben can do *anything*!" he added in an utterly convincing way.

"Now give it back," cried Percy, holding out his hand in alarm. "I'm going to ask mamma to have it framed, and then I'm going to hang it right over my bed," he finished, as Van reluctantly gave up the treasure.

"Did you draw all the time in the little brown house?" asked Van, lost in thought. "How I wish I'd been there!"

"Dear, no!" cried Polly with a little skip, turning away to laugh. "He didn't have hardly *any* time, and — "

"Why not?" asked Percy.

" 'Cause there were things to *do*," said Polly. "But sometimes when it rained, and he couldn't go out and work, and there wasn't anything to do *in* the house, then we'd have — oh!" And she drew a long breath at the memory. "Such a time, you can't think!"

"Didn't you wish it would *always* rain?" asked Van, still gazing at the picture.

"Dear, no!" began Polly.

"I didn't," broke in Joel in horror. "I wouldn't a-had it rain for *anything*! Only once in a while," he added as he thought of the good times that Polly had spoken of.

" 'Twas nice outdoors," said little Davie, reflectively,

238

"and nice inside, too." And then he glanced over to his mother, who gave him a smile in return. "And 'twas nice *always*."

"Well," said Van, returning to the picture, "I do wish you'd tell me how to draw, Ben. I can't do anything but flowers," he said in a discouraged way.

"Flowers aren't anything," said Percy pleasantly. "That's girl's work; but dogs and horses and cars — those are just *good!*"

"Will you, Ben?" asked Van, looking down into the big blue eyes so kindly turned up to his.

"Yes, *indeed* I will," cried Ben. "That is, all I know. 'Tisn't much, but everything I can, I'll tell you."

"Then I can learn, can't I?" cried Van joyfully.

"Oh, tell me, too, Ben," cried Percy, "will you? I want to learn, too."

"And me!" cried Dick, bending forward, nearly upsetting Phronsie as he did so. "Yes, say I may, Ben, *do!*"

"You're too little," began Percy. But Ben nodded his head at Dick, which caused him to clap his hands and return to his original position.

"Well, I guess, we're going to, *too*," said Joel. "Dave an' me. There isn't anybody goin' to learn without *us*."

"Of course not," said Polly. "Ben wouldn't leave you out, Joey."

Phronsie sat quite still all this time on the corner of the table, her feet tucked up under her and her hands clasped in her lap, and never said a word. But Ben, looking up, saw the most grieved expression settling on her face as the large eyes were fixed in wonder on the faces before her.

"And there's my pet," he cried in enthusiasm, and

reaching over the table, he caught hold of one of the little fat hands. "Why we couldn't think of getting along without *her!* She shall learn to draw — she *shall!*"

"*Really,* Bensie?" said Phronsie, the sunlight breaking all over the gloomy little visage and setting the brown eyes to dancing. "Real, true, splendid pictures?"

"Yes, the splendidest," said Ben. "The very splendidest pictures, Phronsie Pepper, you ever saw!"

"*Oh!*" cried Phronsie. And before anyone knew what she was about, she tripped right into the middle of the table, over the papers and everything, and gave a happy little whirl!

"Dear me, Phronsie!" cried Polly, catching her up and hugging her. "You mustn't dance on the table."

"I'm going to learn," said Phronsie, coming out of Polly's embrace, "to draw pictures, all alone by myself — Ben said so!"

"I know it," said Polly. "And then you shall draw one for mamsie — you shall!"

"I will," said Phronsie, dreadfully excited. "I'll draw her a cow, and two chickens, Polly, just like Grandma Bascom's!"

"Yes," whispered Polly, "but don't tell her yet till you get it done, Phronsie."

"I won't," said Phronsie in the loudest of tones, but putting her mouth close to Polly's ear. "And then she'll be *so* s'prised, Polly! Won't she?"

Just then came Jasper's voice at the door. "Can I come in?"

"Oh, do, Jappy," cried Polly, rushing along with Phronsie in her arms to open the door. "We're so glad you've got home!"

"So am I," said Jasper, coming in, his face flushed and his eyes sparkling. "I thought father never would be through downtown, Polly!"

"We're going to learn to draw," said Percy, over by the table, who wouldn't on any account leave his seat by Ben, though he was awfully tired of sitting still so long, for fear somebody else would hop into it. "Ben's going to teach us."

"Yes, he is," put in Van, bounding up to Jasper and pulling at all the buttons on his jacket he could reach to command attention.

"And us," said Joel, coming up, too. "You forgot *us*," Van."

"The whole of us — every single one in this room," said Van decidedly. "All except Mrs. Pepper."

"Hulloa!" said Jasper, "that *is* a class! Well, Professor Ben, you've got to teach me then, for I'm coming, too."

"*You?*" said Ben, turning around his chair and looking at him. "I can't teach *you* anything, Jappy. You know everything already."

"Let him come, anyway," said Polly, hopping up and down.

"Oh, I'm coming, Professor," laughed Jasper. "Never you fear, Polly; I'll be on hand when the rest of the class comes in!"

"And Van," said Mrs. Pepper, pausing a minute in her work and smiling over at him in a lull in the chatter, "I think flowers are most beautiful!" and she pointed to a little framed picture on the mantel of the bunch of buttercups and one huge rose that Van had with infinite patience drawn and then colored to suit his fancy.

"Do you?" cried Van, perfectly delighted. And leaving

the group, he rushed up to her side. "Do you *really* think they're nice, Mrs. Pepper?"

"Of course I do," said Mrs. Pepper briskly, and, beaming on him, "I think everything of them, and I shall keep them as long as I live, Van!"

"Well, then," said Van, very much pleased, "I shall paint you ever so many more — just as many as you want!"

"Do!" said Mrs. Pepper, taking up her work again. "And I'll hang them every one up."

"Yes, I will," said Van. "And I'll go right to work on one tomorrow. What you mending our jackets for?" he asked abruptly as a familiar hole caught his attention.

"Because they're torn," said Mrs. Pepper cheerfully, "an' they *won't* mend themselves."

"Why don't you let Jane?" he persisted. "She always does them."

"Jane's got enough to do," replied Mrs. Pepper, smiling away as hard as she could, "and I haven't, so I'm going to look around and pick up something to keep my hands out of mischief as much as I can while I'm here."

"Do you ever get into mischief?" asked little Dick, coming up and looking into Mrs. Pepper's face wonderingly. "Why, you're a big woman!"

"Dear me, yes!" said Mrs. Pepper. "The bigger you are, the more mischief you can get into. You'll find *that* out, Dickey."

"And then do you have to stand in a corner?" asked Dick, determined to find out just what the consequences, and reverting to his most dreaded punishment.

"No," said Mrs. Pepper, laughing. "Corners are for little folks. But when people who know better do wrong, there aren't any corners they *can* creep into, or they'd get into them pretty quick!"

"I wish," said little Dick, "you'd let me get into your lap. *That* would be a nice corner!"

"Do, mamsie," said Polly, coming up. "That's just the way I used to feel. And I'll finish the mending."

So Mrs. Pepper put down her work and moved the big basket for little Dick to clamber up, when he laid his head contentedly back in her motherly arms with a sigh of happiness. Phronsie regarded him with a very grave expression. At last she drew near. "I'm tired; do, mamsie, take me!"

"So mamsie will," said Mrs. Pepper, opening her arms, when Phronsie immediately crawled up into their protecting shelter with a happy little crow.

"Oh, now, tell us a story, Mrs. Pepper," cried Van. "*Please, please* do!"

"No, no," exclaimed Percy, scuttling out of his chair and coming up. "Let's talk of the little brown house. Do tell us what you used to do there — that's best."

"So 'tis!" cried Van. "*All* the nice times you used to have in it! Wait just a minute, do." And he ran back for a cricket, which he placed at Mrs. Pepper's feet, and then, sitting down on it, he leaned on her comfortable lap, in order to hear better.

"Wait for me, too, till I get a chair," called Percy, starting. "Don't begin till I get there."

"Here, let me, Percy," said Ben, and he drew forward a big easy chair that the boy was tugging at with all his might.

"Now *I'm* ready, too," said Polly, setting small finishing stitches quickly with a merry little flourish and drawing her chair nearer her mother's as she spoke.

"Now begin, please," said Van. "All the nice times you know."

"She couldn't tell *all* the nice times if she had ten years to tell them in, could she, Polly?" said Jasper.

"Well, in the first place, then," said Mrs. Pepper, clearing her throat, "the little brown house had *got to be*, you know, so we made up our minds to make it just the *nicest* brown house that ever was!"

"And it was!" declared Jasper with an emphatic ring to his voice. "The *very nicest place in the whole world!*"

"Oh, dear," broke in Van enviously. "Jappy's always said so. I wish we'd been there, too!"

"We didn't want anybody but Jappy," said Joel, not very politely.

"Oh, Joey, for shame!" cried Polly.

"Jappy used to bake," cried little Davie, "an' we all made pies, an' then we sat round an' ate 'em, an' then told stories."

"Oh, what fun!" cried Percy. "Do tell us!"

So the five little Peppers and Jasper flew off into reminiscences and accounts of the funny doings, and Mrs. Pepper joined in heartily till the room got very merry with the glee and enthusiasm called forth — so much so that nobody heard Mrs. Whitney knock gently at the door, and nobody answering, she was obliged to come in by herself.

"Well, well," she cried merrily, looking at the swarm of little ones around Mrs. Pepper and the big chair. "You *are* having a nice time! May I come and listen?"

"Oh, if you will, sister," cried Jasper, springing off

from his arm of the chair, while Ben flew from the other side to hurry and get her a chair.

Percy and Van rushed, too, knocking over so many things that they didn't help much; and little Dick poked his head out from Mrs. Pepper's arms when he saw his mamma sitting down to stay and began to scramble down to get into her lap.

"There, now," said Mrs. Whitney, smiling over at Mrs. Pepper, who was smiling at her. "You have your baby, and I have mine! Now, children, what's it all about? What has Mrs. Pepper been telling you?"

"Oh, the little brown house," cried Dicky, his cheeks all aflame. "The *dearest* little house, mamma! I wish I could live in one!"

" 'Twouldn't be the same without the Peppers in it," said Jasper. "Not a bit of it!"

"And they had such perfectly *elegant* times," cried Percy enviously, drawing up to her side. "Oh, you can't think, mamma!"

"Well, now," said his mamma, "do go on, and let *me* hear some of the nice times."

So away they launched again, and Mrs. Whitney was soon enjoying it as hugely as the children, when a heavy step sounded in the middle of the room, and a voice spoke in *such* a tone that everybody skipped.

"Well, I should like to know what all this means! I've been all over the house, and not a trace of anybody could I find."

"Oh, father!" cried Mrs. Whitney. "Van dear, get up and get grandpapa a chair."

"No, no!" said the old gentleman, waving him off impatiently. "I'm not going to stay; I must go and and lie down. My head is in a bad condition today; very bad indeed," he added.

"Oh!" said Phronsie, popping up her head and looking at him. "I must get right down."

"What's the matter, Phronsie?" asked Mrs. Pepper, trying to hold her back.

"Oh, but I *must*," said Phronsie, energetically wriggling. "My poor, sick man wants me, he *does*." And flying out of her mother's arms, she ran up to Mr. King and, standing on tiptoe, said softly, "I'll rub your neck, grandpa dear, poor, sick man; yes I *will*."

"And you're the best child," cried the old gentleman, catching her up and marching over to the other side of the room, where there was a lounging chair. "There, now, you and I, Phronsie, will stay by ourselves. *Then* my head will feel better."

And he sat down and drew her into his arms.

"Does it ache *very* bad?" said Phronsie in a soft little voice. Then, reaching up, she began to pat and smooth it gently with one little hand, "*Very* bad, dear grandpa?"

"It won't," said the old gentleman, "if you only keep on taking care of it, little Phronsie."

"Then," said the child, perfectly delighted, "I'm going to take all care of you, grandpa, *always!*"

"So you shall, so you shall!" cried Mr. King, no less delighted than she was. "Mrs. Pepper!"

"Sir?" said Mrs. Pepper, trying to answer, which she couldn't do very well, surrounded as she was by the crowd of little chatterers. "Yes, sir; excuse me, what is it, sir?"

"We've got to come to an understanding about this

thing," said the old gentleman, "and I can't talk much today, because my headache won't allow it."

Here the worried look came into Phronsie's face again, and she began to smooth his head with *both* little hands.

"And so I must say it all in as few words as possible," he continued.

"What is it, sir?" again asked Mrs. Pepper wonderingly.

"Well, the fact is, I've got to have somebody who will keep this house. Now, Marian, not a word!" as he saw symptoms of Mrs. Whitney's joining in the conversation. "You've been good, just as good as can be under the circumstances; but Mason will be home in the fall, and then I suppose you'll have to go with him. Now *I*," said the old gentleman, forgetting all about his head and straightening himself up suddenly in the chair, "am going to get things into shape, so that the house will be kept for all of us, so that we can come or go. And how can I do it better than to have the Peppers — you, Mrs. Pepper, and all your children — come here and live, and — "

"Oh, *father!*" cried Jasper, rushing up to him, and flinging his arms around his neck, he gave him such a hug as he hadn't received for many a day.

"Goodness, Jasper!" cried his father, feeling of his throat. "How can you express your feelings so violently! And, besides, you interrupt."

"Beg pardon, sir," said Jasper, swallowing his excitement and trying to control his eagerness.

"Do you say yes, Mrs. Pepper?" queried the old gentleman impatiently. "I must get this thing fixed up today. I'm really too ill to be worried, ma'am."

"Why, sir," stammered Mrs. Pepper, "I don't know

247

what to say. I couldn't think of imposing all my children on you, and — "

"*Imposing!* Who's talking of *imposing?*" said Mr. King in a loud key. "I want my house kept; will you live here and keep it? That is the question."

"But, sir," began Mrs. Pepper again, "you don't think — "

"I *do* think. I tell you, ma'am, I *do* think," snapped the old gentleman. "It's just because I *have* thought that I've made up my mind. Will you do it, Mrs. Pepper?"

"What you goin' to do, mamsie?" asked Joel quickly.

"I don't know as I'm going to do *anything* yet," said poor Mrs. Pepper, who was almost stunned.

"To come here and live!" cried Jasper, unable to keep still any longer, and springing to the children. "Don't you want to, Joe?"

"To *live!*" screamed Joel. "Oh whickety, *yes!* Do, ma, do come here and live — do!"

"To *live!*" echoed Phronsie, over in the old gentleman's lap. "In this be-*yew*-ti-ful place? Oh, *oh!*"

"Oh, *mamsie!*" That was all Polly could say.

And even Ben had his arms around his mother's neck, whispering "Do" into her ear, while little Davie got into her lap and teased her with all his might.

"What *shall* I do!" cried the poor woman. "Did ever anybody see the like?"

"It's the very best you could possibly do," cried the old gentleman. "Don't you see it's for the children's advantage? They'll get such educations, Mrs. Pepper, as you want for them. And it accommodates me immensely. What obstacle can there be to it?"

"If I was only sure 'twas best," said Mrs. Pepper doubtfully.

"Oh, dear Mrs. Pepper," said Mrs. Whitney, laying her hands on hers. "Can you doubt it?"

"Then," said Mr. King, getting up, but still holding on to Phronsie, "we'll consider it settled. This is your home, children," he said, waving his hand at the five little Peppers in a bunch. And having thus summarily disposed of the whole business, he marched out with Phronsie on his shoulder.

POLLY'S
DISMAL MORNING

EVERYTHING had gone wrong with Polly that day. It began with her boots.

Of all the things in the world that tried Polly's patience most were the troublesome little black buttons that originally adorned those useful parts of her clothing and that were fondly supposed to be there when needed. But they never were. The little black things seemed to be invested with a special spite, for one by one they would hop off on the slightest provocation and go rolling over the floor, just when she was in her most terrible hurry, compelling her to fly for needle and thread on the instant. For one thing Mrs. Pepper was very strict about, and that was, Polly should do nothing else till the buttons were all on again and the boots buttoned up firm and snug.

"Oh, dear!" said Polly, sitting down on the floor and pulling on her stockings. "There, now, see that hateful old shoe, mamsie!" And she thrust out one foot in dismay.

"What's the matter with it?" said Mrs. Pepper, straightening the things on the bureau. "You haven't worn it out already, Polly?"

"Oh, no," said Polly, with a little laugh. "I hope not yet, but it's these dreadful *hateful* old buttons!" And she twitched the boot off her foot with such an impatient little pull that three or four more went flying under the bed. "There, now — there's a lot more. I don't care! I wish they'd all go; they might as well!" she cried, tossing the boot on the floor in intense scorn while she investigated the state of the other one.

"Are they *all* off?" asked Phronsie, pulling herself up out of a little heap in the middle of the bed and leaning over the side, where she viewed Polly sorrowfully. "*Every* one, Polly?"

"No," said Polly, "but I wish they were, mean old things. When I was going down to play a duet with Jasper! We should have had a good long time before breakfast. Oh, mayn't I go just once, mamsie? Nobody'll see me if I tuck my foot under the piano, and I can sew 'em on afterward — there'll be plenty of time. Do, just *once*, mamsie!"

"No," said Mrs. Pepper firmly, "there isn't any time but *now*. And piano playing is *very* nice when you've got to stick your toes under it to keep your shoes on."

"Well, then," grumbled Polly, hopping around in her stocking feet, "where *is* the workbasket, mamsie? Oh, here it is on the window seat." A rattle of spools, scissors, and necessary utensils showed plainly that Polly had found it, followed by a jumble of words and despairing ejaculations as she groped hurriedly under chairs and tables to collect the scattered contents.

When she got back with a very red face, she found

Phronsie, who had crawled out of bed, sitting down on the floor in her little nightgown and examining the boot with profound interest.

"I can sew 'em, Polly," she said, holding up her hand for the big needle that Polly was trying to thread. "I can now truly; let me, Polly, do!"

"Dear, no!" said Polly with a little laugh, beginning to be very much ashamed. "What could you do with your little mites of hands pulling this big thread through that old leather? There, scamper into bed again; you'll catch cold out here."

" 'Tisn't *very* cold," said Phronsie, tucking up her toes under the nightgown, but Polly hurried her into bed, where she curled herself up under the clothes, watching her make a big knot. But the knot didn't stay, for when Polly drew up the long thread triumphantly to the end, out it flew, and away the button hopped again as if glad to be released. And then the thread kinked horribly and got all twisted up in disagreeable little snarls that took all Polly's patience to unravel.

"It's because you're in such a hurry," said Mrs. Pepper, who was getting Phronsie's clothes. And coming over across the room, she got down on one knee and looked over Polly's shoulder. "There, now, let mother see what's the matter."

"Oh, dear," said Polly, resigning the needle with a big sigh and leaning back to take a good stretch, followed by Phronsie's sympathizing eyes. "They *never'll* be on! And there goes the first bell!" as the loud sounds under Jane's vigorous ringing pealed up over the stairs. "There won't be time anyway, *now!* I wish there wasn't such a thing as shoes in the world!" And she gave a flounce and sat up straight in front of her mother.

"*Polly!*" said Mrs. Pepper sternly, deftly fastening the little buttons tightly into place with quick, firm stitches. "Better be glad you've got them to sew at all. There, now, here they are. *Those* won't come off in a hurry!"

"Oh, mamsie!" cried Polly, ignoring for a moment the delights of the finished shoe to fling her arms around her mother's neck and give her a good hug. "You're just the splendidest, *goodest* mamsie in all the world. And I'm a hateful, cross old bear, so I am!" she cried remorsefully, buttoning herself into her boot. Which done, she flew at the rest of her preparations and tried to make up for lost time.

But 'twas all of no use. The day seemed to be always just racing ahead of her and turning a corner before she could catch up to it, and Ben and the other boys only caught dissolving views of her as she flitted through halls or over stairs.

"Where's Polly!" said Percy at last, coming with great dissatisfaction in his voice to the library door. "We've called her and called her, I guess a million times, and she *won't* hurry."

"What do you want to have her do?" asked Jasper, looking up from the sofa, where he had flung himself with a book.

"Why, she said she'd make Van and me our sails, you know," said Percy, holding up a rather forlorn-looking specimen of a boat, but which the boys had carved with the greatest enthusiasm, "and we want her now."

"Can't you let her alone till she's ready to come?" said Jasper quickly. "You're always teasing her to do something," he added.

"I *didn't* tease," said Percy indignantly, coming up to the sofa boat in hand to enforce his words. "She said she'd *love* to do 'em, so there, Jasper King!"

"Coming! Coming!" sang Polly over the stairs and bobbing into the library. "Oh, here you are, Percy! I couldn't come before; mamsie wanted me. Now, says I, for the sails." And she began to flap out a long white piece of cotton cloth on the table to trim into just the desired shape.

"*That* isn't the way," said Percy, crowding up, the brightness that had flashed over his face at Polly's appearance beginning to fade. "Hoh! Those won't be good for anything — those ain't *sails*."

"I haven't finished," said Polly, snipping away vigorously and longing to get back to mamsie. "Wait till they're done; then they'll be good — good as can be!"

"And it's bad enough to have to make them," put in Jasper, flinging aside his book and rolling over to watch them, "without having to be found fault with every second, Percy."

"They're too big," said Percy, surveying them critically and then looking at his boat.

"Oh, that corner's coming off," cried Polly cheerfully, giving it a sharp cut that sent it flying on the floor. "And they won't be too big when they're done, Percy, all hemmed and everything. There — " as she held one up for inspection — "that's just the way I used to make Ben's and mine when we sailed boats."

"Is it?" asked Percy, looking with more respect at the piece of cloth Polly was waving alluringly before him. "Just exactly like it, Polly?"

"Yes," said Polly, laying it down again for a pattern.

"Oh, how *does* this go — that's it, there — yes, this is just *exactly* like Bensie's and mine — that was when I was ever so little. And then I used to make Joel's and Davie's afterward and — "

"And were *theirs* just like this?" asked Percy, laying his hand on the sail she had finished cutting out.

"*Pre*-cisely," said Polly, with a pin in her mouth. "Just as like as two peas, Percy Whitney."

"Then I like them," cried Percy, veering round and regarding them with great satisfaction as Van bounded in with a torrent of complaints and great disappointment in every line of his face.

"Oh, now, that's too bad!" he cried, seeing Polly fold up the remaining bits of cloth and pick up the scraps on the floor. "And you've gone and let her cut out every one of 'em, and never told me a word! You're a mean old hateful thing, Percy Whitney!"

"Oh, *don't!*" said Polly, on her knees on the floor.

"I forgot," began Percy. "And she cut 'em so quick — and — "

"And I've been waiting," said Van in a loud, wrathful key, "and waiting — and *waiting!*"

"Never mind, Van," said Jasper consolingly, getting off from the sofa and coming up to the table. "They're done, and done beautifully, aren't they?" he said, holding up one.

But this only proved fresh fuel for the fire of Van's indignation.

"And you shan't have 'em, so!" he cried, making a lunge at the one on the table, "for I made most of the boat, *there!*"

"Oh, no, you didn't!" cried Percy in the greatest alarm,

hanging on to the boat in his hand. "I cut — all the keel — and the bow — and — "

"Oh, dear!" said Polly in extreme dismay, looking at Jasper. "Come, I'll tell you what I'll do, boys."

"What?" said Van, cooling off a little, and allowing Percy to edge into a corner with the beloved boat and one sail. "What will you, Polly?"

"I'll make you another pair of sails," said Polly, groaning within herself as she thought of the wasted minutes, "and *then* you can see me cut 'em, Van."

"Will you *really*," he said, delight coming all over his flushed face.

"Yes, I will," cried Polly. "Wait a minute till I get some more cloth." And she started for the door.

"Oh, now, that's too bad!" said Jasper. "To have to cut more of those tiresome old things! Van, let her off!"

"Oh, no, I won't! I won't!" he cried in the greatest alarm, running up to her as she stood by the door. "You *did* say so, Polly! You *know* you did!"

"Of course I did, Vanny," said Polly, smiling down into his eager face. "And we'll have a splendid pair in just — one — minute!" she sang.

And so the sails were cut out, and the hems turned down and basted, and tucked away into Polly's little work basket ready for the sewing on the morrow. And then Mr. King came in and took Jasper off with him, and the two Whitney boys went up to mamma for a story, and Polly sat down in mamsie's room to tackle her French exercise.

POLLY'S BIG BUNDLE

THE room was very quiet; but presently Phronsie strayed in, and seeing Polly studying, climbed up in a chair by the window to watch the birds hop over the veranda and pick up worms in the grass beside the carriage drive. And then came Mrs. Pepper with the big mending basket, and ensconced herself opposite by the table; and nothing was to be heard but the tick, tick of the clock, and an occasional dropping of a spool of thread, or scissors, from the busy hands flying in and out among the stockings.

All of a sudden there was a great rustling in Cherry's cage that swung in the big window on the other side of the room. And then he set up a loud and angry chirping, flying up and down and opening his mouth as if he wanted to express his mind but couldn't, and otherwise acting in a very strange and unaccountable manner.

"Dear me!" said Mrs. Pepper. "What's that?"

"It's Cherry," said Polly, lifting her head from *Fasquelle*, "and — oh, dear me!" And flinging down the pile of books in her lap on a chair, she rushed across the room and flew up to the cage and began to wildly gesticulate and explain and shower down on him every endearing name she could think of.

"What *is* the matter?" asked her mother, turning around in her chair in perfect astonishment. "What upon earth, Polly!"

"How *could* I!" cried Polly in accents of despair, not heeding her mother's question. "Oh, mamsie, *will* he die, do you think?"

"I guess not," said Mrs. Pepper, laying down her work and coming up to the cage while Phronsie scrambled off from her chair and hurried to the scene. "Why, he *does* act queer, don't he? P'rhaps he's been eating too much?"

"*Eating!*" said Polly. "Oh, mamsie, he hasn't had *anything*." And she pointed with shame and remorse to the seed cup with only a few dried husks in the very bottom.

"Oh, Polly," began Mrs. Pepper, but seeing the look on her face, she changed her tone for one more cheerful. "Well, hurry and get him some now. He'll be all right, poor little thing, in a minute. There, there," she said, nodding persuasively at the cage, "you pretty creature you! So you shan't be starved."

At the word *starved*, Polly winced as though a pin had been pointed at her.

"There isn't any, mamsie, in the house," she stammered. "He had the last yesterday."

"And you forgot him today?" asked Mrs. Pepper, with a look in her black eyes Polly didn't like.

"Yes'm," said poor Polly in a low voice.

"Well, he must have something right away," said Mrs. Pepper decidedly. "*That's* certain."

"I'll run right down to Fletcher's and get it," cried Polly. " 'Twon't take me but a minute, mamsie. Jasper's gone, and Thomas, too, so I've got to go," she added as she saw her mother hesitate.

"If you could wait till Ben gets home," said Mrs. Pepper slowly. "I'm most afraid it will rain, Polly."

"Oh, no, mamsie," cried Polly, feeling as if she could fly to the ends of the earth to atone, and longing beside for the brisk walk downtown. Going up to the window, she pointed triumphantly to the little bit of blue sky still visible. "There, now, see, it *can't* rain yet awhile."

"Well," said Mrs. Pepper, while Phronsie, standing in a chair with her face pressed close to the cage, was telling Cherry through the bars "not to be hungry, please *don't!*" which he didn't seem to mind in the least, but went on screaming harder than ever! "And besides, 'tisn't much use to wait for Ben. Nobody knows where he'll get shoes to fit himself and Joe and Davie in one afternoon! But be sure, Polly, to hurry, for it's getting late, and I shall be worried about you."

"Oh, mamsie," said Polly, turning back just a minute, "I know the way to Fletcher's just as easy as *anything*. I *couldn't* get lost."

"I know you do," said Mrs. Pepper, "but it'll be dark early on account of the shower. Well," she said, pulling out her well worn purse from her pocket, "if it does sprinkle, you get into a car, Polly, remember."

"Oh, yes, I will," she cried, taking the purse.

"And there's ten cents for your birdseed in that pocket," said Mrs. Pepper, pointing to a coin racing away into a corner by itself.

"Yes'm," said Polly, wild to be off.

"And there's a five-cent piece in that one for you to ride up with," said her mother, tying up the purse carefully. "Remember, for you to ride *up* with. Well, I guess you better ride up *anyway*, Polly, come to think, and then you'll get home all the quicker."

"Where you going?" asked Phronsie, who, on seeing the purse, knew there was some expedition on foot, and beginning to clamber down out of the chair. "Oh, I want to go, too, I *do*. Take me, Polly!"

"Oh, no, pet, I can't," cried Polly. "I've got to hurry like everything!"

"I can hurry, too," cried Phronsie, drawing her small figure to its utmost height. "Oh, so fast, Polly!"

"And it's ever so far," cried Polly in despair as she saw the small under lip of the child begin to quiver. "Oh, dear me, mamsie, what *shall* I do!"

"Run right along," said Mrs. Pepper briskly, "Now, Phronsie, you and I ought to take care of Cherry, poor thing."

At this Phronsie turned and wiped away two big tears while she gazed up at the cage in extreme commiseration.

"I guess I'll give him a piece of bread," said Mrs. Pepper to herself. At this word *bread*, Polly, who was halfway down the hall, came running back.

"Oh, mamsie, *don't*," she said. "It made him sick before, don't you know it did — so fat and stuffy."

"Well, hurry along, then," said Mrs. Pepper, and Polly was off.

Over the ground she sped, only intent on reaching the bird store, her speed heightened by the dark and rolling bank of cloud that seemed to shut right down suddenly over her and envelop her warningly.

"It's good I've got the money to ride up with," she thought to herself, hurrying along through the busy streets, filled now with anxious crowds homeward rushing to avoid the threatening shower. "Well, here I am," she said with a sigh of relief as she at last reached Mr. Fletcher's big bird store.

Here she steadily resisted all temptations to stop and look at the new arrivals of birds, and to feed the carrier pigeons who seemed to be expecting her, and who turned their soft eyes up at her reproachfully when she failed to pay her respects to them. Even the cunning blandishments of a very attractive monkey that always had entertained the children on their numerous visits failed to interest her now. Mamsie would be worrying, she knew; and besides, the sight of so many birds eating their suppers out of generously filled seed cups only filled her heart with remorse as she thought of poor Cherry and his empty one.

So she put down her ten cents silently on the counter, and took up the little package of seed, and went out.

But what a change! The cloud that had seemed but a cloud when she went in was now fast descending in big, ominous sprinkles that told of a heavy shower to follow. Quick and fast they came, making everybody fly to the nearest shelter.

"I don't care," said Polly to herself, holding fast her little package. "I'll run and get in the car — then I'll be all right."

So she went on with nimble footsteps, dodging the crowd, and soon came to the corner. A car was just in sight — that was fine! Polly put her hand in her pocket for her purse, to have it all ready, but as quickly drew it out again and stared wildly at the car, which she allowed to pass by. Her pocket was empty!

"Oh, dear," she said to herself as a sudden gust of wind blew around the corner and warned her to move on. "Now what *shall* I do! Well, I must hurry. Nothing for it but to run now!"

And secretly glad at the chance for a good hearty run along the hard pavements, a thing she had been longing to do ever since she came to the city, Polly gathered her bundle of seed up under her arm and set out for a jolly race. She was enjoying it hugely, when a sudden turn of the corner brought her up against a gentleman who, having his umbrella down to protect his face, hadn't seen her till it was too late.

Polly never could tell how it was done, but the first thing she knew she was being helped up from the wet, slippery pavement by a kind hand, and a gentleman's voice said in the deepest concern, "I beg your pardon; it was extremely careless of me."

"It's no matter," said Polly, hopping up with a little laugh and straightening her hat. "Only — " and she began to look for her parcel that had been sent spinning.

"What is it?" said the gentleman, bending down and beginning to explore, too, in the darkness.

"My bundle," began Polly. "Oh, dear!"

No need to ask for it now! There lay the paper wet and torn, down at their feet. The seed lay all over the pavement, scattered far and wide even out to the puddles in the street. And not a cent of money to get any more with! The rain that was falling around them as they stood there sent with the sound of every drop such a flood of misery into Polly's heart!

"What was it, child?" asked the gentleman, peering sharply to find out what the little shiny things were.

"Birdseed," gasped Polly.

"Is that all?" said the gentleman with a happy laugh. "I'm very glad."

"*All!*" Polly's heart stood still as she thought of Cherry, stark and stiff in the bottom of his cage, if he didn't get it soon. "Now," said the kind tones, briskly, "come little girl, we'll make this all right speedily. Let's see — here's a bird store. Now, then."

"But, sir — " began Polly, holding back.

Even Cherry had better die than to do anything her mother wouldn't like. But the gentleman already had her in the shop and was delighting the heart of the shopkeeper by ordering him to do up a big package of all kinds of seed. And then he added a cunning arrangement for birds to swing in, and two or three other things that didn't have anything to do with birds at all. And then they came out on the wet, slippery street again.

"Now, then, little girl," said the gentleman, tucking the bundle under his arm and opening the umbrella. Then he took hold of Polly's hand, who by this time was glad of a protector. "Where do you live? For I'm going to take you safely home this time, where umbrellas can't run into you."

"*Oh!*" said Polly with a little skip. "Thank you, sir! It's up to Mr. King's, and — "

"*What!*" said the gentleman, stopping short in the midst of an immense puddle and staring at her. "Mr. *Jasper* King's?"

"I don't know, sir," said Polly, "what his other name is. Yes, it *must* be Jasper. That's what Jappy's is, anyway," she added with a little laugh, wishing very much that she could see Jappy at that identical moment.

"Jappy!" said the stranger, still standing as if petrified. "And are there little Whitney children in the same house!"

"Oh, yes," said Polly, raising her clear, brown eyes up at him. The gaslighter was just beginning his rounds, and the light from a neighboring lamp flashed full on Polly's face as she spoke, showing just how clear and brown the eyes were. "There's Percy, and Van, and little Dick — oh, he's *so* cunning!" she cried impulsively.

The gentleman's face looked very queer just then, but he merely said, "Why, you must be Polly?"

"Yes, sir, I am," said Polly, pleased to think he knew her. And then she told him how she'd forgotten Cherry's seed, and all about it. "And oh, sir," she said, and her voice began to tremble, "mamsie'll be so frightened if I don't get there soon!"

"I'm going up there myself, so that it all happens very nicely," said the gentleman, commencing to start off briskly, and grasping her hand tighter. "Now, then, Polly."

So off they went at a very fast pace, she skipping through the puddles that his long even, strides carried him safely over, chattered away by his side under the umbrella, and answered many of his questions, and altogether got so very well acquainted that by the time they turned in at the old stone gateway, she felt as if she had known him for years.

And there, the first thing they either of them saw, down in a little corner back of the tall evergreens, was a small heap that rose as they splashed up the carriage drive and resolved itself into a very red dress and a very white apron as it rushed impulsively up and flung itself into Polly's wet arms.

"And I was so tired waiting, Polly!"

"Oh, dear me, Phronsie!" cried Polly, huddling her up from the dark, wet ground. "You'll catch your death! What *will* mamsie say!"

The stranger, amazed at this new stage of the proceedings, was vainly trying to hold the umbrella over both till the procession could move on again.

"Oh!" cried Phronsie, shaking her yellow head decidedly. "They're all looking for you, Polly." She pointed one finger solemnly up to the big carved door as she spoke. At that Polly gathered her up close and began to walk with rapid footsteps up the path.

"Do let me carry you, little girl," said Polly's kind friend persuasively, bending down to the little face on Polly's neck.

"Oh, no, no, no!" said Phronsie, at each syllable grasping Polly around the throat in perfect terror and waving him off with a very crumpled, mangy bit of paper that had already done duty to wipe off the copious tears during her anxious watch. "Don't let him, Polly, *don't!*"

"There shan't anything hurt you," said Polly, kissing her reassuringly and stepping briskly off with her burden just as the door burst open and Joel flew out on the veranda steps, followed by the rest of the troop in the greatest state of excitement.

"Oh, whickety! She's *come!*" he shouted, springing up to her over the puddles and crowding under the umbrella. "Where'd you get Phronsie?" he asked, standing quite still at the sight of the little feet tucked up to get out of the rain. And without waiting for an answer, he turned and shot back into the house, proclaiming in stentorian tones, "Ma, Polly's come — an' she's got Phronsie — an' an *awful* big man — and they're out by the gate!"

"*Phronsie!*" said Mrs. Pepper, springing to her feet. "Why, I thought she was upstairs with Jane."

"Now, somebody," exclaimed old Mr. King, who sat by the library table vainly trying to read a newspaper, which he now threw down in extreme irritation as he rose quickly and went to the door to welcome the wanderers, "*somebody* ought to watch that poor child, whose business it is to *know* where she is! She's caught her death cold, no doubt, no doubt!"

Outside, in the rain, the children revolved around and around Polly and Phronsie, hugging and kissing them until nobody could do much more than breathe, not seeming to notice the stranger, who stood quietly waiting till such time as he could he heard.

At last, in a lull in the scramble, as they were dragging Polly and her burden up the steps, each wild for the honor of escorting her into the house, he cried out in laughing tones, "Isn't anybody going to kiss *me*, I wonder!"

The two little Whitneys, who were eagerly clutching Polly's arms, turned around, and Percy rubbed his eyes in a puzzled way as Joel said, stopping a minute to look up at the tall figure, "We don't ever kiss strangers — mamsie's told us not to."

"For shame, Joey!" cried Polly, feeling her face grow dreadfully red in the darkness. "The gentleman's been so kind to me!"

"You're right, my boy," said the stranger, laughing and bending down to Joel's upturned, sturdy countenance at the same instant that Mrs. Pepper flung open the big door and a bright, warm light fell straight across his handsome face. And then —

Well, then Percy gave a violent bound and, upsetting Joel as he did so, wriggled his way down the steps at the same time that Van, on Polly's other side, rushed up to the gentleman.

"Papa — oh, *papa!*"

Polly, halfway up the steps, turned around, and then, at the rush of feeling that gathered at her heart, sat right down on the wet slippery step.

"Why, Polly Pepper!" exclaimed Joel, not minding his own upset. "You're right in all the slush. Mother won't like it, I tell you!"

"Hush!" cried Polly, catching his arm. "He's come — oh, Joel — he's *come!*"

"Who?" cried Joel, staring around blindly. "Who, Polly?"

Polly had just opened her lips to explain when Mr. King's portly, handsome figure appeared in the doorway. "Do come in, children — why — good gracious, Mason!"

"Yes," cried the stranger lightly, dropping his big bundle and umbrella as he passed in the door with his little sons clinging to him. "Where is Marian?"

"Why didn't you write?" asked the old gentleman testily. "These surprises aren't the right sort of things," and he began to feel vigorously of his heart. "Here, Mrs. Pepper, be so good as to call Mrs. Whitney."

"*Pepper! Pepper!*" repeated Mr. Whitney perplexedly.

"She's coming — I hear her upstairs," cried Van Whitney. "Oh, let me tell her!" He struggled to get down from his father's arms as he said this.

"No, I shall — I heard her first!" cried Percy. "Oh, dear me! Grandpapa's going to!"

Mr. King advanced to the foot of the staircase as his daughter, all unconscious, ran down with a light step and a smile on her face.

"*Has* Polly come?" she asked, seeing only her father.

"Yes," replied the old gentleman shortly. "And she's brought a big bundle, Marian!"

"A *big bundle*?" she repeated wonderingly, and gazing at him.

"A *very* big bundle," he said, and taking hold of her shoulders, he turned her around on — her husband.

So Polly and Phronsie crept in unnoticed after all.

"I wish Ben was here," said little Davie, capering around the Whitney group, "an' Jappy, I do!"

"Where are they?" asked Polly.

"Don't know," said Joel, tugging at his shoestring. "See — aren't these prime!" He held up a shining black shoe, fairly bristling with newness, for Polly to admire.

"Splendid," she cried heartily. "But where *are* the boys?"

"They went after you," said Davie, "after we came home with our shoes."

"No, they didn't," contradicted Joel flatly, and sitting down on the floor, he began to tie and untie his new possessions. "When we came home, Ben drew us pictures — lots of 'em — don't you know?"

"Oh, yes," said Davie, nodding his head. "So he did.

That was when we all cried 'cause you weren't home, Polly."

"He drawed me a be-*yew*-tiful one," cried Phronsie, holding up her mangy bit. "See, Polly, see!"

"That's the little brown house," said Davie, looking over her shoulder as Phronsie put it carefully into Polly's hand.

"It's all washed out," said Polly, smoothing it out, "when you stayed out in the rain."

Phronsie's face grew very grave at that.

"Bad, naughty old rain," she said, and then she began to cry as hard as she could.

"Oh, dear, don't!" cried Polly in dismay, trying her best to stop her. "Oh, Phronsie, do stop!" she implored, pointing into the next room whence the sound of happy voices issued. "They'll all hear you!"

But Phronsie in her grief didn't care, but wailed on steadily.

"Who is it, anyway?" cried Joel, tired of admiring his precious shoes and getting up to hear them squeak. "That great big man, you know, Polly, that came in with you?"

"Why, I thought I told you," said Polly, at her wit's end over Phronsie. "It's Percy and Van's father, Joey!"

"Whockey!" cried Joel, completely stunned. "*Really* and truly, Polly Pepper?"

"Really and truly," cried Polly, bundling Phronsie up in her arms to lay the little wet cheek against hers.

"Then I'm going to peek," cried Joel, squeaking across the floor to carry his threat into execution.

"Oh, you mustn't, Joe!" cried Polly, frightened lest he

should. "Come right back or I'll tell mamsie!"

"They're all comin' in, anyway," cried little Davie delightedly and scuttling over to Polly's side.

"And here are the little friends I've heard so much about!" cried Mr. Whitney, coming in among them. "Oh, you needn't introduce me to Polly — she brought me home!"

"They're *all* Pepperses," said Percy, waving his hand and doing the business up at one stroke.

"Only the best of 'em isn't here," observed Van rather ungallantly. "*He* draws perfectly elegant, papa!"

"*I* like Polly best, I do!" cried little Dick, tumbling after.

"*Peppers!*" again repeated Mr. Whitney in a puzzled way.

"And here is Mrs. Pepper," said old Mr. King, pompously drawing her forward, "the children's mother, and — "

But here Mrs. Pepper began to act in a very queer way, rubbing her eyes and twisting one corner of her black apron in a decidedly nervous manner that, as the old gentleman looked up, he saw with astonishment presently communicated itself to the gentleman opposite.

"Is it," said Mr. Whitney, putting out his hand and grasping the hard, toil-worn one in the folds of the apron, "is it cousin Mary?"

"And aren't you cousin John?" she asked, the tears in her bright black eyes.

"Of all things in this world!" cried the old gentleman, waving his head helplessly from one to the other. "Will *somebody* have the extreme goodness to tell us what all this means?"

At this the little Peppers crowded around their mother, and into all the vacant places they could find, to get near the fascinating scene.

"Well," said Mr. Whitney, sitting down and drawing his wife to his side, "it's a long story. You see, when I was a little youngster, and — "

"You were *John* Whitney *then*," put in Mrs. Pepper slyly. "That's the reason I never knew when they were all talking of Mason Whitney."

"John Whitney I was," said Mr. Whitney, laughing, "or rather, Johnny and Jack. But Grandmother Mason, when I grew older, wanted me called by middle name to please grandfather. But to go back — when I was a little shaver, about as big as Percy here — "

"Oh, papa!" began Percy deprecatingly. To be called a little shaver before all the others!

"He means, dearie," said his mamma reassuringly, "when he was a boy like you. Now hear what papa is going to say."

"Well, I was sent up into Vermont to stay at the old place. There was a little girl there, a bright, black-eyed little girl. She was my cousin, and her name was Mary Bartlett."

"Who's Mary Bartlett?" asked Joel, interrupting.

"There she is, sir," said Mr. Whitney, pointing to Mrs. Pepper, who was laughing and crying together.

"Where?" said Joel, utterly bewildered. "I don't see any Mary Bartlett. What does he mean, Polly?"

"I don't know," said Polly. "Wait, Joey," she whispered. "He's going to tell us all about it."

"Well, this little cousin and I went to the district school, and had many good times together. And then my parents sent for me, and I went to Germany to school; and when I came back, I lost sight of her. All I could find out was that she had married an Englishman by the name of Pepper."

"*Oh!*" cried all the children together.

"And I always supposed she had gone to England, for despite all my exertions, I could find no trace of her. Ah, Mary," he said reproachfully, "why didn't you let me know where you were?"

"I heard," said Mrs. Pepper, "that you'd grown awfully rich, and I couldn't."

"You always were a proud little thing," he said, laughing.

"Well, but," broke in Mr. King, unable to keep silence any longer, "*I'd* like to inquire, Mason, why you didn't find all this out before, in Marian's letters, when she mentioned Mrs. Pepper?"

"She didn't ever mention her," said Mr. Whitney, turning around to face his questioner. "Not as *Mrs. Pepper* — never once by name. It was always either 'Polly's mother,' or 'Phronsie's mother.' Just like a woman," he added with a mischievous glance at his wife, "not to be explicit."

"And just like a man," she retorted with a happy little laugh, "not to *ask* for explanations."

"I hear Jappy," cried Polly in a glad voice, "and Ben — oh, good!" as a sound of rushing footsteps was heard over the veranda steps and down the long hall.

The door was thrown suddenly open, and Jasper plunged in, his face flush with excitement, and after him Ben, looking a little as he did when Phronsie was lost, while Prince squeezed panting in between the two boys.

"Has Polly got — " began Jasper.

"Oh, yes, I'm here," cried Polly, springing up to them. "Oh, Ben!"

"She has," cried Joel, disentangling himself from the group. "Don't you see, Jappy?"

"She's all home," echoed Phronsie, flying up. "Oh, Ben, do draw me another little house!"

"And see — see!" cried the little Whitneys, pointing with jubilant fingers to their papa. "See what she brought!"

Jasper turned around at that and then rushed forward.

"Oh, brother Mason!"

"Well, Jasper," said Mr. Whitney, a whole wealth of affection beaming on the boy. "How you have stretched up in six months!"

"Haven't I?" said Jasper, laughing and drawing himself up to his fullest height.

"He's a-standin' on tiptoe," said Joel critically, who was hovering near. "I most know he is!" And he bent down to examine the position of Jasper's heels.

"Not a bit of it, Joe!" cried Jasper with a merry laugh and setting both feet with a convincing thud on the floor.

"Well, anyway, I'll be just as big," cried Joel, "when I'm thirteen, so!"

Just then a loud and quick rap on the table made all the children skip and stopped everybody's tongue. It came from Mr. King.

"Phronsie," said he, "come here, child. I can't do anything without you," and held out his hand. Phronsie immediately left Ben, who was hanging over Polly as if he never meant to let her go out of his sight again, and went directly over to the old gentleman's side.

"Now, then!" He swung her upon his shoulder, where she perched like a little bird, gravely surveying the whole group. One little hand stole around the old gentleman's neck and patted his cheek softly, which so pleased him that for a minute or two he stood perfectly still so that everybody might see it.

"Now, Phronsie, *you* must tell all these children so that they'll understand — say everything just as I tell you, mind!"

"I will," said Phronsie, shaking her small head wisely. "Every single thing."

"Well, then, now begin — "

"Well, then, now begin," said Phronsie, looking down on the face with an air as much like Mr. King's as was possible and finishing up with two or three little nods.

"Oh, no, dear, that isn't it," cried the old gentleman. "I'll tell you. Say, Phronsie, 'You are all cousins — every one.' "

"You are all cousins — every one," repeated little Phronsie simply, shaking her yellow head into the very middle of the group.

"Does she *mean* it, grandpapa? Does she *mean* it?" cried Percy in the greatest excitement.

"As true as *everything*?" demanded Joel, crowding in between them.

"As true as — truth!" said the old gentleman solemnly, patting the child's little fat hand. "So make the most of it."

"*Oh!*" said Polly with a long sigh. And then Jasper and she took hold of hands and had a good spin!

Joel turned around with two big eyes on Percy.

"We're *cousins!*" he said.

"I know it," said Percy. "And so's Van!"

"Yes," said Van, flying up, "and I'm cousin to Polly, too — that's best!"

"Can't *I* be a cousin?" cried little Dick, crowding up, with two red cheeks. "Isn't anybody going to be a cousin to me, too?"

"Everybody but Jasper," said the old gentleman, laughing heartily at them. "You and I, my boy," he turned to his son, "are left out in the cold."

At this a scream, loud and terrible to hear, struck upon them all as Joel flung himself flat on the floor.

"Isn't — Jappy — our cousin? I — want — Jappy!"

"Goodness!" exclaimed the old gentleman in the greatest alarm. "What *is* the matter with the boy! Do somebody stop him!"

"Joel," said Jasper, leaning over him and trying to help Polly lift him up. "I'll tell you how we'll fix it! I'll be your brother. That's best of all — brother to Polly and Ben and the whole of you — then we'll see!"

Joel bolted up at that and began to smile through the tears running down the rosy face.

"Will you, *really?*" he said. "Just like Ben — and everything?"

"I can't be as good as Ben," said Jappy, laughing, "but I'll be a real brother like him."

"Phoo — phoo! Then I don't care!" cried Joel, wiping off the last tear on the back of his chubby hand. "Now I guess we're better'n *you*," he exclaimed with a triumphant glance over at the little Whitneys as he began to make the new shoes skip at a lively pace up and down the long room.

"Oh, dear!" they both cried in great distress.

"Now, papa, Jappy's going to be Joey's brother — and he isn't anything but *our* old uncle! Make him be ours more, papa, do!"

And then Polly sprang up.

"Oh! Oh! Deary me!" And she rushed out into the hall and began to tug violently at the big bundle tossed down in a corner. "Cherry'll die — Cherry'll die!" she cried. "Do somebody help me off with the string!"

But Polly already had it off by the time Jasper's knife was half out of his pocket, and was kneeling down on the floor scooping out a big handful of the seed.

"Don't hurry so, Polly," said Jasper as she jumped up to fly upstairs. "He's had some a perfect age — he's all right."

"What!" said Polly, stopping so suddenly that two or three little seeds flew out of the outstretched hand and went dancing away to the foot of the stairs by themselves.

"Oh, I heard him scolding away there when I first came home," said Jasper, "so I just ran down a block or two and got him some."

"Is that all there is in that big bundle?" said Joel in a disappointed tone, who had followed with extreme curiosity to see its contents. "Phoo! That's no fun — old birdseed!"

"I know," said Polly with a gay little laugh, pointing with the handful of seed into the library. "But I shouldn't have met the other big bundle if it hadn't been for *this*, Joel!"

APPLE® *Classics*

Exciting adventures that kids everywhere have loved for a long time...so will you!

☐ MA42035-6 **Alice in Wonderland** by Lewis Carroll
Alice falls down a hole and into a madcap adventure while she meets some very unusual characters! **$2.50**

☐ MA41293-0 **A Christmas Carol** by Charles Dickens
Mean old Scrooge hears the clanking of chains...then a ghost appears! In one terrible hour on Christmas Eve, his life is changed forever. **$2.50**

☐ MA41295-7 **Hans Brinker or The Silver Skates** by Mary Mapes Dodge
Hans really wants to win the big skating race. Does he dare buy new ice skates when his family is poor—and when his father is so mysteriously ill? **$2.95**

☐ MA42046-1 **Heidi** by Johanna Spyri
Heidi, the little Swiss girl, misses the mountaintop home she left behind. Now she lives in a far-off city. Can she ever go back? **$2.95**

☐ MA40719-8 **A Little Princess** by Frances Hodgson Burnett
Sara comes to school with a maid, a pony, and lovely dresses. But Miss Minchin makes her live in a bare, freezing attic! **$2.95**

☐ MA40498-9 **Little Women** by Louisa May Alcott
You'll never forget the March sisters—Meg, Jo, Beth, and Amy. Share their laughter and their tears. **$2.50**

☐ MA41279-5 **Little Men** by Louisa May Alcott
The exciting tale of Jo's school for boys at Plumfield. The sequel to *Little Women*! **$2.95**

☐ MA41269-8 **Pollyanna** by Eleanor H. Porter
"You mean I'll never walk again?" Pollyanna has had a terrible accident. Will she ever be happy again? **$2.50**

☐ MA41343-0 **Rebecca of Sunnybrook Farm** by Kate Douglas Wiggin
The cherished story of young, high-spirited Rebecca in turn-of-the-century Maine. **$2.95**

☐ MA40720-1 **The Secret Garden** by Frances Hodgson Burnett
Mary discovers a secret place all her own, in this story of magic and friendship. **$2.50**

☐ MA41294-9 **The Wind in the Willows** by Kenneth Grahame
Zany misadventures with Toad and his crazy animal pals, Rat, Mole, and Badger! **$2.50**

PREFIX CODE 0-590-

Available wherever you buy books, or use the coupon below.

Scholastic Inc., P.O. Box 7502, 2932 E. McCarty Street, Jefferson City, MO 65102

Please send me the books I have checked above. I am enclosing $_____
please add $1.00 to cover shipping and handling). Send check or money order—no cash or C.O.D.'s please.

Name _____

Address _____

City _____ State/Zip _____

Please allow four to six weeks for delivery. Offer good in U.S.A. only. Sorry, mail order not available to residents of Canada. Prices subject to change.
AC988

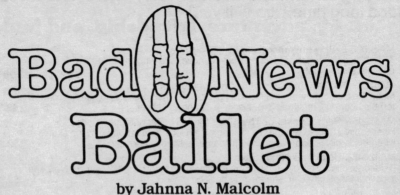